The
Truth-Teller's
TALE

Books by Sharon Shinn

THE SAMARIA NOVELS

ARCHANGEL

JOVAH'S ANGEL

THE ALLELUIA FILES

ANGELICA

ANGEL-SEEKER

THE SHAPE-CHANGER'S WIFE

WRAPT IN CRYSTAL

HEART OF GOLD

SUMMERS AT CASTLE AUBURN

JENNA STARBORN

THE SAFE-KEEPER'S SECRET

THE TRUTH-TELLER'S TALE

MYSTIC AND RIDER

The Truth-Teller's Tale

SHARON SHINN

VIKING

VIKING

Published by Penguin Group

Penguin Young Readers Group, 345 Hudson Street, New York, New York 10014, U.S.A.

Penguin Books Ltd, 80 Strand, London WC2R 0RL, England

Penguin Books Australia Ltd, 250 Camberwell Road, Camberwell, Victoria 3124, Australia

Penguin Books Canada Ltd, 10 Alcorn Avenue, Toronto, Ontario, Canada M4V 3B2

Penguin Group (NZ), cnr Airborne and Rosedale Roads, Albany, Auckland 1310, New Zealand

First published in 2005 by Viking, a division of Penguin Young Readers Group

1 3 5 7 9 10 8 6 4 2

LIBRARY OF CONGRESS CATALOGING-IN-PUBLICATION DATA
Shinn, Sharon.
The Truth-Teller's tale / Sharon Shinn.
p. cm.
Summary: Twins Eleda, who can tell only the truth, and Adele, who cannot
reveal others' secrets, are sorely tested by a newly arrived pair of handsome
dance instructors who seem to harbor a secret.
ISBN 0-670-06000-3 (hardcover)
[1. Twins—Fiction. 2. Mistaken identity—Fiction. 3. Honesty—Fiction.
4. Secrets—Fiction. 5. Courtship—Fiction.] I. Title.
PZ7.S5572Tru 2005
[Fic]—dc22
2005005453

Manufactured in China · Set in Caslon 224 Book · Book design by Jim Hoover

FOR SHEILA
who always tells the truth

AND ALICE
who knows how to keep a secret

WHEN WILL A DREAM BE THWARTED,

NO MATTER WHAT DUES WERE PAID?

WHEN IS THE TRUTH DISTORTED

AND A CONFIDENCE BETRAYED?

Part

One

CHAPTER ONE

hat would you say if I told you there was a time a Safe-Keeper told a secret, a Truth-Teller told a lie, and a Dream-Maker did everything in her power to make sure a wish went astray? Believe what I tell you, for I am a Truth-Teller, and every word I say is true.

No sisters could ever have been less alike than my twin and I. To the casual observer, we looked exactly the same, for we both had wheat blonde hair and exceptionally pale skin, and the bones of our faces had an identical structure. But Adele was right-handed; she parted her hair on the right; her right eye was blue and her left eye was green. I was left-handed; I parted my hair on the left; my left eye was blue and my right eye was green. We each saw in the other the very same face, the very same figure, we saw in the mirror every morning.

You could not blame people for getting us mixed up—until they knew our personalities, and then it should have been easy to tell us apart. For Adele was devious and secretive. She would listen to whispered conversations between

1

strangers and learn all manner of interesting revelations, but never repeat a word. From the time we were quite little, she could lie with utter sincerity, so that you never knew if she was making up a story or concealing a dreadful fact. I, on the other hand, tattled on everyone. If a boy pushed a girl into a puddle, I told his mother about it that very afternoon. If your bow was crooked, your shoes didn't match, or your hair was a mess, I would be sure to let you know. At school, when the teacher asked a question, I could hardly wait to be called on before I would blurt out the answer. Words wouldn't stay inside me, whereas Adele could go days without bothering to make conversation at all. If such a thing were possible, I would have said that I was as transparent as a window—that light and color and information passed through me as if I was not even there—whereas Adele was as opaque and mysterious as a dark curtain motionless before that window on a starless winter night.

She was, in many respects, the most irritating person I knew. If you were ready to leave the house and you called her, sometimes she would not answer. If you wanted her opinion about a dress you were wearing or a boy you liked, she would merely look at you and give you that enigmatic smile. She never told you if she had fallen down and hurt herself or if a girl in school had been mean to her or if she had found out what your parents had bought you as a Wintermoon gift. She could be difficult, obstructive, confusing, and maddening, all without saying a word.

I would not trade her for all the gold in Wodenderry.

The year we turned twelve, we had a brief visit from the

Dream-Maker, who often stayed with us when she came to Merendon. Our parents ran a prosperous inn one block over from High Street, and it was rare that we had more than a room or two open on any night. The Dream-Maker was our guest fairly often, for she traveled constantly between the royal city of Wodenderry and the smaller towns throughout the kingdom. She had to, of course; that was her role in life. She always had to be among people who could tell her their tales or ask for her favor or merely brush by her on the street, not knowing who she was, so that by her very existence she could, now and then, turn someone's deepest desire into reality. There was only one of her in the entire kingdom, and so she always had to be on the move, to touch and change as many people's lives as she could.

I had always been fascinated by Melinda, who had become Dream-Maker a few years before I was born. She was a highborn lady with delicate skin and patrician features; she dressed in the most elegant silks and laces, and her fine white hair was always elaborately styled. It was clear that even after nearly twenty years of dream-making, she had not grown entirely accustomed to her frequent interactions with the rougher folk to be found in the small villages and seaside towns. A certain haughtiness lingered about her still. My mother always said that most Dream-Makers had been sad, lonely women whose lives had been weighted down by their own personal catastrophes, but I could never see any such desolation in Melinda's face. My own theory was that she liked the life of a Dream-Maker very well. Perhaps she had had a dreary life up until the day that power inexplicably passed into her hands, but once she was imbued with the gift of bringing happiness to others, she began to live a life that was rich and pleasant as well.

Whenever she came to my parents' inn, she was greeted with great enthusiasm, for the Dream-Maker meant good business. While she stayed in one of our guest chambers, the taproom would always be full with men hoping to catch a glimpse of the woman who could grant their wishes. The tradesmen promptly made deliveries to our doors; travelers eagerly asked to book a room for an extra night.

And, of course, there was always the possibility that she would bring richer bounty.

Every time she arrived, she and my mother would have the same exchange while my father carried her bags up to the best room. "So, Hannah," Melinda would ask, "any wishes you've been saving up? Any dreams you'd like to see come true?"

And my mother—who looked just like us, except twenty years older and with two blue eyes—would always say, "I'd like my girls to grow up happy and good, and for Bob and me to grow old together."

Melinda would always smile. "Those are the best wishes of all."

This particular summer, Melinda arrived at the inn with great news: Queen Lirabel had had her second baby, this one a girl. The prince had been born fourteen years ago, and the people of the kingdom were beginning to wonder if their much-loved queen would ever have another child. The course of the pregnancy had been followed with great interest throughout the whole kingdom. A traveler could not come from any road that might have intersected Wodenderry without being quizzed on the queen's health and probable due date. Melinda's news was welcome indeed.

"What does she plan to name the little girl? Has that been announced yet?" my mother asked. My father was overseeing the taproom, but Melinda, my mother, Adele, and I were eating around the small table in the kitchen.

"Her official name is Arisande, but there will be a secret name as well," Melinda said, helping herself to some potatoes.

The three of us stared at her. "A secret name?" said Adele. She looked predictably delighted at the concept.

"Oh, yes, just like the prince!" Melinda said. "Here, Eleda, would you pass me that ham?"

I handed her the requested dish. I was frowning. "A secret name?" I said, not sure what that was but knowing already that I disapproved. "What's that? Why would anyone have need of such a thing?"

Melinda shrugged. "Some affectation of royalty, I suppose. Prince Darian has a secret name, too—and so does Lirabel, for all I know. They are kept in the royal record books and inscribed on the tombstones, but no one ever calls the members of the royal family by those names. Well, they're secrets."

"I have a secret name," Adele said.

"Yes, it's *Liar*," I shot at her.

"Girls," Mother reprimanded.

"There will be a great naming ceremony in a week or

two and then—well, now, Hannah, you and your girls would be interested in this—then there will be a full year when Lirabel will invite Truth-Tellers and Safe-Keepers from all over the kingdom to come in and visit with the little girl. She did the same thing when Darian was born. You can't believe the number of Truth-Tellers who announced, in the most pompous way, 'This boy will be brave and strong and true. He will grow to be a young man of exceptional honor.' That sort of thing. As if you could know such a thing about a baby."

"What did the Safe-Keepers have to say?" Mother asked.

Melinda gave a rather unladylike snort. "Well, of course, they never say much, do they? I suppose they were all watching him with their eyes half closed and storing up little bits of information, and in twenty years when he turns out to be demented or ill-favored or just plain odd, they'll nod their heads and say, 'I knew when he was in the cradle.'"

I was giggling. Adele looked amused, but in a pitying way, as if Melinda was too obtuse to understand some great and obvious truth. My mother said, "My, it sounds like you have a low opinion of Safe-Keepers."

Melinda shrugged her thin shoulders in her fashionable dress. "Not at all. You know my own daughter is a Safe-Keeper, or she used to be, and she is the dearest girl. But I do always wonder how much these people really know, and how much they pretend they knew after a secret has already been revealed. It does not seem like it would be so hard to nod your head wisely and say, 'Ah, yes. I knew it all along.'"

"They really do know," I said regretfully. It pained me to

admit that anyone could willingly swallow knowledge and hold it inside himself for days or weeks or decades, but I simply knew it was true. "And it's harder than you would think to keep a secret."

"*You* couldn't do it," Adele said in a taunting voice.

I stuck my tongue out at her. "*I* wouldn't want to," I replied.

"Anyway, so I thought you and Bob might be taking the girls into Wodenderry in the next few months," Melinda said. "I can make sure you're introduced to the queen, if you like, for I know everyone at court. But you'd be welcome without my introduction."

All three of us were staring at her with our blue and green eyes.

Melinda put down her fork, an arrested expression on her face. "What?" she demanded. "What did I say?"

My mother also laid down her silverware, as if it had suddenly become very heavy or very breakable. "Why would you think Bob and I should take the girls to Wodenderry to meet the princess?" she asked in a careful voice.

Melinda looked surprised. "Because Adele is a Safe-Keeper, of course, and Eleda is a Truth-Teller. They're still really too young to be practicing, I realize—indeed, it's rare that they would even show signs of their talent at this age—but it won't be long now before they're hiding secrets and announcing truths. I think Lirabel would be charmed to have such fresh, young faces at the palace."

My mother was still staring. "My daughters? Are—they are—such special people? But are you sure?"

Melinda looked even more surprised. "Well, of course I'm sure. Do you mean to tell me you didn't know?"

And then it was as if all the thoughts inside my head went into a dizzying whirl, spinning around three times before yielding up a bright, tiny nugget of light. It was as if knowledge burst inside me in a star-colored pinwheel. Suddenly I had a piece of information I had not had before—and it was certain, it was absolute.

"Oh!" I said, and I knew I sounded amazed. "Melinda's right! We are—it's just like she said. I'm a Truth-Teller. Adele's a Safe-Keeper. She's right. It's true."

My mother looked at me, uncertain but hopeful. "Well— if you say so. I've never known you to tell a lie, not ever. But does that mean—if you're a Truth-Teller—you couldn't lie, even if you wanted to."

"But I never want to," I said, a little too earnestly. Adele giggled.

My mother turned her doubtful eyes on my sister. "And does that mean Adele—"

"She's a Safe-Keeper," I said a little grumpily. Because now that she had an official *sanctified* reason never to tell me anything I asked, Adele would be even more insufferable.

"Well, isn't this excellent news!" my mother said, puffing up a little with pleasure. "Melinda, you'll never have to ask me again what I'm wishing for. This is better than a dream come true!"

Melinda looked from me to Adele. "Are you happy? Or are you shocked at the news?"

"I'm quite happy," I said—and then, to be scrupulously

honest—"though I admit I am a little shocked."

"And you, Adele?" the Dream-Maker asked. "Are you surprised as well?"

Adele gave us all her most annoying smile and said, "I knew it all along."

You would have thought my father had been told his daughters were next in line to take the throne. There had never been a Safe-Keeper or a Truth-Teller on either side of the family, and he could not have been prouder. He told all of his acquaintances; he told guests who checked into the inn for the night; he managed to work the information into every conversation he had with friends or strangers. My father in general was a hearty, happy, genial man who thought his life had been blessed beyond his desserts; his ruddy face was always creased in a smile, and his big hands were always reaching out to pat someone on the back or offer help in some task. To him, this was just further proof of the overwhelming goodness of the world.

Within two days of learning the news, he had written to the royal arboretum and ordered two full-grown trees to plant in the green area behind the inn. One was a kirren-berry, the tree of silence. Sit beneath it in spring or summer and its limbs, with their flat dark leaves, would stretch noiselessly above you; in autumn or winter, you would hear no rustle from its slim branches as they shook in a frenzied breeze. It was traditional for Safe-Keepers to plant a kirren-berry tree on their property so that anyone desperate to tell a secret would know where to go to speak in safety.

A few yards away from the kirrenberry, he planted a chatterleaf, the tree that Truth-Tellers had taken as their emblem. This was a species that was never silent at all. Its lime-bright leaves made silky whispery sounds during any light spring breeze; even in the dead of winter, its bare twigs and branches rattled against one another like sticks in a drummer's hands. Birds of all types were drawn to its lush greenery, and once settled on its springy branches they would commence to sing endless arias. Crows and ravens made their nests among its upper reaches and engaged in unending gossip. A whistle from a chatterleaf would yield a deep and satisfying sound, like a foghorn in Merendon harbor or the bellow of a small, angry animal.

I loved that chatterleaf tree more than I could say. I loved the varying sounds it made depending on what kind of wind stirred its branches—a shushing susurration if the breeze was faint and the leaves had almost all dropped away; a clattering, jabbering, conversation when wilder winds whipped up off the ocean; and a rich, sad, moaning when spring storms lashed through Merendon, shaking all the rafters and bending the trees nearly double.

But during no storm and no season did the kirrenberry tree make a sound.

The first person to come by the inn and inspect our new acquisitions was Roelynn Karro, daughter of the wealthiest merchant in town. She was our age exactly, because she had been born when we were only three days old, and she had been our best friend ever since we could remember. She had dark hair of a rich chestnut hue, and her eyes were a complex hazel. In personality, she fell somewhere between

Adele and me. She could keep her counsel, if she felt like it, but she was never so happy as when she was discussing some friend or recent event. Though she was the richest girl in the city of Merendon, I often doubted that she was the happiest. Her mother had died when she was quite young, and her father was a gruff and greedy man whom everyone respected but no one liked. His first name was Delton, but you had to think hard to remember that; everyone in the entire town referred to him simply as Karro. Her older brother, Micah, seemed to have assumed the task of raising her, though he did a slipshod job of it, as you might expect from a boy of fifteen. The result was that Roelynn was as wild as a summer bramble and just as prickly.

She admired our new greenery, though. "Very nice," she said, putting her hand on the smooth bole of the chatterleaf tree and swinging around it in one complete revolution. "And I thought the new sign out front looked quite pretty."

Adele giggled. In honor of our new status, our father had rechristened our inn the Leaf & Berry and had just hung the plaque this morning. "We must have the only inn in the kingdom with that particular name," my sister said.

Roelynn swung around the tree a second time, rattling the trunk enough to send a few of the resting crows off in search of more stable perches. "Listen to those birds!" she exclaimed. "Are they never quiet?"

I shook my head. "The nightingale sings till dawn, and the songbirds call out the entire day."

"Something to listen to, then, when you wake up in the middle of the night," Roelynn said. "Or when you don't want to think too much during the middle of the day."

I gave her a sharp look. "What wouldn't you want to think about?" I demanded.

She shrugged. "Oh—anything. All the little problems of the day. I like your tree, Eleda."

But she liked Adele's equally well, and the two of them sat on the ground beneath its thin branches for a good ten minutes, neither of them saying a word. I grew restless and went inside the inn to see if there were any tarts to spare. When I came back outside, Adele and Roelynn were sitting on the green bench that was situated midway between the two trees. I sat beside Roelynn and shared the treats.

"So the two of you are professional women now," Roelynn said. "Will you have customers come to call? How much will you charge? Will your parents set aside a room for you to hear secrets and pronounce truths?"

Adele and I looked at each other across Roelynn's figure. These were questions neither of us had thought to ask yet. "I suppose we will eventually," I said at last. "But—I mean—we're twelve years old. Who's going to trust us with important news?"

"I would," Roelynn said.

Adele gave her a searching look. "Do you have important news?"

I felt that squeeze on my heart that I had learned meant the truth was obvious. "Yes," I said. "She does. Roelynn, what is it?"

"My father has made a deal with the queen," she said. She didn't sound very excited about it. "He's going to handle all the royal shipments that go through the port of Merendon. He's going to become a very wealthy man."

"He's already a wealthy man," I said dryly.

Roelynn nodded. "He'll be almost as rich as the queen herself, or so he says. He thinks maybe one day she'll grant him a title and he'll become a nobleman. It's all he can talk about."

"I'd like to be rich," Adele commented.

"Me, too!" I replied. "But, Roelynn, you don't sound happy about it at all."

She sighed and leaned against the back of the bench. "He says he wants Micah and me to start behaving like gentry. He doesn't want us to go to the Merendon school anymore—he wants us to have private tutors. He wants us to dress in better clothes and—and—"

"He wants you to make different friends," I said.

She nodded glumly. "He says you're daughters of tradesmen."

"Well, we are," I said.

Roelynn tilted up her small, pointed chin. "I don't care," she said. "You're my *friends*."

Adele was smiling. "We'll still be your friends," she said. "Nothing will change that."

Roelynn hesitated before speaking again. "And so I hope," she said. "But there's something else, something that might take me away from Merendon forever."

We both leaned forward and spoke in matching voices. "What?"

"My father has decided I should marry the prince."

We both stared at her.

Roelynn nodded, even more glum. "It's true. He thinks this new shipping contract is just the beginning. First, he'll get all that money. Then he'll win a title. Then he'll propose to the queen that she should marry her son to me."

There was a moment of silence. "That's ridiculous," I said flatly. "Prince Darian will be married to some—some— highborn lady of Wodenderry. Or even a foreign princess! I love you dearly, Roelynn, but you're just a merchant's daughter."

"You might speak a little more kindly," Adele murmured.

Roelynn sighed. "No, she's telling the truth. Of course. And yet my father seems to think that my future is all but assured. Maybe he has even discussed it with the queen already, I don't know. Maybe that's why she gave him the shipping contract. But I don't want to marry the prince! I don't even know him. I want to fall in love with a handsome man, and marry him, and live in Merendon the rest of my life. Why shouldn't I be allowed to do that?"

"You should," Adele said firmly.

Roelynn nodded and then crossed her arms over her chest. She looked very small and very, very stubborn. "Well, I can tell you this right now, and you can repeat it as the truth or hide it as a secret, but I will not marry the prince at my father's command."

I smiled a little. "I don't think that's something I'll need to announce just yet."

And then Adele asked a strange question. "What about

Micah?" she said. "Does your father intend for him to marry the baby princess?"

I gave her a frowning look, because who cared about Micah? He was tall and thin, with Roelynn's dark hair and fine features; he was always in a hurry and always appeared to be struggling with greater cares than he could really handle. I had never liked him all that much.

Roelynn shook her head. "I don't know. He hasn't said so. My guess is that my father would want Micah to marry the daughter of some rich merchant in Lowford or Movington. Expand the freighting lanes, you know."

"Does Micah always do what your father wants?" I demanded.

"No," Roelynn said, smiling faintly. "More often than I do, but not all the time. They have terrible fights sometimes."

I shook my head. I wanted to say, *Your father is a dreadful man,* and I can tell you that I wasn't the only person in Merendon who thought so, but it seemed to be one of those truths that didn't have to be spoken aloud. "Well, I don't suppose there's anything you *or* Micah can do just now," I said practically. "So I wouldn't worry about the prince or anything else at this moment."

Adele came to her feet. "No," she said. "Let's just go buy ourselves some ribbon and make bows for our hair. We'll talk about all this some other day."

Though it would be years before we did.

CHAPTER TWO

wo months after Melinda brought us the news of Princess Arisande's birth, a more official announcement went out. Messengers traveled down all the main roads of the kingdom on behalf of the queen and her husband. *Truth-Tellers welcome. Safe-Keepers requested. Come see the new royal infant.*

Even so, my mother probably would not have had the nerve to present her daughters at the royal palace—she had been outside Merendon only twice in her entire life—but my father thought it would be the event of a lifetime for us, an opportunity not to be overlooked. They discussed it for a few days in private, while Adele lingered near doorways and crouched by keyholes trying to overhear, and then refused to tell me what she'd learned.

In the end, though, we did go to Wodenderry.

My father's uncle watched the inn while the four of us traveled to the royal city. Never had I seen such a spectacular place! The streets were wide enough to let two traveling coaches pass in different directions; the buildings were all

16

grander than the house that Roelynn lived in, and that was the biggest building in all of Merendon. There were so many people out, night or day, that the streets were never empty and the air was never still. I did not think even a kirrenberry tree would be able to cast a silent shadow anywhere over those crowded boulevards and abbreviated lawns.

We stayed at a small, respectable inn that Melinda had recommended, and my mother made friends almost immediately with the matronly woman who managed the place. We hadn't been on the premises more than half an hour before she and my mother were comparing notes about cooking, cleaning, and caring for customers. My father had already braved the few blocks closest to the inn and come back to report on the wide variety of shops and restaurants he had discovered.

"You three girls will want to go shopping," he said. "After we come back from our visit with the queen."

It was hard to believe that Adele and I were actually in Wodenderry to make our curtsies to Queen Lirabel. It was hard to believe even as, the next day, we essayed the crowded streets and made our way directly to the royal palace.

It seemed like there were hundreds of people at the palace before us—guards in formal livery, noblemen and -women in the finest clothes imaginable, and gawking peasant folk who stood outside the wrought-iron fence and peered inward. Our own little party was somewhere in the middle, respectable but hardly well-to-do. The guards at the gate asked our business and waved us inside when my father explained.

"Go to the blue parlor," they told us. "That's where the others are gathered."

It took another twenty minutes and consultations with another seven or eight guards to locate the blue parlor. This was a large, pretty room with floor-to-ceiling windows and furnishings of blue, yellow, and ivory. Five others had arrived before us—none of them young enough to be accompanied by their parents. Excitement had sustained me this far, but I began to wonder what business Adele and I really had among such exalted company. Two twelve-year-old girls come to make their pronouncements over the newborn princess? It was laughable, really. It was hard to believe that even my optimistic father would have ever thought this was a worthwhile idea.

None of the others spoke to us while we waited. I amused myself by trying to guess which ones were Safe-Keepers, which Truth-Tellers. The old, grim-looking woman with the hot blue eyes was clearly a Truth-Teller; all the others stayed as far from her as they could, not wanting to have their clothes critiqued or their motives examined aloud. There was a tall, heavy man who sat by himself in the corner. His face looked both watchful and sharp; I thought he could be one of those rare Truth-Tellers who kept as many secrets as he pleased. Across the room from them sat two women and a man, laughing and talking in low voices. Safe-Keepers all, I thought, for it was strange but true: Safe-Keepers, at least the ones I knew, all seemed sociable and at ease with the world, despite all the dreadful secrets they knew and must keep buried in their hearts. Truth-Tellers, who could release their burdens aloud every day, were often nasty-tempered and fierce, and many of them were friendless.

I couldn't honestly say that I would rather be a Safe-Keeper than a Truth-Teller, but I certainly did not want to end up feared and unloved. I vowed at that very moment to be the kind of Truth-Teller who knew how to make friends as well as offer unpopular revelations. I did not expect the task to be an easy one.

We had waited perhaps an hour before we were joined by an entourage. A pair of footmen entered the room, so sumptuously dressed that at first I thought they must be royalty themselves. One clapped his hands for silence, the other announced the arrival of the queen. They folded back to stand on either side of the door, and then three women entered the room at a rather more leisurely pace. It was easy to spot Queen Lirabel, not just because her image was stamped on all the coins of the realm, but because of her majestic carriage. She held herself very straight; the gold crown circling her black hair never looked to be in danger of falling off. She was dressed in a stiff purple gown embroidered in gold, and rings sparkled on most of her fingers.

Beside her walked a fair-haired woman with an easy smile and a Safe-Keeper's guarded eyes. I knew this must be Fiona, close advisor to the queen. I did not know the whole tale, but there was some mystery about her. She had been discovered only fifteen or sixteen years ago in some backwater village, but had come to Wodenderry when it was discovered she was related to the queen. I thought she looked interesting and full of secrets.

Behind them walked a nursemaid carrying a baby. The nurse was plainly dressed and older than the other two women—clearly someone who had had much experience raising children and would not go wrong with such a precious charge. The baby herself was dressed in the most elaborate gown of white silk and ribbons; its hem practically dragged the floor. She was wide awake and curious, her dark blue eyes taking in the sights of the room, her tiny fist pressed against her rosebud mouth. Her cap of fine hair was as black as her mother's.

The nine of us were all on our feet and curtsying or bowing as our gender dictated. I peeked up from under the fall of my hair to see Queen Lirabel nodding graciously.

"Thank you. I'm so pleased you are here. Thank you for taking the time to come to Wodenderry and offer your insights to the princess," she said.

All of us straightened again and watched her. The footmen brought over three chairs, and the women sat, but the rest of us remained standing. The queen looked meditative. I saw Fiona's bright eyes pass over the others in the room and then come to rest on Adele and me. Unconsciously, I reached for my sister's hand and found hers already outstretched, seeking mine.

"How shall we do this?" the queen asked, as if speaking to herself.

"Let us proceed by age," Fiona suggested, "and do the greatest honor to our oldest guest." She nodded at the mean-eyed old woman leaning on her cane.

"Let us do so," Lirabel said, and the crone shuffled

forward. The nursemaid positioned the baby in her lap so that the child's grave eyes seemed to look up at the intent old woman. I thought such a scrutiny might make me cry even at the age of twelve, so I was impressed that Arisande did not seem to be unnerved in the least.

"She will be a good girl, loyal and true," the ancient Truth-Teller proclaimed at last. "She will be the jewel of your court when she is a young lady, and she will support her brother when he becomes king. You need have no fears for this one."

Lirabel looked pleased, but she merely inclined her head in a regal manner. "Thank you. Your words are greatly appreciated. The footmen will show you to the door and give you a small gift for your trouble."

Adele's fingers tightened on mine. *Gift?* We had not expected any recompense for our troubles. Merely being in the presence of royalty was honor enough for us.

Next to approach the queen's tableau was the heavy man with the unreadable face. He, too, studied the tiny princess a moment before making an observation. "She has a kind heart," he said at last. "Many people will love her."

This made Fiona smile, though Lirabel seemed less delighted by promised kindness than prophesied loyalty. "Thank you," she said nonetheless. "Your words are welcome. The footmen will take care of you now."

He left; one by one the Safe-Keepers presented themselves to the women and the baby. Safe-Keepers don't tell you what they're thinking, of course. They merely nod, and look enlightened, and then offer those irritating, enigmatic smiles. Fiona's amusement increased as she watched them, and the queen's expression grew more stony. My guess was that a three-month-old baby had very few secrets to impart and that the Safe-Keepers really had no role here, and everybody knew it, and nobody wanted to say so. Still, the queen thanked all of them for taking the trouble to travel to Wodenderry, and one by one they curtsied again and exited through the door.

More quickly than I would have thought possible, my family members were the only visitors left in the room. By now, Adele and I had our hands locked together so tightly that I began to wonder if we would ever be able to disentangle our fingers. When the queen looked our way, I felt my entire body turn to stone.

But she was looking at our parents, not us. "And which of you has come with your family to offer some thoughts on my daughter's future?" she said.

Beside her, Fiona was smiling. "Not the adults, Lirabel," she murmured, "the little girls."

The queen's gaze dropped and flicked between Adele's face and my own. Her expression softened. "So?" she said, her tone of voice a question. "These small ones are—what are they, then? Safe-Keepers or Truth-Tellers? They seem very young."

"Sometimes it's the sort of thing one knows at a very young age," Fiona answered. She pointed at Adele. "That one is a Safe-Keeper, I believe, and her sister is most assuredly a Truth-Teller."

"Is that so?" the queen demanded.

Adele nodded. I was too frozen to make even that much of a motion.

"Well, then," the queen said, "come forward and greet my daughter."

Adele, of course, immediately dropped my hand and did just that. I followed her more slowly, marveling that even feet made of ice could be forced to walk across a palace floor.

By the time I had arrived beside Arisande and the nursemaid, Adele had lost all her shyness. She was bending down and cooing at the serious little face, and she laughed out loud when the miniature hand reached out as if to touch her. Without even asking permission, she extended her own hand, and the tiny fingers curled around her thumb as if they would never let go.

"She likes me!" Adele exclaimed, glancing over her shoulder to beam at the rest of us. "Do you see that? She likes me! Hello, little princess," she crooned. "Aren't you the pretty one? Don't you look just like your mama? Oh, yes, that's a lovely smile. Show me that smile again. Oh yes, you like me, you do."

I was embarrassed for her—such a display!—but I heard the queen and Fiona laugh. "I imagine most people like you," the queen said, and her voice was far warmer than it had been when she addressed the others. "What is your name, child?"

"Adele. I'm a Safe-Keeper. My family and I are from Merendon." It must have been the effect of royalty; Adele never volunteered so much information at once.

The queen transferred her gaze to me, and I found that she was not so frightening after all when she smiled. "And your name?" she asked.

"Eleda," I replied.

She continued addressing me, since all of Adele's attention had gone back to the baby. "And you and your sister are identical twins?"

I shook my head. "We're mirror twins. We are the same in every way, except reversed. Even our names are the same, except they're backward."

The queen looked much impressed by this small detail, arching her black brows over her dark eyes. "Very clever," she approved. "And are you close to your sister?"

There were days I hated her and days I wanted to protect her and days I thought she was the most exasperating human being in the entire kingdom. But I could never be less than truthful. "As close as sisters can be," I said.

She nodded, pleased by this as well. "Cherish her," she said. "A sister is the finest gift you can ever have."

Fiona was laughing. "I quite agree."

By now, Lirabel's face was open and friendly. I thought maybe she liked children. "So you are the Truth-Teller," the queen said. "Do you have any comments to offer me about my daughter?"

I assumed what I thought was a more professional expression. "Let me look into her face," I said, and stepped next to Adele. She moved over to make room for me, but didn't drop her hand, and so I studied Princess Arisande while she clung to my sister's thumb and made small nonsense sounds. What can you really tell about a baby, after all? Her face was soft and unformed, and even her smile seemed involuntary, more an attempt to practice moving her facial muscles than a signal of delight at the world around her. But there was a great sweetness in the shape of her head, a lingering contentment in the rhythm of her heart. It was impossible to forecast anything but happiness for such a serene little spirit.

"She will be a loving child and a delightful woman," I said, and I could tell as the words left my mouth that they were true. "And she will be an obedient daughter. You will certainly have less trouble with her than you do with your son."

There was a sudden blank silence in the room. It was a moment before I realized that my words had created the chill—and what exactly my words had implied. I felt myself blush a hot and uncomfortable color as I turned to face my queen.

"I'm sorry. I didn't mean—the words just came out," I stammered. I couldn't bring myself to look at her. But I couldn't bring myself to unsay the words, either.

Queen Lirabel's voice came, thoughtful and far from angry. "Do you even know Darian?" she asked. I shook my head and still refused to look up. "Do tales of him get carried all the way to Merendon?"

"No," I whispered. "It's just that—I can tell—he is a difficult young man. He's wayward, and he's reckless, and sometimes you despair of controlling him."

"All those things are true," she said.

I glanced up at her. She did not look any angrier than she sounded. I continued with a little more strength in my voice. "But he is a good person, too. You don't have to fear for him."

She raised her eyebrows again, and then she smiled. "That is most excellent news," she said. "For sometimes he does make me worry."

"I think that's what boys do," I said. "Make their mothers anxious."

Now Fiona laughed aloud, and the queen's smile grew wider. "And girls are not always so easy either," Fiona said. "But I am glad to hear that Arisande will be a docile child."

The queen looked over at Adele, who was reluctantly freeing her hand from the baby's grip. "And have you formed any secret impressions about my daughter that you will take home and keep to yourself for the next twenty years?" Lirabel asked.

Adele smiled and nodded. "I do wish I could know something, though."

"What is it?"

"I wish I could know her secret name."

"Adele!" I exclaimed, for her request was even more shocking than my comments. The queen looked taken aback, but the woman beside her was smiling.

"I think that's a secret you can be trusted with," Fiona said, and she motioned my sister forward. When Adele was close enough, Fiona leaned over and whispered in her ear. Adele nodded solemnly—and then, when Fiona whispered something else, nodded again. Then Fiona sat back in her chair, and Adele stepped away.

"Thank you very much for coming," the queen said, reverting to the formal tone she had used when she spoke to the others. I knew that our audience was over. "I've enjoyed your visit very much. The footmen will see you out and bestow a small gift on you."

"It was our pleasure," I said, curtsying in tandem with Adele. Our parents—who, all this time, had remained motionless across the room—now came hurrying up to collect us. They made their own bows and curtsies, and we were almost immediately out in the hall. One of the footmen closed the door behind us. The other handed each of us a small velvet box that we were probably supposed to wait to open until we were out of the palace and back in our rented rooms. But neither Adele nor I had such patience. We pulled off the tight-fitting lids and then oohed at the treasure revealed inside—a small, hand-painted miniature of the sleeping princess Arisande. It was hung on a red cord and intended to be worn as a necklace, although of course such a thing was too fine ever to be paraded in public. It would go in a locked cabinet and be brought out on special days, and worn, perhaps, around the house for five minutes at a time before it was reverently returned to its place of safety.

I received the pendant five years ago, and I have it to this day, its condition as pristine as the hour I got it. I imagine I will have it till I die.

CHAPTER THREE

ver the next two years, the folk of Merendon gradually began to turn to my sister and me when they needed a Safe-Keeper or a Truth-Teller. There were others who provided such services, for Merendon was a fairly large city and its many souls had much need of both frankness and discretion. But we were popular both because of our location—in the heart of the business district—and our novelty. Who could resist the allure of seeking help from a set of twins? And we never disappointed. I gained a reputation for being fearsomely honest, while Adele grew more watchful and close-mouthed with every passing year.

You have to understand, sometimes these traits worked against us.

Adele became quite recalcitrant in school, for instance, often refusing to answer teachers' questions about math or literature because she considered her opinion to be "a secret." I continued to infuriate my fellow students by virtuously reporting cheaters and liars. Nonetheless, we each had our share of friends. The young girls all wanted Adele as their confidante, so they could pour out their silly tales of adolescent love and betrayal. The boys relied on me to impartially referee games and honestly determine who had won a race.

All our classmates knew us and accepted the skills we had to offer. It was outside of the schoolhouse that we sometimes got into trouble. Or others got into trouble because they could not tell us apart.

I remember one incident from the summer we were thirteen, when we had gone to the dressmaker's shop to get fitted for Summermoon dresses. My mother was standing with me in the back room as Lissette, the shop owner, pinned me into the shell of a lavender frock. Adele was wandering through the bolts of saffron and indigo in the front. I heard the door open, and a few people exchanged greetings. Then I heard a woman say, "Are you the Truth-Teller?" and my sister reply, "Yes."

If I have failed to mention it before, let me just say here that Adele hid a wide streak of mischief behind her demure demeanor. Whereas I find it impossible to tell a lie, Adele finds it fatiguing to tell the truth. It was entirely typical of her to make such a response to such a question.

I jerked away from the dressmaker's fingers. "I have to go," I said, trying to pull the half-finished gown over my head. "Someone needs me in the shop."

Lissette and my mother each clamped their hands around me. "You stay right here," my mother said. "We'll be done in just a minute."

"But you don't understand—Adele—someone has asked for me—"

"Adele will do just fine," my mother said calmly. "You hold still."

And though I tried to squirm away, I couldn't break free without tearing the dress—and it really was a lovely dress. By the time I was able to step out of the purple frock, don my own clothes, and hurry out into the front room, the only people there were Adele and the shop assistant.

"Who was that?" I asked my sister. "Who was here?"

She gave me an innocent stare from those wide eyes, one green, one blue. "No one was here. Just me."

I stamped a foot. "I *heard* someone come in. You told her you were me."

"Oh," Adele said. "I can't tell you what she said."

I turned to the assistant, a colorless girl a year or two older than we were. "Did you see who it was whispering to my sister a few minutes ago?"

The girl nodded, uninterested. "It was Widow Norville. I didn't hear what she asked about, though."

I looked back at Adele, my face full of surprise. "The Widow Norville? I've never spoken to her in all my life."

"I know," Adele said cheerfully. "She doesn't usually talk to people like us."

"What did she want?"

"She had a question. I gave her an answer. You don't need to be concerned."

And that was all she ever said about it.

I spent some energy trying to determine what the Widow Norville could have wanted to ask of me. Though I never could say definitively, I eventually assumed she had wanted some information about old man Haskins, who had recently lost his own spouse and clearly had been trying to find himself another one. Maybe Widow Norville wanted to know if he was a kind man; maybe she was asking if he was really as rich as he seemed to be. The answers to those questions, in order, were *yes* and *no,* and so I would have told her. I have no idea what Adele said to her, but three months later the two of them wed, and from that day on they seemed to be very happy together. My guess was that Adele had somehow obtained secret information about old man Haskins—that he harbored a great fondness for the widow, perhaps, and that he was desperately lonely—and she used this information to tailor her reply to the Norville woman. Though I greatly disapproved of her methods, I could hardly fault her results. And, as I would come to realize time and time again, even if I could not trust Adele's truthfulness, I could trust her good heart. She would never deliberately see someone come to harm. If she lied, it was with a purpose, and usually toward a good end.

I, of course, never lied, even with those motives.

From time to time, people would approach me on the street or in the market square and ask me if I was the Safe-Keeper. "No," I would always reply quite roundly, and then they would beg my pardon and back away and go off in search of someone a little more discreet. But sometimes they failed to pose the question the right way, and then they got a different kind of counsel than they bargained for.

For instance, Joe Muller came up to me one day as I waited for my sister outside the bakery and said, "I need to talk something through with someone," he said. "Do you have a minute?"

"Certainly," I said.

He hesitated, running a hand through his thinning brown hair as he attempted to formulate his thoughts. "I've been thinking about buying the old Windemere place," he said. "I might buy some sheep and see if I can get a little flock going. Karro said he'd ship the wool for me at cost for the first two years, and then I'd pay him double for two years. I haven't told anyone about it, because I know Ralph Haskins is thinking about buying the place, too."

I couldn't believe it. "Are you mad?" I demanded. "There are more sheep farms near Merendon than there are boats in the harbor. If you're going to buy the place, that's fine, it's a good property, but think of something else to do with it. And *never* make any deal with Karro or *anyone* that means you have to pay twice the going rate at *any* point in the future. Can't you do basic math? You don't have to worry about old man Haskins, though. He doesn't have enough money to buy the Windemere place. I don't think anyone does but you. You can probably get a better price than the one you were offered."

Joe stared at me with his mouth hanging open. It was a full minute before he was able to speak again. "I guess you're not Adele," he said at last.

"No," I said in a huffy voice. "I guess I'm not."

Now he began to smile. "But maybe that's not such a bad thing. So you don't think I'm much of a businessman, do you? But you approve of the Windemere property?"

"I think you should be a little more careful about the deals you make," I said, a bit embarrassed and trying to repair some of my damage. "But I do think you should buy the Windemere place."

"What should I pay for it? What's it worth? And what should I do with it if I don't run sheep?"

We talked over his options for a few more minutes, until Adele came out of the bakery carrying a bag of bread. "Hello, Joe," she said with a quick smile. "Were you looking for me?"

I surmised that they had had some conversation in the past when he mentioned he might want to confide some of his business decisions to her.

He was grinning broadly now. "No," he said. "I think your sister has helped me figure it all out. Thanks, girls. I'll be in touch."

Adele watched him thoughtfully as he walked away, then turned her head so she could inspect me. I couldn't keep the smug expression from my face. "I suppose you gave him some good advice," she said at last.

"I suppose I did."

I expected her to be irritated, but that was the thing about Adele. She never seemed to feel such uncharitable emotions, or else she knew how to hide them. "Good," she said. "Let's go home."

For the most part, the residents of Merendon did not make the same mistake that Joe Muller and Widow Norville had. They did not want to risk talking to the wrong sister. Most people realized pretty quickly that they could not simply ask "Are you the Truth-Teller?" or "Are you the Safe-Keeper?" because Adele was capricious and I wasn't always around to give a straightforward answer. After some trial and error, the townspeople settled on one particular question that seemed guaranteed to net the appropriate response: "Is it safe to tell you a secret?" Adele always answered yes to that, and I always answered no. I believe strangers who were sent looking for us were also told to use this password, and I know our parents generally warned their overnight guests to ask us something of the sort before they began to pour out their hearts. So after a while we had fewer incidents of mistaken identity and interesting conversations at cross-purposes.

Those who knew us really well, of course, had no need to ask meaningful questions to try to determine who we were. Our mother, for instance, never got us confused, not once, not for a second. Our father would sometimes start to speak to one of us, hesitate, study her face more closely, and then continue on or change his tone, depending on how right he had been in his first impression. Every once in a while, Adele tried to fool him, but he was never caught for more than a minute or two.

I, of course, never attempted such deception.

The one person besides our mother who never got us mixed up was Roelynn Karro. If she came upon my sister sitting under the chatterleaf tree, she would drop to the ground beside her and say, "Hello, Adele." If she encountered me in an uncharacteristic moment of silence, she would say, "Good morning, Eleda. What are you thinking about?" She didn't even appear to be scanning for the telltale physical signs—the placement of the hair part, the arrangement of the mismatched eyes. She just seemed to know which sister was which.

The summer we all turned fourteen was an unhappy one

for Roelynn. Her father, who had already begun to restrict her free time, watched her even more closely. He hired tutors to instruct her in foreign languages, governesses to teach her how to behave in society, and seamstresses to dress her in all the finest clothes of the season. It was a rare afternoon when she could find a few hours to slip away and visit the old friends she had been forbidden to see.

One week, Karro took Roelynn to Wodenderry so that she could meet the queen and be introduced to all the gentry. We knew before she left that she was dreading the trip, for she crept to our house in the middle of the night and threw chatterleaf pods at the window of our third-story bedroom. I was the first one to wake up and peer down at the shadowy yard.

"Who's there?" I demanded. "Go away or I'll call my father."

"Shh! Eleda! It's Roelynn."

"What are you doing out so late?" I made no attempt to hide my astonishment. "You shouldn't be here! At this hour!"

"I want to talk to you. Wake up Adele and come down."

It was against my nature to sneak out of the house, but I did poke Adele in the ribs and tell her who waited below. The two of us made our way with some caution down the steps and out the kitchen door. Roelynn had already taken a seat on a blanket she'd spread under the kirrenberry tree. That meant that whatever she wanted to talk about was something that I would have to do my best not to discuss later, with anyone except Roelynn or Adele.

"What's wrong?" Adele asked as we dropped to the ground beside her.

"My father's taking me to Wodenderry tomorrow," she said.

Both of us nodded. We had not had a chance to visit with Roelynn for at least two weeks now, but that news had been on the lips of everyone in Merendon. "And what will you do while you're there?" Adele asked.

Roelynn hunched her shoulders. "Meet all his merchant friends, I suppose, and all the gentry folk he's managed to scrape an acquaintance with. Oh, and be introduced to the queen and her husband."

Adele and I exchanged glances by insufficient moonlight. "And Prince Darian?" I asked.

Roelynn shrugged again. "I don't know! I would think so! Although maybe the queen wants a chance to look me over first and decide if I'm good enough for her son. Or maybe the queen doesn't even know that the prince is destined to marry me, and this is all some grand fiction made up in my father's head. In any case, we're to have tea at the palace one day, and then we're going to some formal dinner there another day. It will be dreadful."

"What are you going to wear?" Adele asked.

Roelynn cheered up a little at that. "Oh, the most beautiful new dresses! I wish you could come by the house and see them. One is a very deep pink with flowers embroidered all along the bodice, and the other is a pale green edged in antique lace. And I have all sorts of new hats and gloves and ribbons to wear when I'm *not* out dining with the queen."

She relapsed into depression. "But it will still be horrid. The whole trip. I don't want to go."

Adele looked thoughtful. "We could—aren't there some herbs you can take that would make you sick? You could swallow them as soon as you got home tonight. You'd have a fever by morning."

I stared at my sister. "*Pretend* to be sick? Of course she can't do that!"

Adele ignored me. Roelynn said, "Yes, I thought of that, but I don't have any such herbs. And I hardly have time tonight to run out and find an apothecary who might stock them."

"Anyway, your father would just make you wait a week or two and then reschedule the trip," I said. "You can't be sick all summer."

"Maybe it won't be so bad," Adele said. "I rather liked the queen when we met her two years ago."

"You'll probably see Melinda," I said. "I think she's in Wodenderry right now."

"I don't want to go to Wodenderry," Roelynn said in a stubborn voice. "I want to stay right here."

There was a strange tone in her voice that caught my attention. "What's so special about right here?" I asked suspiciously.

Roelynn drew her knees up to her chin and loosed a dramatic sigh. "The most wonderful man," she said in a dreamy voice. "Roger. Who would want to have tea with a stupid old prince when Roger is right here in town?"

"Who's Roger? Where did you meet him?" I asked.

"He's—he's tall and he's beautiful and he speaks with this accent—north country, I think it is—and he has the kindest smile. He can ride any horse in the stables. All the dogs love him, and the stable cats, the ones who won't go near anyone, will sidle up to Roger and ask to be fed from his hand."

I raised my eyebrows, because this didn't exactly sound like the description of a wealthy tradesman's son. "Where did you meet him?" I asked again.

"In my father's stables."

"Does he *work* there?" I demanded. "Is he a *groom*?"

"A groom does an honest day's work," she said, ruffling up in anger.

"So he does, and so does a blacksmith, and so does a cobbler, but you're not going to marry any of those," I said briskly. "Even if you don't make a match with Prince Darian, your father would never allow—"

"My father! I am so sick of my father!"

"Well, I don't blame you; he's a very difficult man. But if you think he would ever, *ever,* allow you to carry on any romance with a stable hand—"

"My father can't tell me what to do," she said mutinously.

Adele and I exchanged glances again, because that was patently untrue. Adele spoke up for the first time in quite a few minutes. "Well, certainly you can carry on a romance with this Roger in secret, at least for a while," Adele said in a comforting voice. "Eleda and I will help you."

I almost said *No, I won't,* but I realized that Adele was doing her best to calm Roelynn down, and that this might not be the best time to be blatantly factual. Adele continued, "But I think if you don't do some of what your father says, he'll never let you out of the house again. You'll have to be very careful if you want to keep seeing Roger. You'll have to act like a very dutiful daughter. Then he might not watch you quite so closely."

"Yes—you're right—that's true," Roelynn said, thinking it over. She brightened a little. "So if I go to Wodenderry—"

"And behave very well," Adele interpolated.

"Then, when I come home, I'll have lots and lots of time to spend with Roger," Roelynn said happily. "Yes, I think you're right. I'll have to go to Wodenderry after all."

Since it was already obvious that she would have to go to the royal city, we were both relieved when she reached this conclusion. We spent the next twenty or thirty minutes discussing what sights she might see in the city, what exotic foods she might try, and whether or not she would really get a chance to meet the prince. We might have talked that way for the next two hours, for all I know. But suddenly—right in the middle of a debate about plain satin slippers versus embroidered linen ones—a voice spoke out of the darkness.

"Roelynn? Is that you? It better be, because this is the last place I'm looking."

We all stiffened under the silent shadows of the branches, but none of us felt any apprehension. It was a voice we all recognized, belonging to Roelynn's brother, Micah.

Roelynn glared in his direction, not bothering to stand up. "Yes, it's me," she said in a surly tone. "Why are you looking for me? Go home!"

He pushed his way through the trailing branches, which parted soundlessly beneath his hands. It was hard to see his face in the poor light, but the tone of his voice made it easy to guess its expression: weary and annoyed. That was generally how he looked, in any case, when dealing with his sister. "I'm looking for you because your maid came looking for *me* and said you weren't in your room, and she was going to go wake our father. I said, 'No, don't bother, I know right where she is, let me go find her.' But if I'm not back in another few minutes, I imagine she'll wake the household, and then I suppose you realize what kind of nightmare you're in for when you do bother to wander home."

Roelynn gathered her skirts in her hand and jumped to her feet. Adele and I followed suit. "Yes, indeed! How awful that would be! Let's go home right now."

Micah put his hand on her arm as if to pull her out from under the tree, and then he paused and looked back through the darkness. It was the strangest thing. It was as if he spoke to Adele and none of the rest of us were there. "I expect Roelynn to behave like a little fool, but I thought I could count on you," he said, and now he sounded weary and disappointed. "I would have thought you would have taken care of her for me."

I stared at him in blank astonishment, but Adele seemed entirely composed. "I helped you more than you know," she said. "Don't be angry with me."

Roelynn was tugging on her brother's arm, anxious to get home before her father was alerted. "Good-bye, Adele! Good-bye, Eleda!" she called once she was out from under the encircling branches of the tree. "I'll come find you when I'm back and tell you all about my adventures! And about—about—anyone else I happen to talk to."

Adele laughed. I frowned. Within seconds, Roelynn and Micah were lost to darkness.

I turned on my sister. "What did *that* mean?" I demanded.

She was tranquil. "What?"

I waved a vague hand. "Micah. And you. And how he thought he could count on you. When have you ever even *spoken* to Micah? Why would you?"

She laughed again. "You don't have a very high opinion of him."

"Well, he's so—I mean, all he ever does is bustle about on his father's business. He's always busy. He's always frowning. He always looks worried. I mean, what would I have to say to him? What would anyone?"

"He's a very good brother," she said.

I waited, but she had no more to offer. "That still doesn't make him interesting to talk to."

She shrugged. "Well, it was kind of him to come looking for Roelynn," she said.

"It will be interesting to hear what kind of adventures she has in Wodenderry," I said.

Adele laughed. "Oh, I think it will."

CHAPTER FOUR

oelynn was gone a week. I thought about her every day, but I didn't have much time to wonder how her trip was going. The inn was always very full during the summer travel season. Merendon was a popular destination, for it was a large city built along a harbor, and merchant ships brought all manner of exotic merchandise to the local shops. There were other amenities to be found on the crowded streets—several very fine restaurants, one theater that performed classic dramas, any number of pubs and dress shops and jewelers. Situated as it was on a well-traveled road, near the stables, a celebrated pub and a dozen shops, our inn was considered an excellent place for a traveler to spend a few nights in comfort and style.

Whenever we weren't in school—which we weren't in the summer—Adele and I were pressed into service as maids, laundresses, cooks, clerks, and accountants. My father was more likely to have me count the money, knowing I would be scrupulously exact as I tallied the sums; Adele more often greeted customers when they first arrived, since she was less likely to point out that their boots were muddy and their clothes disarranged from travel. Both of us were reasonably good cooks, though Adele was apt to be creative with a recipe, while I followed all instructions. However, neither of us liked to clean.

I was extremely displeased one day that week to find five guest rooms in need of cleaning and my sister nowhere in sight. I changed the bedsheets and swept the floors and dusted the furniture in all five rooms before Adele returned. I heard her footsteps going past me on the stairs to our third-floor bedroom, so I dropped my broom and hurried up after her. I was just in time to see her closing the bottom drawer on the old dresser located on her side of the room.

"Where have you been?" I asked furiously. "I've been cleaning all afternoon! Five whole rooms!"

She turned quickly, her back against the dresser, and gave me that unreadable smile. "I'll clean tomorrow," she said. "Or I'll do all the dishes tonight. Your choice."

I came a step closer, instantly alert. "Where have you been?" I asked again.

"Out."

"Running errands?"

"Yes."

"For Mother and Father?"

She didn't answer that. She rarely lied to me outright, since I could always tell when she wasn't telling the truth. She just found ways not to tell me what I wanted to know.

"What kinds of errands?" I said. When she was still silent, I added, "You may as well tell me. I can see you've put something in the drawer. I'll just look for it as soon as you're gone. And if you move it somewhere else," I continued, "I'll just keep looking and looking until I find it. You know how good I am at finding things."

She hesitated a moment, then sighed and nodded. She knelt on the floor and I knelt beside her as she pulled out the bottom drawer. There, under her best undergarments, most precious ribbons, and the velvet box containing the painted miniature of Princess Arisande, she had hidden a small cloth bag. I opened my hands, and she shook a few dried leaves into my palms.

"What is this?" I said. "Some kind of herb, I can tell that, but what does it do?"

"It makes you sick," she said. "It gives you a fever and turns your stomach."

I looked at her, astonishment holding my whole body rigid. "Like you were telling Roelynn about the other night?" She nodded. "But why would you want any herbs like this? We don't need to trick her father anymore."

Adele shrugged and carefully picked the withered leaves from my hands. Placing them back into the bag, she set the cloth into the drawer and closed it tight. She didn't stand up, though. "There might come another time," she said softly, "when someone needs to feign illness. When it seems like the right answer to a wrong situation."

"I can't imagine such a time," I said, frowning.

She came to her feet, shrugged again, and smiled. "No. Well, you wouldn't," she said. "Come on. We'd better go down and help Mother with dinner."

~ ✕ ~

The first news we obtained about Roelynn's trip to the city came from Melinda. After the Karros had been gone for a week, the Dream-Maker arrived at our inn, having just left Wodenderry a few days before.

It was some time before we could ask her how Roelynn was faring. First she had to be lionized by all the guests already staying at the Leaf & Berry, who confided in her their deepest desires. Then she had to spend a few hours catching up with all her special friends from Merendon, who seemed to know exactly when to drop by. It was well past ten o'clock at night, and Adele and I were just finishing up the dinner dishes, when Melinda made her way back to the kitchen to visit with the family.

"Well, Hannah, I hardly need to ask you how things are going," the Dream-Maker greeted our mother, who was reviewing her ingredients for tomorrow's meals. "The inn looks prosperous, as always, and your girls are growing up to be the most remarkable young ladies. I would think you're very proud of them."

"Indeed, Bob and I both are, but they're still young enough to make mischief now and then," Mother replied. Mother loved us, but she didn't think we were perfect, as Father did.

"Anything else you'd wish for?"

"Bless me, I can't think of a thing."

"I know what *I'd* wish for, and I know you can grant it," I said, laying down my dish towel and going over to sit beside Melinda at the small family table. Adele sat beside me. "Information about Roelynn! How is she doing in Wodenderry?"

Mother joined us at the table, bringing a pot of tea and four cups. "Yes, do tell us," she urged. "Everyone in Merendon is dying to know."

"Did she meet the prince? Are they going to make a match of it?" I asked.

Melinda rolled her eyes and shook her head. "Indeed, no, she did *not* meet the prince, and Lirabel was quite angry about it, too," the Dream-Maker said. She accepted a cup of tea from my mother's hands and sipped it with such daintiness you would have thought she was in the queen's dining room that very moment. "She was *supposed* to meet him, you understand. Lirabel had arranged two quite ordinary events at the palace during which both Darian and Roelynn could be present. They would get a chance to say hello, and it would not be very awkward, and no one would know that Roelynn had been carted down to Wodenderry for the prince to look her over as if she was some kind of mare he was considering purchasing for the stables—"

"Melinda!" our mother exclaimed.

Melinda sniffed. At times like this, her noble features seemed very pronounced. "Well, that's how it always seems to me, like some kind of breeding competition. You should have seen the men the old king paraded through the palace when he finally decided it was time to marry off Lirabel. And then, wouldn't you know, she ended up marrying a young man she'd known since childhood—noble enough, but hardly a great match—and her father was not at all pleased about it. But you couldn't change her mind, and I didn't blame her. Better pick a man you can be sure loves you than a man who will treat you badly, even if he does come dripping in gold and owning half the shipping rights to the kingdom."

"But what about Roelynn?" Adele said gently, not at all interested in these old tales but more diplomatic than I would have been. "And the prince."

Melinda made a sound that, in a less-refined woman, would have passed as a snort. "The prince. Well, he failed to show up for the tea party that had been arranged first. Lirabel sent the servants up to his room to find him, but he was nowhere in sight. Naturally, quite a hue and cry ensued—because, well, he's the prince. And even though he's got to be sixteen years old by now, I suppose Lirabel always fears that someone could kidnap him or do him some kind of harm."

"And was he kidnapped?" my mother breathed.

I was fairly certain that, if that had been the case, the whole kingdom would be aware of the event by now. So I was not surprised when Melinda shook her head. "No. If you please, he and his cousin had taken it into their heads to go off to the boat races along the southern shore, and they'd left that morning. He'd written his mother a note—he just had managed to make sure it didn't get delivered to her until he'd been gone for half the day."

"His cousin," my mother said. "Now who exactly would that be?"

"Tobin is the son of the king's brother," Melinda said.

"Charming as they come, but completely feckless. Darian never gets into trouble that Tobin's not right by his side, cheering him on. I would think Lirabel would have him barred from the palace, but she loves him too much, and she's the type who holds tight to such family as she has."

"So Tobin and Darian went off to these boat races," Adele prompted. "Wasn't the queen furious?"

Melinda grinned. "Well, she *was*, but it was all her fault to a certain degree. She had been very casual about how she was going to introduce Roelynn—she didn't want Darian to suspect that she was bringing in a prospective bride—so she hadn't really told him that special company was on the way and he had to be present. And apparently he scoots off like this all the time on some lark or another. She could hardly think he'd done it on purpose to spite her."

"I'll bet Karro was mad, though," I said.

Melinda looked unconvinced. "Not as much as you might have expected," she said. "He was really more focused on Lirabel and making sure *she* had a good impression of Roelynn. Because if the queen doesn't like the match, you know, it has no hope of going forward."

"That seems unfair," I remarked. "If the queen herself got to marry for love."

Melinda smiled a little grimly. "It's only fair when it's happening to *you*," she said.

"So did she?" my mother asked. "Did the queen approve of Roelynn?"

"Oh, yes," Melinda said. "Roelynn was on her best behavior."

"Which, you know," I said, "wasn't something we could really count on."

Melinda laughed. "Indeed, no! But she was having the most wonderful time. It's not every day a fourteen-year-old gets to go to the royal palace and have tea with the queen and a dozen other nobles, and have everyone tell her how beautiful she is, and have the queen sit right beside her and talk to her like an important lady. You couldn't blame her if she preened a little. She behaved very prettily, and she looked quite lovely, too, and I could see the queen was quite taken with her. And the next night, at the ball—"

"Was the prince there that night?" I asked.

"No! Still off at the races! Anyway, at the ball, Roelynn was besieged with suitors. She was allowed to dance only a few times—as were all the other young girls who had been permitted to attend—but she looked so adorable and danced so well that everyone who watched her couldn't help smiling. And everyone watched her. Karro was very proud," Melinda added in accents of distaste. "It was almost enough for me to wish Roelynn would suddenly become very vulgar, just to spite him."

Adele and I could not help giggling at that. My mother was more interested in the central point. "But then—it's settled?" Mother asked. "They've made the match?"

Melinda spread her hands in a delicate gesture of uncertainty. "Let us say, the queen seems very well-disposed toward Karro," she said. "But as far as I know, no actual deal was struck. No dower agreements were discussed, no betrothal was set. But as I understand it, the queen will not be actively looking elsewhere for a bride for her son."

"And how did Roelynn react to that?" I wanted to know.

Melinda shook her head. "I don't know. I didn't get any of this from Karro or Roelynn, you understand. I only know what I observed and what Fiona told me afterward." She gave me a sharp look, and then sent an equally pointed one in my sister's direction. "I'd imagine the two of you would have a better idea of how young Roelynn would feel about such an arrangement."

"Who wouldn't want to marry a prince?" our mother said, blue eyes at their widest. "And go live in the palace and know that one day you will be queen?"

"Roelynn isn't like other girls," Adele said with a little smile.

I turned on her in exasperation. "Oh, and I suppose *you'd* want to move to Wodenderry and leave behind everyone you know and try to figure out how to govern the whole kingdom? Not that *I* ever heard you say!"

Melinda was laughing. "Adele isn't like other girls, either."

I felt a little sulky. "The truth is, it would be hard to be bartered off to someone you don't know and leave behind all your familiar life, even if you would be rich and powerful once you got married," I said. "I think it would be very hard to be queen. I suppose it's just as much work as it is glamour, and not much fun on most days."

"And yet Lirabel likes being queen," Melinda said. "And perhaps Roelynn would, too."

Mother sighed. She was quite the romantic, and she

liked to believe that all princes were charming and all young maidens were happy to be swept up into the royal embrace. "Well, I suppose we'll just have to see what happens next," she said. "I for one would very much like to see our little Roelynn marry the prince."

Adele smiled that secretive, infuriating smile. "I don't think we're likely to see anything like that for a while yet."

It was three more days before we received Roelynn's report on the week in Wodenderry, but it basically tallied with Melinda's. She had had a wonderful time; the queen had been most incredibly gracious, and Roelynn had met the handsomest young men who had said the nicest things to her and made her feel quite beautiful. She would like to go spend a season in Wodenderry sometime—attend all the spring fetes, all the summer balls—and become much better acquainted with some of the young men and women she had met.

"And would Roger be going with you during this visit?" Adele asked in an innocent voice.

We were sitting under the chatterleaf tree at the time— well, Adele and I were. Roelynn was swinging in circles around the trunk. At Adele's words, she stopped for a moment and stared. "Who?" she said, and then she blushed a color deep as summer roses. "Oh! *Roger!* Yes, of course, I will always want Roger with me, wherever I go—except, I don't know, perhaps while I'm in the city he might be here in Merendon, minding the house and the business, you know—"

"Oh, for goodness' sake, we all know Roger is just some boy you're flirting with to flout your father," I said crisply. "Tell us more about Wodenderry."

Roelynn scowled for a moment, then allowed herself to forget my last unflattering remark. She recited the rest of her tale, and spoke in great detail about one of the attractive young noblemen who seemed to have spent the majority of his time at the ball telling her how beautiful she was. In fact, this enterprising young man had succeeded in stripping away one of her very expensive gloves so that he could kiss her on her bare wrist, and then he had insisted on keeping the glove as a memento of their encounter.

"He said he will write me every day," she concluded rather dreamily. "I've told him that I can't possibly write back so often, but he said he will live for the one or two letters I manage to get off to him without my father's knowledge."

I couldn't bring myself to look at Adele. I knew she would be smiling. "And I suppose you've brought one of those letters with you today?" my sister asked. "So that we can post it for you?"

"Yes!" Roelynn replied. "I knew you wouldn't mind."

"But what about the prince?" I asked impatiently. Clearly it was pointless to ask again after Roger. "Melinda says you didn't meet him. Did you form any impression of him by what other people said? Did you spend any time thinking what it might be like to live at the palace?"

"Oh—the prince," Roelynn said, waving a hand. "I don't think I have to worry about him for a while yet. He wasn't even *there* during my visit. And the queen scarcely mentioned his name to me. I don't really think she's looking for a bride for her son yet. I could tell my father was very happy about how the visit went, but I don't think they came to any kind of arrangement, or he would have been crowing about it the whole way back in the carriage. And he didn't. He just sat there and looked greedy and pleased."

"So then," Adele said, "tell us more about this handsome young nobleman you met at the ball."

CHAPTER FIVE

It wasn't quite the end of Roger, though. Proximity proved to be more compelling than penmanship, and as the weeks passed and the notes from the young nobleman grew less frequent, Roger began to seem more appealing again to Roelynn. We heard about their assignations only sporadically, for we were back in school and much of our home time was claimed by chores, so we were not often free to meet with Roelynn, even when she could sneak away to look for us. Still, there were a number of whispered conversations late at night under the kirrenberry tree. Thus we learned how Roger had summoned the nerve to hold Roelynn's hand, the courage to kiss her, the temerity to touch her breast through the fine cotton of her dress. I was a little shocked at his forward behavior, but Adele, who was never shocked, merely recommended that Roelynn think very, very carefully before she allowed Roger to take any more liberties.

"You're a smart girl, and you know what can happen if you continue along this way," Adele said. "Do you really want to explain to your father that you're carrying the groom's baby? I don't think you'll like your life much if that's what happens next."

Roelynn was inclined to be indignant. "As if I would do something like that!"

Adele shrugged. "You're wild enough," she said calmly. "Don't do something stupid and then pretend you had no idea what the consequences might be."

Shortly after that exchange, Roelynn stormed away. I gave my sister an appraising glance. "For a moment there, you sounded like a Truth-Teller," I said. "I'm not used to hearing you talk like that."

"Well, it would be hard to keep the secret if she really did become pregnant by him," Adele said dryly. "A little plain-speaking now might save years of future heartaches."

We didn't see Roelynn for more than a week after that conversation, and when we did, it was rather an adventure. We had headed to the dressmaker's shop to pick up our new wool dresses. Autumn was well on the way, and we had outgrown last year's good winter clothes. As we entered the shop, I idly noticed a tall, broad-shouldered groom loitering outside, holding the bridle of a lady's horse. Adele saw him, too—Adele noticed everything—but she put it together more quickly than I did.

"Roelynn must be here," she whispered. And sure enough, Roelynn was the first person we saw as we stepped through the door. Only then did I realize that the handsome groom must be the beloved Roger.

Roelynn seemed to have forgotten her pique. She

greeted us with smiles and dragged us to a counter where the seamstress had laid out lengths of deep sapphire velvet and contrasting ribbons of palest blue. "Don't you think this will be the most beautiful gown ever? I can wear it at Wintermoon."

We admired the color and asked about the cut. Lissette handed me my new dress as well as Adele's, and I carried them both to the back room to try mine on. I had just stripped down to my chemise when I heard a commotion out front and the violent sound of a door being wrenched open.

"Roelynn!" a man shouted, and he sounded as if he could not have summoned more rage if he had been falsely accused of treason. "*Roelynn Karro!* Are you in here? Your horse is out front, so you cannot hide from me. Come face me, you shameful, wicked girl!"

It was her father, of course. I clutched my dress and peered out through the crack of the door to see Karro prowling through the rows of fabric. He was a thickly built man, not particularly tall, with dark hair and swarthy skin and heavily marked features. His head always seemed too large for his frame, and when he was angry, he would swing it from side to side in a manner that made me think of a furious bull. At this particular moment, his face was enraged and his big hands were balled into threatening fists.

Roelynn stepped from around a counter and faced him with absolute coolness. "I'm right here, Father," she said. "I wasn't hiding at all. What's wrong?"

"What's wrong? *What's wrong?*" he bellowed. "You've

gone off with that sly, scheming stable boy, haven't you, after I expressly forbade you to see him again! I'll have him horsewhipped out of Merendon, see if I don't—yes, and I might take the whip to your back, too, you wretched girl! Consorting with gutter trash—acting like the most common woman—I raise you like a queen, I treat you like a princess, and this is how you behave the minute my back is turned—"

Roelynn took the verbal abuse—and what looked like the imminent possibility of physical abuse—completely without flinching. "That's not true, Father," she said, as soon as she had a chance to speak. "I've never consorted with stable boys, as you say. I've never done anything improper. I don't know why you would accuse me of such a thing."

"Don't lie to me!" he roared. "You're sneaking off to the stables at all hours—you think I'm too dull to see you, but I know what you're doing—hugging and kissing men who ought to be fawning on the ground at your feet—"

She spread her hands. "Father! What are you *talking* about? I go to the stables when I want to ride. I'm friendly to all the servants and grooms at the estate—which is more than I can say about you, with the way you yell at everyone for no reason at all! I'm not—I wouldn't—I'm horrified that you would say such things about me! That you would even think—" And here her voice trembled a little and she pulled out a handkerchief to cover her face.

"Are you telling me—do you mean—but you're off with the grooms every day! And that boy out front—yes, that one outside right now, holding your horse!—every time I go looking for you and you're gone, he's gone as well!"

She lifted her tear-streaked face from her handkerchief. "You *told* me," she said with great dignity. "You made me promise I would not go off riding alone. I thought you *wanted* me to bring someone with me when I came into town. All the other grooms are too busy to dance attendance on some young girl, but Roger has always been kind enough to come with me when—"

"Ha! Roger! You call him by his name?"

"I call all of them by their names," she said coldly. "Marcus and Hal and Jim and Roddie. Do *you* know any of their names? Do you ever speak to them at all—except to shout at them when they haven't saddled your horse quickly enough?"

Karro's dark face flushed darker, but he seemed to be losing some of the hot edge of his temper. He wanted to believe her, that was certain. He didn't want to think his only daughter, his jewel, his Roelynn, had been sullying herself with inferior men in the stalls in the back of the barn. "Are you telling me the truth?" he demanded, staring down at her composed face. "Or are you just saying what you think I want to hear?"

Roelynn pointed, and Karro's eyes lifted in the direction she indicated. "Ask Eleda," she said. "She'll tell you the truth."

I had to stuff my fingers in my mouth to keep from crying out. Adele stepped forward tranquilly and gave Karro a little curtsy. Lissette and the two other customers in the store did not move or say a word.

"Good afternoon, sir," Adele said in a soft, demure voice. "What did you want to ask me?"

"Are you the Truth-Teller?" he barked. "Or are you that other one?"

"I'm the Truth-Teller," Adele said.

"Then is my daughter telling me the truth? Has she been spending time with this—this groom when my back is turned? Or is she merely behaving as any good gentle-woman should and making sure she is accompanied any time she rides out?"

Adele managed to make her voice sound both scandalized and respectful. "Spending time with a groom, sir? Roelynn? Oh, no. Absolutely not. Roelynn has never done anything improper, with a groom or with anybody."

"Hmph. Well. All right. If you say so," Karro said, appeased and mollified. He patted Roelynn awkwardly on the back and spoke in a gruff voice. "I'm sorry I accused you, then. But you're such a tricky thing. No one can keep track of you."

"I don't try to be difficult, Father," Roelynn said, sounding wounded.

"No. I'm sure you don't. It's just that you—but there. We've said enough about this. What do you say to a little treat, hey? Do you see some pretty ribbons you like? A yard of lace, maybe? You pick out something you want, and I'll buy it for you. Don't be angry with your old bear of a father. I just want what's best for you."

"I know you do, Father," she said in a quiet voice. "And you don't have to buy me presents."

"Of course I do! My only daughter! I'll buy you every-thing in the whole shop if you want it."

"Well, then—" she said and looked around. "There was this beautiful flowered silk. I saw it when I came in—"

Karro wasn't much interested in shopping, it turned out. He merely motioned Lissette over and stuffed a few coins in her hand, with the admonition to "let me know if this doesn't cover it." Then, with his characteristic heavy step, he stalked back to the door and out onto the street. I couldn't see well enough to notice if he exchanged a few sharp words with the offending groom or not.

I couldn't scramble into my clothes fast enough. "Roelynn!" I squealed, running back out to the front of the shop and grabbing her hands. "How frightening! What a ter-rifying man your father is! But you were so calm!" I turned to look at my sister. "And you—"

Adele pursed her lips and nodded at me, clearly enjoin-ing silence. I abruptly shut my mouth. All her good work would go undone if the other women in the shop realized that the wrong twin had proclaimed Roelynn's innocence to her father.

"You were very brave," I ended lamely.

"I am only glad we were able to reassure him," Adele said. "But Roelynn—and forgive me, but I must speak the truth—I think it is time your behavior was more circum-spect. I know, I know, you have done nothing wrong, but perhaps you should be more careful of the impression you give your father. You don't want to give him additional rea-sons to suspect your actions. You would hardly want to see such an unpleasant scene reenacted in a more public place."

"No, you are quite right," Roelynn said, sounding both more subdued and more sincere than I heard her in quite some time. "I must be better. I *will* be better. I do not want such a thing to happen ever again."

And that really was the end of Roger. But it was hardly the end of Roelynn's illicit romances with unsuitable men. But then, none of us had really believed it would be.

As it turned out, Roelynn did have a chance to wear the blue velvet gown over Wintermoon. Most folk celebrated the cold, year-end holiday with traditional bonfires and small family gatherings, but Karro did things up in a much grander style. So he planned a lavish dinner party for Wintermoon night and invited the richest families from Merendon and the neighboring towns.

Adele and I were not on this list, of course, but we were intimately informed of all the details of the event as they were finalized, because Roelynn came by every day or two to fill us in. We knew who had accepted the invitation, who had declined, what the menu would include, and how the house would be decorated. In fact, we helped gather some of the greenery for those decorations on a frosty expedition one winter afternoon. Roelynn and a stablehand (not Roger) came by in a well-sprung cart to pick up Adele and me in front of the inn, and we set out for the wooded acres that could be found a few miles outside the city limits. The three of us sat in the back under a heavy quilt and chatted while the driver made his way down the frozen, rutted lanes to the outskirts of the forest.

"I can't take the cart no farther," the driver announced at length. "I'll sit here and make a fire, and you girls run in and chop down what you like."

We scrambled out of the cart and chased each other into the woods. We really didn't have much to hunt for, since our father had gathered most of the spruce ropes and oak branches that would be used to weave the Wintermoon wreath for the inn, while servants had performed the same function for the Karro household. But everyone wanted to add something special to a Wintermoon wreath—a sprig of holly, a spray of rowan, a raven's feather, a river stone. Every year since we'd been seven or eight, Adele and Roelynn and I had searched for truelove vines; every year we had failed to find them. We continued to look for those and other treasures.

According to tradition, every household designed its own Wintermoon wreath and displayed it for a week or two during midwinter. The basic form of the wreath would be braided from evergreen and oak, and then it would be decorated with all manner of additional items, all of them representing something—holly for joy, a cornstalk for plenty. Adele and I usually pulled a few twigs from the kirrenberry and chatterleaf trees and wound them around the wreath, signifying our commitment to our professions. Our mother always attached a few dried plums and apricots, to represent a full pantry and a well-stocked cook pot. Father usually went to Lissette's shop to buy a length of gold thread to tie everything together—and to call down riches on our home.

Roelynn chose something different every year to bind into her father's wreath—bird feathers (for lightheartedness), dried roses (for love), once even a snakeskin that we had found abandoned in the woods. Adele and I had refused to touch it, but Roelynn had snatched it up with a cry of pleasure.

"What is *that* supposed to represent?" I had said rather sharply.

"I don't know. A new skin. A new life. Casting off old things," she had said.

"What do you want to leave behind?" Adele had inquired.

Roelynn had laughed. "I'll know when it's gone."

But she had never told us what that might have been.

This year we moved rather quickly through the spindly upraised arms of the winter-bare trees. It was cold, and the wind had a bitter edge to it, and none of us wanted to stay out for long. As always, we looked for the heart-shaped leaves of truelove, but we couldn't find the vines anywhere. The woods offered many other interesting finds, though— ropes of ivy, still blood red with autumn's coloring; wing feathers from half-a-dozen birds; the stems of dried wildflowers; a tiny fossilized claw from what might have been a squirrel or mouse. Roelynn and I squealed and turned away, but Adele picked it up and seemed to like it.

"Strength," she decided, and added it to her bag of trophies.

Down by the stream that was so small it sometimes

meandered off to nothing during droughts, we found a long, swooping red feather. Roelynn ran forward with a little cry and snatched it up.

"From the tail of a tasselback," she exclaimed. "Isn't it beautiful?"

Adele came forward to look. The quilled scarlet edges were decorated with random streaks of black and gray. "That's the bird in the royal crest," Adele said. "It's painted on all the coaches and embroidered in all the livery."

"I know," said Roelynn. "The royal bird. I'll have to put this in my wreath."

"What for?" I asked rather tartly.

Roelynn laughed and spun around in a circle, holding the bright feather like a candle under her chin. Just like a candle, it seemed to illuminate her face with its own particular colors and characteristics. "For saying farewell to royalty," she said. "I'll tie this feather to my father's wreath, and then when we throw it in the bonfire, the feather will burn away, and I'll be forever free of any fear that my father will marry me off to the prince."

"That's not usually how the Wintermoon wreath is supposed to work," Adele said in a dry voice. "What you bind into the wreath is what you want to draw your way."

"Or what you want to see go up in smoke and drift away," Roelynn said firmly. "What really matters is your intention as you attach the object to the greenery."

"So I suppose you'll tell your father why you're sewing a tasselback feather into his Wintermoon wreath?" I said.

Roelynn looked thoughtful. "No. I'll tell him—what you

said. That it's a way to bring me the attention of the prince."

"He'll be glad to hear that, I imagine," I said. "He'll have you back in Wodenderry before the bonfire's even cold."

"Hmmm. You're right," Roelynn said. "Well, I just won't mention the feather to him at all. Or I'll just tell him—that I found it in the woods. That I don't know what it represents. I just thought it was pretty."

"Micah will know what it is," Adele said. "Won't he say something?"

Roelynn made a small sound of exasperation. "Micah! You're right. Well, then I'll just—I know! I'll bind it into *your* Wintermoon wreath, and then I'll come down to the inn at midnight and be there when you throw it into the fire."

She often crept away from her house during her father's festivities and came to join us at the Leaf & Berry, so this seemed like a fairly workable plan. Adele held out her hand, and Roelynn rather reluctantly laid the feather on her palm.

"It seems almost too pretty to burn," Adele remarked. "Are you sure that's what you want to do?"

Roelynn took it back. "I'm sure. I'm very glad I found it."

The wind swooped low through the trees, and I shivered where I stood. "I'm cold," I said. "Let's go home."

We made our way out of the forest, back to the road, and we found that Karro's admirable groom had indeed built a fire while we were gone. He had also made us hot chocolate, which we gratefully drank, and warmed up a few bricks in the small bright flames. So we were almost warm and definitely happy as we headed back to town, our packs full of treasures and our minds full of Wintermoon dreams.

CHAPTER SIX

intermoon is the time for old troubles to die and new hopes to rise. It is a time when the whole world sleeps under a still, white patina of frost till it wakes to the fresh dawn of spring. Wintermoon is the time to take stock, look forward, make plans, shrug off the past. It is my very favorite time of year.

The inn was always very crowded the few days before and after Wintermoon, as people stayed for the night while journeying to and from the homes of their loved ones. But the day of Wintermoon itself, there was hardly ever anyone staying with us. Everyone wanted to be with their families. This was not a holiday you would choose to spend with strangers.

Even so, there were sometimes one or two travelers staying overnight at Wintermoon—usually people visiting Merendon friends whose houses were already overfull. Now and then there would be lonely old widowers or bony spinsters who had nowhere else to spend the holiday, and who checked in at the Leaf & Berry, pretending they were late for their own joyous gatherings. Once we had an entire family staying with us—father, mother, six children—unable to complete their journey because the mother had gone into early labor with her seventh child. The baby was born at midnight on Wintermoon, a most mystical time of year. The father carried the infant down to the bonfire and, with his other six children, tossed pinecones and holly berries into the flames. Plenty and joy. I thought the omens could not have been more propitious.

This year, the Dream-Maker was our only guest, and a most welcome one she was. She had been invited to Karro's dinner party, but I didn't think she had come to Merendon specifically to attend it. She just liked to settle into some big town over the winter holidays so that large numbers of people could brush past her during the course of the day and have some hope that their dreams might come true in the following year. It was easier to believe in magic on Wintermoon; it was easier to think that your secret desires might finally be fulfilled sometime in the coming months.

"Well, Hannah, any particular dreams in your life these days?" Melinda greeted our mother as she always did.

Our mother, as always, shook her head. "I've got everything I could ever wish for."

Melinda glanced at Adele, who was taking her coat, and me, as I bent to pick up her luggage. "What about you girls?" she asked. "You're old enough to have some dreams and wishes."

"Old enough to know better than to talk about them aloud," Adele said with a laugh.

"Old enough to know which ones are never going to come true, even with years' worth of wishing," I added.

Melinda's perfect eyebrows rose. "Old enough to be true cynics," she said. "Give yourselves time. One day you'll have dreams that are bigger than you are."

Adele and I helped get her settled in her room, then carried up hot water so she could clean and dress for the party. When she came downstairs, attired in a lovely rose-pink gown that made her white hair seem to glow, we exclaimed over her elegance and beauty.

"Well, I thought if it was good enough for dinner at the palace, it was good enough for dinner at Karro's," Melinda said, pulling on long, fine gloves. "I don't plan to stay late, though. I'd rather celebrate the bonfire here. When will you be throwing your wreath into the flames?"

"We'll wait till you get back," promised my father, who was ready to drive her to Karro's in our little gig. "We'll be up all night, of course. We don't need to burn it at midnight."

"Goodness! I hope I'm back before then."

"Should I send Bob to fetch you?" my mother asked.

Melinda grinned rather wickedly. "No. I'll make Karro find someone who wants a favor. I would think any number of people would be happy to drive the Dream-Maker anywhere she wishes on Wintermoon night."

We all laughed, and the two of them left. Mother and Adele and I busied ourselves in the kitchen, cooking all our favorite foods and relishing the simplicity of making a meal for four instead of for the ten or twenty who might ordinarily be staying at the inn. After Father returned and we'd all eaten, Mother cleaned the kitchen while Father and Adele and I went outside to start the fire.

By this time it was completely dark and quite cold. Father had stacked cords and cords of wood in a cleared space behind the inn—an area between the toolshed and the vegetable garden. It was far enough from the two trees to be certain no stray sparks would catch the bare limbs on fire, but close enough to the house to allow us to run back inside if we got too chilly. Father carefully built the piles of kindling and put the bigger logs on top, then started the fire with a coal brought from the kitchen. So small, at first—a flicker, a tendril of yellow, a fugitive lick of untamed gold—and then a fire, and then a blaze, and then, as more logs were added, a true inferno. Its heat sent us scampering back toward the house until cold beat us back toward the fire's hungry embrace. My face and my hands were hot enough to seem fevered, but my feet were numb against the icy winter ground.

"That's pretty, that is," my father said, admiring the leaping, twisting flames. "That'll last all night."

I turned to view what I could of the neighboring buildings. A few of the merchants situated nearby had houses in other parts of town, but most of them lived in quarters above their businesses. So up and down our street I could see an almost unbroken string of similar fires, scarlet and saffron against the velvet night. Once I had climbed to the roof of the inn to look out over the Wintermoon landscape, and counted nearly fifty separate bonfires before I lost track.

Father yawned hugely. It was only eight or nine o'clock, and we would be up till dawn—and the next day's customers would probably start arriving by noon. "I think I'll go in and sleep for a bit," he said. "Will you girls keep the fire going?" We gave quick assents. "Wake me up when Melinda gets back," he said, "and we'll throw the wreath in."

Father went in, and Mother never came out—but that, too, was a tradition on Wintermoon Eve, at least at our house. The two of them napped together, or perhaps took a couple of hours to love each other, while Adele and I stayed outside and watched the fire. I tended to be cautious with the logs, putting on a fresh one only when the blaze looked as if it might die down; Adele would add them with abandon, piling on three, five, six new ones while there was plenty of fuel still on the fire. It didn't matter. There was always more wood than we needed to see us through the coldest night.

Shortly before midnight, I was kneeling by the fire when I saw Adele turn her head and seem to listen to the wind. "Someone's coming," she said, though it was hard to hear much through the crackling of the wood. Sure enough, a few minutes later, I caught the clop of shod hooves on the cobblestoned road—and a few minutes after that, I heard the mixed sounds of a man's voice and women's laughter.

"Melinda's back," I said, coming to my feet. "It sounds like Roelynn is with her."

"And Micah," Adele said. "He must have driven them here."

I wouldn't have recognized Micah's low-pitched voice late at night when I was thinking about other things, but that was Adele for you. She never overlooked anything.

Sure enough, the three shadowy figures coming around the corner of the inn stepped into the firelight and revealed themselves to be Roelynn, Micah, and Melinda.

"How was the dinner?" I asked. "Was it grand?"

"Very elegant," Melinda said. "The food was excellent, and all the guests were deeply impressed. Quite a success, I would say."

"It was so *very* dull!" Roelynn gave as her own critique. "But everyone complimented me on my gown. And the food *was* really good. I'm sure my father will want to have another dinner next year—and the next year and the next."

Adele looked at Micah, whose thin face seemed even thinner and more sober by firelight. "And you?" she asked. "What did you think?"

"Oh, well, Micah got to sit by all the pretty girls and act all lord of the manor," his sister answered for him. "I thought Allea Marsters was going to forget all decorum and sit right in his lap. He didn't seem to mind, though. She was wearing a most—revealing—gown. And my father thought *I* was showing too much skin!"

"Allea was behaving quite properly, I thought," Micah said stiffly. "She seems like a very pleasant young lady. She showed more decorum than you did, at any rate."

Roelynn tossed her head. I looked at Micah in some surprise. "Really? The girls were flirting with you? The young women from Lowford and Movington, I suppose?"

"Of course they were," Roelynn said, answering for him again. "Micah's quite a catch, you know. I'll inherit some of

Father's money, but Micah will inherit the business. He'll be a very rich man, and you'd better believe all the girls know it. He might be quiet and a little dull, but that doesn't matter much in a husband if he's got a lot of money."

"I don't want to marry a girl who wants to marry me for my money," Micah said.

Melinda looked over at him with a little smile. The firelight made her look like some old-fashioned full-length portrait of a noblewoman from a bygone age, all styled white hair and poised elegance. "And what *do* you want?" Melinda asked him. "What are the dreams of Micah Karro?"

Micah looked uncomfortable to be asked that question in front of his sister and her friends. "I want what anyone wants," he said in a low voice. "I just want a good life."

"I think you'll have to be more specific than that," the Dream-Maker replied.

Before Micah could respond, the back door opened, and my father called out, "Is that Melinda? Are you back? Hannah, Melinda's here. I'll go fetch the wreath."

In a few minutes, he came out, holding the huge circle of decorated greenery. It was so large that he could scarcely support it, and Micah hurried over to help him carry it to the fire. Kind, I thought, a little surprised. Mother was right behind them, wrapped in a heavy shawl that she'd thrown over her head to keep her ears warm.

"Brrr! I don't remember a Wintermoon so cold for ages," Mother commented as she joined us before the fire.

"Are we all ready?" my father asked, casting a quick

look around. "Anything else you want to tie to the wreath? Roelynn? Micah? You girls?"

"My feather's already on there," Roelynn said.

"It's not my wreath," Micah said.

My father grinned at him. "Well, you can wish on any wreath you like, can't you? Here at the inn, at least, everyone's welcome to join their wishes to ours."

"Did you tie your stone to Father's wreath?" Roelynn asked him.

He shook his head. I thought he looked a little embarrassed. "I didn't feel like explaining it to him."

"What stone?" my mother asked.

He turned his head courteously to address her. "I was out at the harbor one day, overseeing one of my father's ships. And I found a white stone, worn almost flat, with a hole in the middle. When I picked it up, the sea captain told me it was a lucky symbol—a whole circle, beginning and end, the sign of a full and complete life. I thought it might be something to throw into the Wintermoon fire."

My father, who had been sharing the weight of the wreath with Micah this whole time, now pulled it from Micah's hands and eased it down to rest on the ground. "Well, tie it on, then! Do you have it with you?"

Micah nodded and pulled the stone out of his pocket. I couldn't see much, but it looked quite ordinary to me. "I don't have anything I can use to bind it to the wreath, though."

Without saying a word, Adele pulled a white ribbon from

her hair and handed it to him. Micah thanked her gravely and, while we all watched, tied the stone to the wreath.

"There now," my father said, sounding satisfied. He always loved it when people added personal items to the Wintermoon greenery. "Is that it? Any more last-minute contributions? No? Micah, if you would—"

The two men worked together to lift the ring of greenery to shoulder height. All the women, fearing shooting sparks, took a few paces backward. Micah and my father heaved the wreath into the fire and it crashed with a satisfying shower of fire onto the steepled logs. The scent of fire was suddenly haunted by the sharp tang of spruce.

"That's a good Wintermoon bonfire," Melinda said in approval.

"We'll let that burn a little, then we'll add some more fuel," Father said.

"Who'd like some hot chocolate?" Mother asked. "I've got the kettle on in the kitchen."

Roelynn said yes, but Micah frowned her down. "My sister and I have to be getting back," he said. "We left my father with a houseful of guests. We were only supposed to be gone long enough to deliver the Dream-Maker."

"You can stay for hot chocolate, surely," Mother said.

But Micah was adamant. While he was making his earnest good-byes to my parents, Roelynn looked at Adele and me, her face a study of irritation and resignation, but she followed him meekly enough when he led her back to the Karro carriage. The rest of us enjoyed Mother's hot chocolate and stood around the fire for another hour or so.

Melinda went in first, Adele and I a little later. As always, my mother and father got out a blanket and sat together before the fire until dawn. At least, I assume they did—I was sound asleep.

In the morning, rather late, I woke while Adele was still sleeping. Dressing quietly, I put on shoes and a shawl and crept downstairs. Out the back door, out to the fire, to sift through the cinders and see if anything remained. If you tied coins or glass or metal scraps to the wreath, often they would remain, charred but whole, after the bonfire burned down. It was considered lucky to retrieve such items, for they were imbued with Wintermoon magic and had tremendous power during the coming year. Usually Adele and I came down together to search through the coals and see what the ritual had left behind, but she had looked to be deeply asleep, and I was too impatient to wait.

This year, I couldn't find anything of interest. Everything we had attached to the wreath appeared to have been flammable—all our vines, all our wildflower stalks, even Roelynn's feather. I searched for nearly half an hour and never found anything to keep.

Just as I had decided to give up, my mother's voice called from the back door. "Eleda! Time for breakfast! Go wake up your sister and come eat!" I ran inside, snatched a biscuit from the stove, and ate it as I bounded upstairs. Adele was still sleeping in our room, lying on her side, her hands curled up on the pillow beside her cheek.

I came a few steps nearer and bent over, studying her fingers. They were faintly streaked with soot; a line of black showed under her right thumbnail. For a moment, I could not imagine what the fastidious Adele could have been doing to get her hands dirty in the middle of the night. And then I realized: She must have woken up earlier than I did, sometime after our parents had gone to bed, and crept downstairs without me to inspect the remains of the bonfire.

She had found something, too. The state of her hands attested to that. I stared at her another few minutes, wondering what treasure had been so important to her that she had lain awake all night to be sure she would be the first one to rise and go through the coals of the Wintermoon fire so she could find it and keep it for herself.

CHAPTER SEVEN

pring came; the world was sweetly green; Adele and Roelynn and I all turned fifteen. Melinda came to town right before the spring planting. The day after she left, a local farmer found a cache of old gold buried in his fields and instantly became the second richest man in Merendon. Joe Muller, who had indeed bought the Windermere property a couple of years ago, purchased additional land and began raising racing horses. He was soon the third richest. Roelynn's father took her to Wodenderry for another week of splendor, and she came back even more infatuated with the city and, this time, with a young guardsman who served the queen.

Again, the prince had been scheduled to be there for this visit, but he and his cousin Tobin had taken off for the southern parts the night before Roelynn arrived. The reason was unclear but seemed to have something to do with attending the hasty wedding of a rapscallion friend.

This was the year I learned about the perils of falling in love, although danger of any sort was far from my mind when I first met Edgar. He came with one of the acting troupes that traveled throughout the kingdom, putting on plays in small towns and performing private productions for the very wealthy. His troupe—as well as companies of mimes, jugglers, peddlers, clowns, and singers—had come for the Summermoon festival that was the highlight of the hot season. In fact, Edgar and his friends had arrived in the city three weeks before the festival itself to get themselves settled into their quarters, build a makeshift stage on the edge of town, practice their lines, and market their plays. They gave comedic performances three times a week, put on a drama once a week, and promised that the play they planned for Summermoon would be extraordinary.

Edgar would enact the romantic lead in this production. Of course he would—he was a beautiful young man. He was not particularly tall, but he was well built, with wide shoulders and a muscled physique. He had dark blond hair that fell most winsomely across his forehead, and his face was sculpted into the shape of perfect masculine beauty. He had a smile that was irresistible and an easy way with all kinds of women—from little girls to dowdy old ladies, all agog to meet a true actor. If I believed in magic, I would say he cast a spell of enchantment over any woman he met. Certainly he cast a spell over me.

I was running errands for my mother when I first came across Edgar. He was standing in the dressmaker's shop, glancing between four bolts of similar fabric, and looking full of a comical panic. Lissette herself had no time to spare for him—though I'm sure she wanted to give him all her

attention—because the shop was full of women ordering fin-
ery for the Summermoon events. The stranger's expression
of rueful helplessness made me smile, and I approached him
rather boldly.

"You look lost," I said. "Do you need some help?"

He turned to look at me, and I was instantly lost in the
dazzle of his smile. "Oh, I so very much need help," he said
gratefully. "I was sent here to buy ten yards of striped blue
cloth, which sounded easy enough, but now I see that there
are dozens of choices that seem to answer that very description, and I haven't the slightest idea what to choose."

His voice was extremely attractive—low-pitched and
lilting, with a trace of an accent I could not place. He
might have been from foreign parts, or just some corner of
the kingdom that I didn't know well. "Well, it depends on
what you want the fabric for," I said. "Clothes? Curtains?
Upholstery? Though none of these are really suitable for
upholstery, I have to say."

"Clothes," he said. "A lady's gown and a man's waistcoat."

I raised my eyebrows, because it would seem a bit odd
for a man and woman to go about dressed in matching
garments, but I didn't say anything. "And will these be
everyday clothes that will see a great deal of wear, or will
they be special-day clothes that will be brought out only
once a year? Because *this* fabric, though it costs more and
is a little prettier in finish, is not nearly so sturdy as *this*
fabric and will not do at all if you're going to expect it to
stand up to much use."

He smiled again. "I suppose you'd call it everyday wear. We'll be dressing up in these outfits every time we perform *Killed by a Kiss*, which is two or three times a week—and we're hard on our clothes, we are."

"Every time you perform—why, then, you're with one of the acting troupes that's come to town?" I asked. I could tell I sounded excited as a little girl. But really, what could be more glamorous than an actor's life? I would be a dreadful actress, of course; I couldn't even speak a quick lie, let alone spend a couple of *hours* pretending to be someone I wasn't. But I had a secret love for theater.

The fair young man swept me a very elegant bow. "Indeed I am. Edgar Beauman at your service, of the Harst and Hope Regional Traveling Company. Though you could just as truthfully call me Dirk Daggerhand or Handsome Joe Hamilton and half-a-dozen other names I could give you."

"But those are only parts you play," I said, "and not really you."

He laughed. "I play them so often sometimes I think I am more Dirk than Edgar."

"And you have come to town for Summermoon?"

"Yes, this is our third or fourth trip to Merendon. It's our favorite city to play! Just the right size—big enough to fill the house every night, but not so big you get lost when you try to find your favorite shops from last year. And I've always found the people most friendly." He grinned.

I grinned back, something I rarely did. It was so obvious he meant *I find the women most friendly.* "What play will you be performing over Summermoon?" I asked.

"I just told you—*Killed by a Kiss*. It's a romance and a mystery, and there's a great bit with sword fighting right in the middle. You'll have to come see it."

"Oh—I wish I could," I said. "But I'm usually working on Summermoon."

"Working?" He glanced around the dress shop, which was getting more crowded by the minute. More than one woman had cast curious and envious glances my way while I stood there chatting with Edgar Beauman, and I must confess that this made me feel extraordinarily pleased with myself. The handsomest man who had ever been seen in Merendon, and he was talking to *me*. "Are you one of the seamstresses here, then?"

"Oh, no! My parents own the Leaf and Berry Inn down the street. Summermoon is one of our busiest times of the year, because so many people come to town for the festival. I'd never be able to get away to see a play."

"Well, but, we'll be putting on performances for the next three weeks," he said in a wheedling tone of voice. "Couldn't you get away one night, at least? You could see *Rebecca's Revenge* or *The Lost Kingdom*—though I wouldn't recommend that one, to be honest—or *The Devil of a Time*. That one's fun, and we're putting it on tomorrow night. I'll give you a free ticket if you say you'll come."

I laughed. He was probably handing out free tickets all over town—I understood that was a very common ploy entertainers used to swell their audiences—but it was still most flattering to be coaxed. "I might be able to come tomorrow night," I conceded, "but I'd have to have two tickets. My parents would never let me go to such a thing alone at night."

He promptly presented me with two slips of paper, hand-printed with tomorrow's date and the title of the play. "Who will you bring with you?" he asked. "Your brother? Your beau? Maybe I don't want you to come after all if you're going to bring your beau." He pretended to try to snatch the tickets back.

I quickly put my hands behind my back, the tickets safe in my fingers. "No, I'll bring my twin sister. I'll bet you won't know which is which."

He took a moment to study my face, smiling as if the task was a pleasurable one. "I bet I will. Does she look so much like you?"

"Most people can't tell us apart. Though there are distinguishing characteristics."

He held up a hand. "Don't tell me! I want to prove to you that I know who you are. Though I—" He paused, and suddenly that comical expression crossed his face. "Though I don't know what your name is, precisely."

I could not help laughing at that. "Eleda," I said.

"And your sister's name?"

"Adele."

He thought about that a moment. "Eleda. Adele," he said. "Am I right in guessing that your names are the same, except that one is the other backward?"

I caught my breath. No one had ever realized this before until one of us had pointed it out. How could he be so sensitive, so attuned to every detail? "Yes," I said. "We mirror each other exactly."

"Then I must suppose she is as pretty as you are, though I find it hard to believe," he said.

"I must suppose you say things like that to every woman you have a conversation with."

He put his hands to his chest as if to feel for the jeweled hilt of a dagger. "Stabbed through the heart!" he exclaimed. "You scarcely know me, and already you accuse me of inconstancy."

I was enjoying myself hugely. "I am a very truthful girl," I said demurely. "And the truth is, you seem to me to be an unregenerate flirt."

"Ah, well, every man must employ his own particular talents," Edgar said in a philosophical voice. "A blacksmith uses his strength—a barrister uses his intellect. I'm an actor, and all I have is charm. You can't fault me for using it."

"Not at all," I said politely. "In fact, I compliment you on your skill."

He burst out laughing. "You *are* a funny one!" he said, but he seemed delighted, not offended, so I smiled. "No girl has ever talked to me that way before."

My smile went slightly awry here. "Yes, well, I'm often accused of being—blunt."

"But I like it," he insisted. "You're an original. So will you come to the play tomorrow?"

"I will try very, very hard."

He turned back to survey the selection of fabric before

him. "And will you tell me which of these materials I should buy? Because I've already forgotten what you recommended."

I gestured at the bolt I considered the best bargain. "You might ask Lissette if she'll give you a better price if you buy twice as much as you planned," I said. "Sometimes she'll give a quantity discount—and if you're going to wear those clothes so often, you might need to replace them quicker than you think."

"Excellent advice!" he said. "I can't tell you how glad I am that I ran into you."

I smiled. "I am happy to have pleased you."

He laughed at that. "Oh, you please me very much, Eleda the innkeeper's daughter. And I'll see you tomorrow night? You promise?"

I never made promises I wasn't sure I could keep. "I'll try," I said again. "Thank you for the tickets."

He held out his hand, and for a moment I thought he wanted the tickets back. But then I realized he wanted to shake my hand to seal the bargain. It was probably a bit too familiar on such short acquaintance, but we were in a public place, and he was a delightful man, and I rather wanted to discover what it would feel like to touch him. So I put my hand in his, and he bent down and kissed my knuckles.

Excitement ran like a ribbon of fire from my fingers straight to my heart.

I snatched my hand back. "*Mister* Beauman!"

He was laughing as he straightened up. "*Miss* Eleda!"

I was confused and blushing, but I have to say I was not at all upset. On the contrary. But there were consequences to such behavior. I knew that more than one woman, shopping in the store, had witnessed the playful gesture and would be reporting it to my mother before the hour was much older. "I have to go home now," I said, backing away from him and edging toward the door. "Good luck with the rest of your purchases."

"Thank you for all your help. I'll see you tomorrow night," he said, raising his voice as I made it to the threshold so that absolutely everyone in the shop could hear what he said.

"You're welcome," I said, and fled out the door. My cheeks were still hot with embarrassment and excitement when I reached home.

Adele was most willing to accompany me to *Devil of a Time*, and my mother merely laughed when I breezily related to her the encounter in the dress shop. "Actors," she said complacently. "They behave most scandalously. I was courted by an actor once."

Adele and I both stared at her with complete astonishment. "You *were*?" Adele said faintly. It was one of the few times in my life I could remember that Adele didn't claim she had always known something that heretofore had never been whispered aloud by anyone.

"Oh, it was before I met your father, of course," Mother said. She touched a hand to her cheek and smiled. For a moment, she looked exactly the way Adele did when she was contemplating some sweet secret. "Such a romantic boy. And utterly *striking*. But so unsteady. Hardly to be relied upon. Nothing like your father." She smiled again and then shook her head a little as if to shake free of strong memories. "Well! That was a long time ago."

Adele turned to look at me, her blue and green eyes at their widest. "I suppose this actor of yours is unsteady and unreliable as well," she said.

I shrugged a little pettishly. "Not that it matters. I'll probably never even speak to him again. I'd just like to go to this play, is all."

"Yes," Adele said, "I'd love to go."

Since our parents didn't object, and we worked hard during the next afternoon to get our day's chores done, Adele and I actually did attend *Devil of a Time* the following night. We wore the dresses that we had commissioned last year for the Summermoon festival—fine enough for an outdoor summer play, but no longer the most elegant outfits in our wardrobes—and walked the two miles to the edge of town, where the theater had been set up. The streets of Merendon, in winter so empty at this time of day, were still full of tourists and townspeople enjoying the late sunshine and fine weather. We knew at least a third of the people who joined us in the rather rickety stands built three-quarters of the way around the makeshift stage. We had arrived early, so we secured excellent seats—in the center of the fourth row. We would be able to see everything.

And it was a wonderful play. Oh, it was silly and melodramatic and every once in a while the actors would deliver a particularly ridiculous line. At that point, they would turn to glance at the audience as if to say, "It is not my fault this is such a nonsensical play!" which only made everyone in the audience laugh even harder. The heroine was so pretty and so engaging that I would have hated her for standing up there onstage, flirting with Edgar (the hero), except that her quick asides to the audience made it clear that she thought he was a big overgrown boy who was not nearly as interesting as most of the men in the stands probably were. Edgar himself, even when he was down on his knees proclaiming undying love to her, managed to make it seem as if he was laughing at his own lines without diminishing the power of the play in the least. More than once, when he was supposed to be making some impassioned speech to his ladylove, his eyes were scanning the crowd, and it was clear he was telling the audience, not the actress, who really owned his heart.

All in all, a most impressive performance.

He saw me the very first time he came onstage. I know, because even while he spoke his part, his gaze was restlessly roving over the stands, searching for someone. He stopped looking when he saw me. A small smile touched his mouth, even though his character was not, at that particular moment, supposed to be happy; his hand went surreptitiously to his heart. As soon as his speech was over and the other actors were engaged in a long-winded argument, his eyes came back to me; the smile returned. And then he glanced away from me, to Adele, and back to me. The smile widened. I felt myself blushing in the incomplete darkness of the stands.

Perhaps it was no wonder that I thought the play

the most marvelous entertainment I had ever seen.

It lasted nearly three hours and was still too short. The minute it ended and the ill-rigged curtain came clumsily down, the crowd erupted into applause. "That was certainly enjoyable!" Adele called into my ear as we rose to our feet, clapping and stamping along with everyone. "And how beautiful your young man is!"

"He's not my young man!" I called back.

She laughed. "He certainly seemed most enamored of you!"

"Can we wait a little bit?" I asked. "To see if the actors come out? I'd like to tell him how marvelous I thought his performance was."

"I wouldn't even dream of leaving without meeting him," she said, sounding amused.

Many of the rest of the audience members had the same idea, but the stands had almost emptied by the time the actors came ducking out from under the curtain. The heroine was instantly surrounded by a coterie of adoring young men; no wonder she had not seemed so moved by Edgar's scripted professions of love. Even the older actors, who had played outrageous characters, had their share of supporters. I was willing to bet that all the young women who had lingered in the stands had done so with the sole purpose of expressing their admiration to Edgar . . . but none of them got a chance. He swept aside the curtain, vaulted over the edge of the stage, and hopped up the first two sets of steps. He came to a halt one row below us.

"Eleda," he said, taking my hand and bowing over it

very low. He had not even seemed to hesitate for a moment before deciding if I was the correct twin. "I'm so happy you're here tonight! What did you think of the play?"

"I thought it was very silly and very fun," I said, laughing and pulling my hand away. "You make the most convincing hero. I imagine you have quite a following in the towns you play at on a regular basis."

"That may be," he said. "But more and more I find myself wishing to play for a smaller and smaller audience—the same one every night—and a most faithful audience at that."

Adele laughed, reminding me of her existence. I said, "Edgar, let me introduce my sister, Adele, to you. She enjoyed the play, too."

He bowed over her hand with as much flourish as he'd displayed to me, but he dropped her fingers instantly, whereas he had shown a disposition to cling to mine. "Thank you so much for coming to my play with your sister," he said.

Adele smiled. "Thank you so much for the tickets. It was quite a treat."

"I suppose you don't often get a chance to attend the theater and watch people make fools of themselves?" he asked.

She was smiling still. "Oh, you'd be surprised at how often people can be found playing one role or another," she said. "And not always on the formal stage."

That made me raise my eyebrows, but Edgar didn't seem to notice the barb. "What was your very favorite part?" he said, directing the question at both of us.

"The scene where the heroine hid the diary," said the Safe-Keeper.

"The scene where the villain was unmasked," said the Truth-Teller.

He glanced between us, smiling again. "I don't think, for sisters, you are very much alike," he said.

"But we are closer than most people realize," Adele said.

"Will you be able to come back sometime in the next three weeks?" Edgar asked. "We have two more plays in our repertoire even before we open *Killed by a Kiss*. You could come see them all."

I wanted to, of course. But it would not be such an easy thing to do. "Oh—I don't know," I said. "There's so much to do to prepare for Summermoon! It's a very rare night our parents can spare both of us together."

"Then come by yourself," Edgar said.

I laughed. "I don't think that's likely to happen."

"I'll give you passes," he pressed. "Good for any night. Come whenever you like."

"We'll see," I said.

I could have stood there for hours listening to him beg for my attendance, but just then a man swept the curtain back and called out. "Edgar! Someone back here looking for you! Says it's important."

Edgar spread his hands dramatically as if conceding there were powers that could not be ignored. "It seems I must go," he said, digging into his pocket and pulling out a few scraps of paper. "The passes. I hope you will use them."

He bowed again, kissed his hands to me, and with incomparable grace skipped down the bleachers and back onto the stage.

Well. I could not help a sigh.

"What a wonderful night," I said, as Adele and I more cautiously made our way out of the stands. "And didn't you think Edgar was just the handsomest man?"

"Indeed I did," she agreed.

"And charming?"

"He has so much charm it's criminal," she said.

"And he's a very fine actor, too," I added. "Even in such a silly play. I wonder what the historical play is like. More serious, I would suppose. I wish I could see him in that."

"You might be able to get away one night."

"Yes, but I couldn't go alone!"

"I'm sure Roelynn would find a way to join you."

Oh, yes, Roelynn would be the perfect companion for a trip to the theater to swoon over a dashing young actor. But. "Yes, but Roelynn is so much more beautiful than I am! And wealthy and delightful. What if Edgar liked her more than he liked me?"

Adele smiled. "I imagine Edgar meets many young women at least as delightful as Roelynn on a pretty regular basis. If you can't feel easy introducing him to your friend while you're standing there watching, you could hardly relax a moment once he was out of your sight meeting fetching young women all over the kingdom."

That made me frown. I did not like the picture she conjured up of Edgar going from town to town, dallying with all the prettiest girls. Not that I didn't realize it was true. I just didn't like to think about it. "Well, maybe I won't take Roelynn," I said a little childishly.

"Oh, why not? Isn't she all caught up in some intrigue of her own right now? The sailor Micah introduced her to—the one who's working on one of her father's ships?"

I cheered up instantly. "Yes! She talked about him for hours last time we saw her. She wouldn't be interested in Edgar. Anyway, Edgar wouldn't be interested in her. I mean, he's not even interested in me, really. He's just flirting. It doesn't mean anything."

"It means he finds you attractive," she said. "That's always nice to know."

"Yes, and isn't he just the handsomest man?" I said again. I went through all the adjectives one more time as we walked down the dark and mostly empty streets of Merendon. Adele agreed to them all: *charming* and *entertaining* and *talented* and *worldly*. And just as we'd rounded the corner on our street, and the inn with all its lighted windows was only a block away, I said, "And you really liked him, didn't you?" and she said, "Yes, I did."

And I stopped dead and peered at her in the dark because I could tell she was lying.

She stared back at me, her face impassive, and neither of us spoke for at least a minute. And then I said, in a much different tone of voice, "Why don't you like him?"

She looked as if she was considering another lie, but then sort of shrugged and gave it up. "Because he's handsome and charming and delightful, and I think he's probably the most faithless man in the kingdom. And I don't know why he would find it amusing to romance a fifteen-year-old girl, when he's obviously twenty-five or more. I suspect his motives and distrust his honor." She shrugged again.

I was absolutely furious. "How can you say such terrible things? You don't know anything about him! He could be the kindest man in the world! You don't like him because he's an actor—and you're a snob, you're like Mother and Father and even Roelynn's father, you think people have to have some kind of respectable, boring profession to be worthwhile—"

She tried to interrupt me numerous times. "I didn't say that—I didn't say any of that—well, *you're* the one who's usually more judgmental than I am, so this is just a little funny—" I wouldn't let her complete a sentence. I wouldn't listen to what she had to say. I put my hands over my ears and ran the last few yards to the inn. Then I yanked the door open and darted upstairs, past my mother, who stood there gaping at me. I dashed into the room and flung myself on the bed before I remembered that this was Adele's room, too. Then I jumped up, locked the door, and threw myself back on the bed and cried for an hour.

I suppose Adele spent the night in one of the guest rooms or on the sofa in the parlor downstairs. She didn't even come upstairs and twist the handle on the door. I have no idea what she told our parents. Certainly nothing about Edgar, because they didn't come seeking me out the next day to tell me in no uncertain terms to have nothing to do with such a man. No, Adele was a Safe-Keeper, not one to tell other people's stories.

But I did not appreciate her discretion. I could not forgive her for the things she had said the night before. From
that day until Summermoon, I went out of my way to avoid
speaking to her at all. You would have thought this would
have been difficult, particularly as there was no way to bar
her from her own room after that one night, and we spent
the next three weeks sleeping only a few feet apart. But
Adele had a great gift for silence. If you did not want to talk
to her, that was perfectly fine with her. She never felt the
necessity of initiating any conversation at all.

So I did not tell her how my romance with Edgar progressed. I did not tell her how, so many days when my
mother sent me out on errands, I was able to swing by the
southern edge of town and visit the Harst & Hope Regional
Traveling Troupe. I did not tell her about the night Roelynn
and I went to see *Rebecca's Revenge*, and stayed nearly two
hours after the performance had ended, while I flirted with
Edgar, and Roelynn quickly established friendly relations
with the young man who handled horses and heavy lifting
for the actors. I did not tell her about the stolen kisses, the
quick embraces, the whispered pleas for me to stay another
minute, another hour, there's a little room right behind the
stage where we could be quite private. . . .

I told no one but Roelynn that I had agreed to meet him
very late on Summermoon, after *Killed by a Kiss* had closed
and all the chores at the inn were done. I knew that no one
would miss me till very late the following morning, for
Mother and Father would sleep in, and Adele, if she did not

sleep late, would see my empty bed and assume I had risen early. I thought it would be my one chance to find out if he truly loved me, as he said he did. I wanted to know, but I did not want anyone else to know about my desperate assignation.

I had learned to be my own Safe-Keeper. I found I rather liked it. There is nothing so exhilarating as a secret, particularly a dangerous one. Nothing so exhilarating . . . and nothing so deadly.

CHAPTER EIGHT

ummermoon is such a different celebration from Wintermoon. Much more lighthearted and frivolous, full of activities and distractions. Wintermoon is a time to think about the months past and what you would like to leave behind, and to look forward to the year ahead and plan to make better use of your time. Wintermoon is a time for reflection and soul-searching and coming to terms with your dreams. Summermoon is simply about delight.

Our entire street had been decorated with ribbons and pennants and floral wreaths since the week preceding the holiday. Restaurants set out chairs on the sidewalks, and minstrels strolled by. It was said that the city beggars earned half their year's income on Summermoon alone, for generous (and often drunken) revelers would toss them dozens of coins as they passed by. The Leaf & Berry was full of guests, some rooms holding two or three more people than the accommodations usually allowed, and there was so much work to do that I had very little time to enjoy the pleasures of the festival. But everyone was in such a good mood that it was hard to complain about the extra sheets to wash, the extra food to prepare, the additional cleaning that had to be done to keep the front parlor looking inviting.

Besides, I knew that once midnight rolled around on Summermoon, my responsibilities would be done, and I could creep out the back door and head down to the edge of town for my romantic tryst with my handsome actor.

"Are you really going to meet him tomorrow?" Roelynn whispered to me the afternoon before that much-anticipated day. She had come to the inn with Micah to collect some of our guests, who would be attending dinner at her father's house that evening. Karro's house was quite large, but his circle of acquaintances was even larger, and he could not accommodate them all overnight.

"Yes, I am," I said. "I'm going to wear that dress you lent me—you know, all gauze and pink ribbons. I've hidden it in the back of my armoire."

"And are you going to—when you're alone with him, are you going to—" She hesitated, saw my scowl, and plunged forward. "Are you going to allow him to make love to you?"

"No," I said right away. And then, "I don't know. I haven't decided. I'm not sure that's what he wants."

"Oh, I'm certain that it is," she said in a knowing tone of voice. "But is that what *you* want? You should know now, before you meet him, so that you aren't tricked or coerced into doing something you don't intend to do."

"Tricked! Coerced! What kind of opinion do you have of him, anyway?" I demanded.

She shrugged. "Persuaded, then. You know what I mean. You should not allow the excitement of the moment to cause you to do something you don't want to do."

"I never do what I don't want to do," I said.

"Well, not usually," she replied. "But with a man—particularly with a man like Edgar—it's different. Sometimes your will is not as strong as you'd like. Just be sure that what you do is what *you* want to do."

I was so annoyed with her that I couldn't wait for Micah to reappear with the guests in tow. "And have you sometimes been tricked and coerced into doing things you didn't want to do?" I snapped.

She nodded, looking sad. "I have."

Now I stared, and my whole attitude changed. "Roelynn! Tell me!"

"Oh—not now—it was a while ago. But it won't happen to me again. So promise me you'll be careful tomorrow, Eleda. Promise me."

"You make it sound like I'm going to an execution, not a rendezvous."

"I just want you to be happy."

We had no time to talk anymore because now, when I least wanted them to appear, Micah and the guests came out the front door. Roelynn hurried over to greet them in her best rich-man's-daughter voice, and I went back inside. I was instantly drawn into the day's calamity—a dinner roast ruined, should we substitute with baked chicken or perhaps another meat pie?—and didn't have another minute to think about Roelynn or my own situation until nearly midnight.

When I fell into bed and instantly tumbled into sleep, I did have one final thought before dreams overtook me: *Tomorrow at this time I will be with the man I love.*

I woke the next morning feeling as if someone had scraped out my stomach with a trowel. My guts clenched and twisted with a sort of quivering horror, like a housekeeper who'd spotted a mouse in her kitchen and shook from an excess of revulsion. I managed to stagger up and dress myself, but after my third visit to the chamber pot, I could not move again. I lay myself gingerly on my bed and prayed for the world to end.

My mother found me about an hour later when she came bursting into my room in a fit of temper. "Eleda! What are you doing still in bed? There are the breakfast dishes to be done and the lunch to be started, not to mention the cakes and pastries to be prepared for tonight—"

One more word about food and I certainly would have vomited right at her feet, but just then her voice stopped, and she fluttered across the room. "What is it? Are you sick? Oh, poor thing, look at you, you're as white as milk." More food references. I actually groaned. She put her hand on my forehead. "A fever? Maybe, a little one. I can't tell. When did you get sick? Last night?"

"This morning," I whispered.

She made a *tsk*ing noise. "Oh, dear. Let's see. I can—I

can send Adele to Mary Percy and see if she can help out this afternoon—and then I can send your sister up to take care of you—"

"I don't need taking care of," I managed. "I just want to lie here and die."

She laughed very softly. "Yes, no doubt, but *I* don't want you to die. And on Summermoon! How sad to die on such a happy day. Have you been able to keep anything down? Water? Shall I bring you some tea? Come on, let's get you out of these clothes and into your sleeping shift—"

She fussed over me another twenty minutes or so, easing me out of my day clothes and back under the sheets. There is really nothing like having your mother nearby when you're sick to make you feel as if the world is not quite such a miserable place. She was so busy she would scarcely have time to wash her own face and braid her own hair, yet she stayed beside me long enough to do both those chores for me, and then kissed me on the cheek.

"I'll come back every so often and check on you," she said. "Call out if you need me, and one of us will come running upstairs."

"I'm just going to sleep," I said, and closed my eyes.

I don't remember much of that horrid day, except that I felt much worse before I felt any better. The fever built over the next three hours, so that Adele had to go fetch ice from the dairy and lay packs of it around my face and chest. My father came in twice to look down at me fearfully and make me recite my name, my birthday, and my recent history. Nothing could convince him that you were really in danger until you began to hallucinate and forget your identity, so each time he left me, he seemed completely reassured. My mother blew in about once an hour, checked my temperature, made me drink some water, and told me I would be just fine in a day or so.

I slept intermittently, and every time I woke up, Adele was sitting there watching me. She never said much, but as soon as she saw my eyes open, she stood up and offered me something to drink. Once, after I choked on a glassful of tepid water, she brushed the back of her hand against my cheek.

"I'm so sorry," she said in a soft voice.

"I hope that it's not the sort of thing everyone else is going to catch," I whispered.

"No one else seems to feel sick. Yet," she replied.

I closed my eyes. "I wouldn't wish this on anyone," I said.

I expected her to say *Neither would I,* but she was silent. Or maybe I had fallen asleep before she even had a chance to speak. Before I knew it, I was dreaming again.

It was dark before I remembered how I had planned to spend this Summermoon Eve.

I groaned and tried to push myself out of bed, but I was so weak I fell back on the covers before I could even achieve a sitting position. Edgar! What would he think when midnight arrived and I was nowhere to be found? Would he suppose I had grown fearful and reluctant? Would he assume that my parents had found out about my plan and locked me in my room? Would he think I had been teasing him all along and had never had the intention of showing up for our rendezvous? How long would he wait? Would he worry? Would he be angry? Would he forgive me when I was finally able to make my excuses in person, two or three days from now?

Would the troupe even still be here? Would I ever see him again?

Anxiety and despair made me feel even worse, and I fretted on my bed, turning my head from side to side and tangling myself in the sheets. When my mother next entered the room, she found me fevered and hysterical. "Adele!" she called down the stairs, and a few minutes later, my sister appeared in the door. Between them they convinced me to drink a dreadful-tasting tea that I knew had been doctored with some kind of soporific herb.

"No," I wept, trying to push the cup away. "I don't want to sleep. I want to get *up*. I have to *go*. I don't want that, I don't want it—"

But though I spilled half of it down the front of my nightshirt, half of it did go down my throat, and I lay back on the hot pillows, sobbing. "I'm getting worried now," my mother said.

"I'll sit with her awhile," Adele replied.

"Yes, I think that would be best."

I suppose she did stay; I was asleep within ten minutes. I don't think I stirred again for another three or four hours. I woke with a peculiar lightheadedness, as if my brain had been siphoned from my skull and the whole interior cavity was now empty. My body felt weightless and strange, as if all the bones had been similarly hollowed out. I was fairly certain that if I could navigate to the dark window and push myself out, I would float down to the ground in a gentle, pleasant swirl.

I tried to sit up and managed to do so, though the movement made me dizzy for a moment. Once my head cleared, I attempted to climb out of bed. I had to stand there a minute or two, swaying on my bare feet, but eventually I was able to straighten and take a few cautious steps. And, since I was still on my feet, I kept walking till I arrived at the window situated between my bed and Adele's. I glanced at her bed, which was empty. It was either sometime before midnight, or she had chosen to sleep elsewhere than the sickroom.

I knelt on the floor before the open window and leaned out to smell the fresh air. It was deep summer, and so the breeze was full of summer scents—the green smell of cut grass, the dense smell of hot brick, the rich, heavy perfume of a myriad of flowers. Even at this late hour, traces of smoke lingered in the air; I could catch a whiff of spilled wine and stale bread. The streets were almost empty, though. Close by I could hear the quick tapping sound of running footsteps— farther away, the clustered tread of two or three people walking together. A light laugh drifted through the air. But the streets were dark. The common torchlights were extinguished, and no light spilled from the windows of the houses and shops as far up and down the street as I could see.

Past midnight, then. Only an hour or two till dawn.

Summermoon was over, and I had missed my appointment with Edgar. I lay my head on my crossed forearms and wept again.

In the morning, I felt remarkably better. I had crawled back to my bed sometime after my last bout of tears and curled up in a tight ball under my sheets. I had assumed that grief would kill me off before sunrise, so I was actually a little surprised to find myself still alive when I opened my eyes. Alive, free of fever, clearheaded, and hungry.

I sat up in bed and looked around. There was a tray of fresh water and juice on the chair by my bed. The window was open and bright sunshine streamed into the room, making me feel almost cheerful. Adele lay fully dressed on the other bed, curled up on her side facing me. When I made some small noise as I poured juice into a glass, she stirred and sat up.

"Good morning," she said, inspecting me with those mismatched eyes. "You look like you feel better."

"I do feel better," I said. "I feel good. Whatever that sickness was, it seems to have passed in a day."

"Do you want something to eat?"

The glass to my mouth, I nodded as vigorously as I could without spilling anything. "Oh, yes," I said, after I'd swallowed half the contents. "I'm starving."

She swung to her feet. "I'll tell Mother."

A few minutes later, Mother arrived, bearing a tray of fruit and toast and scrambled eggs. Adele helped her set it up across my lap, and the two of them watched closely to see how well I would retain my food. But I was ravenous. I ate everything she'd brought and glanced around to see if there might be more.

Mother smiled. "Now, this is encouraging. You act as if you're completely well."

"May I get up, then?" I asked. It was a rule of our house that you had to stay very quiet for at least a day after you had been sick, so that you did not misjudge your strength and suffer a relapse. But I really felt perfectly fine. "There's so much I wanted to do yesterday that I would like to do today—" *Go see Edgar. Tell him why I failed him the night before. Promise him I would come to meet him tonight or tomorrow night or some other night while the troupe was still in town.*

Mother reached out and smoothed the lank hair back from my forehead. I could not help glancing at Adele, who looked tired after her long day yesterday, but whose hair was at least clean and combed. She looked gravely back at me but didn't say anything. "I think you'd better stay in for today," Mother said. "You can come downstairs, though, and sit quietly in the kitchen."

"I want to go out," I said pettishly. "I want to see Roelynn. I want to see my friends."

Mother looked unexpectedly grim. "At least one of your friends is in no condition to be seen," she said.

"What do you mean?"

Before speaking, she glanced at Adele, who apparently already knew this story. "Something terrible happened last night to your friend Eileen Dawson," Mother said at last.

105

Eileen wasn't really a friend of ours—she was our age, and she had been in all our classes when we were younger, but she was the daughter of a wealthy shipowner, and she considered herself too fancy to associate with innkeepers' daughters. What made her easier to dislike was that she was not only haughty, she was beautiful, and she believed all the young men in town were secretly in love with her. Roelynn was forced to socialize with her fairly often, because Eileen's father and Karro did business together, but for myself, I would never have considered Eileen a friend.

Still. Clearly there was interesting news about her. "What happened?" I asked, leaning forward in my bed.

"She had a tryst last night with a young man—an actor who was in town for the festival," Mother said. "Apparently he—well, he was not the kind of man she thought. He took advantage of her—and used her very badly—"

She seemed to be having difficulty finding the words that would convey the horror of what had happened without upsetting me too badly. I frowned and looked over at Adele. Who said flatly, "He raped her, and beat her, and left her bleeding on the side of the road. Someone found her this morning and thought she was dead, but she's not. They think she'll recover in a day or two."

Mother stroked my hair again. "I can't believe that such wretched, cruel people exist," she said.

I felt a tight pressure building up in my chest. "Do you know—did she say—who did this to her?" I choked out. "You said—it was—an actor, but—"

My mother nodded. "They had built a stage down on the

south end of town. The Harst and Hope Regional Traveling Troupe. I can't remember the young man's name—"

"Edgar," Adele said entirely without inflection.

"That was it. Edgar Beauman. Of course, Eileen's father and uncles went off immediately to find this dreadful man, but he was gone. The whole troupe had packed up and left town sometime in the middle of the night."

My stomach twisted beneath my rib cage. I looked around wildly, grabbed the pitcher from the tray, and retched up all of my breakfast. I kept vomiting and vomiting long after my stomach was empty.

So I slept most of that day, too. When I finally came downstairs around dinnertime, I was listless and sad. Mother and Adele were busy making and serving dinner to the many guests who still remained at the inn, so I sat alone in the kitchen, picking at my toast and spooning up a few mouthfuls of chicken broth. My father sat with me for twenty minutes, speaking in the loud, hearty voice he thought was most likely to cheer up an invalid, and then had to hurry out to help a new arrival with luggage. I took another bite of toast, thought I might gag as I tried to swallow it, waited a moment, and was able to choke it down.

I had never felt so miserable and stupid in my life.

How could I have been so mistaken? How could I not have seen through the mask of charm and beauty that was Edgar's outer self to the dark soul underneath? I was a Truth-Teller—it was automatic with me to know when someone was lying, when someone was presenting a false face to the world. Why had the counterfeit timbre of his voice rung true to me? What had prompted me to believe a man who spent most of his life dissembling? Why had I, usually so suspicious, become so credulous and simpleminded in his presence? Was it just that I had wanted to hear someone tell me he loved me? Was it just that the words he spoke, the vows he swore, were so freighted with sweetness that they would have seemed true no matter who spoke them? Everyone wants to be loved. Everyone wants to be beautiful. Perhaps lovers' vows are always believed, no matter how insincere the speaker is. Perhaps they have a magic so potent that they trick anyone who hears them. Or perhaps it is darker than that. Perhaps lovers' vows are always so false that no one can be expected to hear the lie. They just must take on faith that the lie is always there.

I ate a little more soup, then set down my spoon. I wasn't hungry. I didn't think I would ever be hungry again. I didn't think I would ever be anything except lost and sad and shaken.

My mother came in through the door that led from the dining room to the kitchen, Adele right behind her. "Have you eaten something? Good," Mother said. "Can I get you anything else?"

I shook my head. "I just want to go upstairs and sleep. Forever."

She grinned. "I imagine you'll feel better in a day or so. Actually, considering how sick you were yesterday, I'm surprised you're doing so well today. What kind of strange illness was that? Almost as if you ate something that made you sick, and once you washed it out of your system, you were fine."

"Almost," I said. "Like I accidentally swallowed poison or some tainted food . . ." My voice trailed off and I stared at my sister across the room. She was standing at the stove, ladling soup into a tureen, but she looked up when she felt my gaze on her face. Her eyes met mine, blue eye staring into blue, green eye staring into green, but her expression didn't change. After a moment, she returned her attention to the ladle and the serving dish.

"Well, I'd hope you didn't swallow any poison," my mother said briskly. "I put down some powder now and then for the rats, but you'd never take something like that by mistake."

"No," I said. "No, I don't think I took anything by mistake."

Adele put the lid back on the tureen, stepped away from the stove, and pushed through the door back to the dining room. She hadn't said a word since she'd walked into the kitchen.

"More soup? Just a little bit?" my mother said in a coaxing voice. "I'm so glad to see a little color back in your cheeks. How about some tea? Doesn't that sound good?"

When I'd finally eaten enough to please my mother, I sat outside for a little bit on the bench between the kirrenberry and chatterleaf trees. The air was still warm this late at night, but the breeze was fresh and felt good on my skin. I'd scrubbed my face but hadn't bothered to bathe or wash my hair, and I felt sticky all over. Tomorrow. Tomorrow I would wash away two days' worth of dirt, the remnants of my ill-ness, the memories of the last three weeks, all thoughts of Edgar. Tomorrow I would be clean and whole again.

I waited a long time before Adele finally came out of the inn and sat beside me on the bench. It was completely dark by then, and the moon, one night past full, had risen fairly high in the clear night sky. I was tired but not exactly sleepy. I was prepared to wait as long as it would take for her to join me.

Once she sat, though, we passed another ten minutes in silence. The chatterleaf tree whispered and murmured in the light wind, but the kirrenberry waved its full summer leaves without making the slightest sound.

"How did you know?" I asked presently.

That could have meant almost anything, but she chose to answer the question I had intended. *How did you know what I was planning to do last night?* "Roelynn told me," she said. "She was worried about you."

"Why didn't you tell me you knew?"

"You weren't speaking to me. And I didn't think any-thing I said would stop you."

I sighed heavily and leaned against the back of the bench. We were quiet for a few more minutes. Then I asked in a low voice, "How did you know about Edgar?"

"Last year. When the troupe was in town. Something of the same sort occurred. Except the girl wasn't so badly hurt, only humiliated. She told me about it."

"And why didn't you tell me *that*?" I demanded.

She looked at me, her face very grave. "The story was

told to me in confidence," she said quietly. "I couldn't repeat it, even to you."

"Stories like that," I said in a stern voice, "should be shouted from the rooftops. Everyone should know those kinds of tales."

"Eileen has chosen to tell hers," Adele said. "Now everyone does know."

I had only a few more questions. "You gave me some of that herb you got—the stuff you hid in your bottom drawer," I said. "Didn't you?" Adele nodded. "What did you put it in? When did you give it to me?"

"In your potatoes the night before. I mixed it in your gravy."

"Did you *know* how terrible it would make me feel?"

A small smile for that. "Yes. I'm sorry. But I knew that if you weren't really, really sick—"

"You're a strange sister," I said.

"I'm sorry if you hate me," she said. "I had to do something."

I scooted forward a little on the bench so I could lay my cheek on Adele's shoulder. I was so tired. My stomach seemed fine now, but my head still hurt. My chest felt bruised and my arms and legs felt weighted, but those symptoms, I thought, were not left over from the drug my sister had administered. Those were the lingering aftereffects of heartache and betrayal, and it would take more than a day or two before they finally disappeared. "I couldn't hate you," I said. "It just seems very odd to be poisoned for love, when a few well-chosen words would do."

"Words can carry their own poison," she said. "The truth can be toxic."

"But secrets can be deadly."

I heard the smile in her voice. "Well, you at least were not meant to keep secrets," she said. "Promise me this will be the last time you try."

"All right, but I will expose you sometime if I think it will be good for you," I said drowsily. "I won't keep your secrets, either."

She laughed. "What makes you think I would try to have any secrets from you?"

I yawned and sat up, shaking my head. It did no good; I still could not think clearly. "Because you have secrets from everybody."

"But I don't let them hurt anyone," she replied.

I looked at her in the dark. "So far."

CHAPTER NINE

utumn was fiery and golden; winter was a fierce and unrelenting white. Karro held another Wintermoon dinner party so lavish it required the services of half the townspeople. The inn was overflowing with guests from Wodenderry and smaller towns, and Adele and I could not keep ourselves from gawking at their gorgeous, expensive clothes and their calculated, affected gestures. The prince had been invited to attend the event, and had accepted the invitation, but two days before Wintermoon his mother sent a curt message that he had broken his leg in a careless sporting accident. He would be unable to travel for at least six weeks.

The news amused and delighted Roelynn, who had been quite glum at the prospect of finally meeting young Darian. Her father and the queen had just renewed their shipping contracts, and Karro had spent another week in Wodenderry currying the royal favor. While an official betrothal had never been formalized, it was clear that the queen was seriously considering the idea. In Karro's mind, there was obviously no doubt that the marriage was all but sealed, and he told anyone who had not already heard the news that one day his daughter would be queen. For her part, Roelynn still maintained that she would never marry to suit her father's notions of politics—but she said such things only when she was alone with Adele and me.

Which was why she was so pleased at the prince's most recent round of misfortune. "He's not coming, he's not coming!" she sang, dancing around the chatterleaf tree. It was too cold to sit outside and talk, and so I told her, but neither Roelynn nor Adele seemed to mind the bitter chill.

"He must have broken his leg on purpose so he wouldn't have to come here," Adele said. She and I were standing more sedately just under the bare, shivering branches. I had my arms crossed over my chest in the hopes of generating some body heat, but Adele just lounged there with her coat unbuttoned and her thumbs hooked over the edges of her pockets. "I don't think you're *ever* going to meet him, if he has anything to say about it."

Roelynn stopped dancing and clapped her gloved hands together. "Yes! That's what I think, too! *He* doesn't want to marry *me* either! A merchant's daughter from Merendon— he must surely think his mother can make a better match for him than that! Or perhaps he's fallen in love with some- one wholly ineligible—a seamstress or a kitchen maid—and he is going to all these desperate shifts to avoid being mar- ried off to anyone. I don't know, maybe he's had boat races and broken bones every couple of weeks for the past ten years as the queen has attempted to introduce him to a whole array of fashionable and boring young women."

I didn't see much point in romanticizing rude behavior. "I think he just sounds selfish and careless," I said. "You're better off not marrying someone like that, even if he is the prince."

"I don't want to marry the prince," Roelynn said dreamily. "I'd rather marry Steffan."

Adele and I looked at each other. I was frowning; Adele was laughing. "Steffan?" my sister repeated. "I don't believe we know about him."

Steffan, as we learned, was the younger son of a successful wool weaver in Movington. This made him more respectable than many of the men Roelynn had fallen in love with to date, but he was still hardly likely to be on Karro's short list of approved prospects for his daughter. What added to his unsuitability was that he was uninterested in his father's business and wanted to make a name for himself as a poet. Roelynn proceeded to recite for us one of the sonnets Steffan had written expressly for her. Adele stopped me with a quick, meaningful look before I could voice my opinion of his talent.

"Very nice," Adele said. "Will he be at the Wintermoon dinner party?"

Indeed he would, as would so many other people of consequence (except Prince Darian). The Dream-Maker had already arrived in town and was staying at the Leaf & Berry. Even though we could have sold the room five times over for three times the price, my parents had held it for Melinda, and I was very glad. It was hardly Wintermoon without her.

The days leading up to the holiday were exceedingly busy, as our Wodenderry guests were quite demanding, but we enjoyed being involved in all the bustle. As always, despite the preceding chaos, Wintermoon itself was a coldly serene day followed by a still, watchful night of contemplation and renewal. Adele and I fed the fire while our parents followed their tradition of sleeping until nearly midnight. Silently we made our own wishes as we poked new logs into the flames. I prayed for steadiness and clearer insight and the perspicacity that would prevent me from ever being fooled by a man again. It was impossible to guess what Adele might wish for.

As had become another tradition in our household, Micah and Roelynn accompanied the Dream-Maker back to our bonfire once the formal dinner was over. "It's too *cold* out here," Melinda complained. "I'm going in to put some boots on and then I'll come back out with your parents."

"How was the party?" I asked the other two once she had gone inside.

"Quite nice," Roelynn said. This meant she had had a chance to talk with Steffan half the night and had received a fair number of compliments from many of the other high-born guests. The years when her current flirt was not invited to the dinner were the years she stigmatized it as a dull, interminable affair. "I was a little sorry to leave, actually."

"Don't bother to stay just to please us," I said tartly.

She laughed. "Silly. It's not Wintermoon unless I burn the wreath with you."

"Did you enjoy the dinner?" Adele asked Micah, always trying to draw him into the conversation when years of casual acquaintance should have told her he never had much to say.

"It's an important event for my father," he replied. "I don't particularly enjoy it, but I do what I can to make it successful."

Roelynn rolled her eyes. "He had to dance with all the old dowagers and the silly young debutantes," she said. "But you didn't mind the pretty girls, did you?"

He smiled slightly and looked at Adele. "Silly is the right word," he said. "I find I don't have much to say to them."

"Well, really, you don't have much to say to anyone," I said, trying to sound encouraging. Adele gave me a look of reproach. Roelynn laughed.

Micah, unexpectedly, looked amused. "Someday, Eleda," he said, "you may find I am more interesting than you always thought."

I tried to look as though I found this possible. Roelynn said, "Oh, good, there are Melinda and your parents. What a beautiful wreath you have this year! It's enormous!"

My father smiled broadly and dropped the wreath to the ground to rest against his knee. "Does everyone have their special wishes ready to tie to the wreath?" he inquired. "It's time for burning."

All of us pulled something out of our purses or pockets, even Melinda, and Adele handed around bits of ribbon. I had hunted through the woods all last week until I found a dried-up bush of carraphile. It bore a leaf often harvested for use in herbal teas, and I thought it might be expected to confer equanimity. I'd crushed the leaves and gathered them in a little gingham bag, and now I tied the bag to the wreath. I didn't bother to specify what I was wishing for, and neither did any of the others. But I could tell that Roelynn's contribution was a lacy sachet filled with dried petals—probably pulled from roses bestowed by the romantic Steffan—and that Melinda's was sewn into a bag of velvet. A request for a soft life, perhaps, or an easy year. Whatever items Adele and Micah attached to the wreath were remarkably similar in size and shape, and they tied these pieces to the wreath with matching red bows. As always, Mother and Father added strands of dried fruit tied with gold braid. A well-provisioned home blessed with material riches.

When everyone was done, Micah and Father lifted the wreath and tossed it into the fire. "Mercy!" Mother exclaimed as the flames shot up almost as high as the roof, and then died down in a shower of drifting sparks. Someone's little packet had held a mix of spices, because the baking scents of cinnamon and nutmeg were very strong. Domestic scents. Possibly Roelynn had wished for marriage when she tied Steffan's roses to the wreath.

"Very lovely," Melinda pronounced. "Happy Wintermoon to you all. May every dream you wished for come true."

In the coming months it seemed that at least one or two residents of Merendon saw their deepest desires realized. The Widow Norville, now Mrs. Haskins, reconciled with her long-estranged son and had a chance to meet her granddaughter. Karro sent a laden ship into a foreign port and traded for the most fabulous goods ever seen in our kingdom; he made a fresh fortune selling these in cities from Wodenderry to the coast. He even allowed Micah to set sail on some of those trading ships, which Roelynn said was her brother's wish come true. Eileen Dawson spent the spring with her grandmother in Lowford and came back talking shyly of a handsome, smiling young man with kind manners and excellent family connections.

I recovered from my melancholy and again began to think the world a pretty good place.

Roelynn broke off relations with Steffan when she discovered he was an abysmal horseman and had no interest in improving, but since she immediately took up with a coachman who traveled the Merendon-Wodenderry road, she didn't stay unhappy for long.

It was hard to know what exactly all these individuals had wished for when they stood around their Wintermoon bonfires, but some of them, at least, had to be glad of the way their fortunes turned. Mrs. Haskins and Eileen Dawson certainly credited Melinda with making their dreams come true.

But certain wishes no one thinks to make. The small ones, the ordinary ones, the ones that say, "Let life continue on this way forever, with no misfortune, no despair. Turn tragedy aside and let me remain, if not ecstatic, then content."

I didn't wish that, at any rate. I would have been willing

to bet that neither Roelynn nor her father had put such dreams into words. So we were all horrified when news came back from the harbor one spring afternoon: One of Karro's ships had gone down a hundred miles off a foreign coast and all hands on board were believed lost.

Roelynn's brother Micah had been aboard the ship.

There was no way to comfort Roelynn. I was not good at comforting anyone, anyway, because I could never see the value of offering false words of hope or reassurance. But in those first awful days following the news of Micah's disappearance, I wished fervently that I had learned how to shape the conventional phrases of consolation and encouragement. *There, there. You'll be fine.* Or, *Everything will seem better in the morning.* Or, *All things happen for a good reason.*

I could not imagine that any of these things were true. And so I could not say them. I could only run up to Roelynn, when she appeared weeping at our back door, and throw my arms around her, and push back her dark disheveled hair, and tell her how very, very sorry I was.

I had never been particularly fond of Micah, it was true, but Roelynn was, and I could not imagine anything worse than losing a sibling. Anything. I hugged her, and let her cry, and shuddered at the strange, terrible events a life could hold.

As might be expected, Adele was much better at this sort of thing than I was. She spent much of her time away from the inn, at Karro's house, sitting silently beside the grieving Roelynn. Or at least I assumed that they sat there in silence—Adele never bothered to say. When Roelynn came to the inn, looking for solace, more often than not she and Adele would end up outside together, curled on the ornamental bench, their arms around each other's shoulders, their faces solemn with pain. Not for the first time, I marveled at my sister's gift for wordless empathy. I was so much more likely to try to *do* something to make the situation better. Nothing could improve this particular circumstance, but I found myself bustling just the same. I stitched a black silk shawl for Roelynn and embroidered it with Micah's initials; she wore it every day during the month after we heard the news. I worked in the kitchen to make the special dishes that I knew were Roelynn's favorites, and I carried them to the kitchen door of the great mansion, hoping to tempt her into eating. Karro must have employed three cooks and any number of scullery maids, so it wasn't as if they needed my contributions to the dinner table, but I felt better just for making the effort. And Roelynn appreciated it, I knew, for she always made a point of personally returning the serving dishes and thanking me profusely for my gifts.

How Karro took the news of his son's disappearance I could only guess, for I never saw him. But new ships that he had commissioned to be built sat unfinished in the harbor; merchants who came to town to renew contracts with him waited for days at the Leaf & Berry and were never admitted into his presence. Roelynn said that he would sit by himself for hours in his private office, and whether he drank or whether he wept or whether he merely stared out the window and mourned, she had no idea.

It occurred to me that, now that she was Karro's only heir, Roelynn would be an even richer catch in the marriage market, and the queen might lose whatever final disinclination she might have shown toward the match with her son. I felt guilty for even having the thought, and I did not make this observation aloud.

It was probably three weeks after we had gotten the dreadful message that I began to notice something was wrong with Adele.

It had always been hard to tell when Adele was sick, unless she had a rash or a hacking cough, because she never bothered to mention it when she didn't feel well and her behavior did not change at all. She was so often reserved or withdrawn that you could not tell when her silence was the result of a fevered lethargy or merely her current mood. When we were children, every time I fell ill, my mother just assumed Adele would do so as well, and dosed her with whatever drugs had been prescribed for me. Now and then, even when I was healthy, my mother would pause and lay her hand across Adele's forehead to check for heat. Once we learned she had sprained her ankle only when we noticed her very slight limp and the way she leaned against the wall with her heel slightly raised.

I've never understood people who won't speak up when they're in trouble. I always want whatever sympathy and aid is available, the minute I start to feel miserable. I am not interested in bearing wretchedness alone. But I think concealment is such a habit with Adele that she sometimes is not even aware she is practicing it.

At first, this time, I could not imagine what Adele might be hiding. At first, I was not even sure I was reading the symptoms right. But then I started watching her more closely at dinner. She put small portions on her plate and pretended to eat, but mostly she just moved food around and then covered the whole mess with a napkin when the meal was over. Or she ran errands right at lunchtime and came back claiming to have eaten with Roelynn or to have purchased a pie from a street vendor. She began to wear her hair in a new style so that when my mother said, "Your face looks thinner," she could reply, "It's the way I've got my hair pulled back." She wore her long-sleeved dresses and her high-necked blouses even in the warmth of early spring.

It was another week before I became certain that Adele was trying to starve herself to death.

The longer I watched her, the more I became convinced that she was barely eating enough to keep a child alive. Her cheekbones had acquired a gaunt prominence, and when she put on her nightclothes and hurriedly slipped into bed, I could tell that her arms and her legs had grown painfully thin. In such a short time. I woke once in the middle of the night to hear her slipping soundlessly from the room, so I rose and followed her with equal stealth. I saw her duck out the back door and vomit in the garden, clutching her stomach as if she was in so much pain that she expected her body to tear itself in half.

I cannot describe the terror that took hold of me that night as I peered out a small round kitchen window and watched my sister try to throw her life away.

The minute she turned for the door, I ran back upstairs and flung myself in bed. I pretended to be sleeping as she crept back into the room and arranged herself on her own mattress. I lay awake the rest of the night trying to decide what to do.

In the morning, Adele was the first one up, dressed, and downstairs. I supposed she had given up sleeping as well as eating. As soon as she left, I scrambled up and began searching her possessions. Neither of us had that many places where we could hide things—and I rarely bothered to hide things, anyway—so I didn't have that many places to look. Her armoire. Her dresser. A few small boxes cached under her bed. The pockets of her various gowns and jackets. I figured that surely I would find something, anything, that would give me a clue as to what had made my sister so sad.

It took me almost an hour, and the whole time I was jumpy, expecting her to walk in on me at any moment and demand to know what I was doing. I found the most amazing items among her store of secret treasures, things I could not believe she had kept. The painted miniature of Princess Arisande, of course. A letter from Melinda, written to us one year at Summermoon when we were quite small. A wooden baby rattle that must have been ours when we were infants, though she could certainly have no memory of holding it. Two thin, gold-blonde braids—one from my head, one from hers—cut when we were six years old. A sketch of the palace in Wodenderry, acquired when we had gone to the royal city four years ago. A newly minted gold coin with an excellent profile of the queen. A ring that Roelynn had given her one year. Inch-long strips of ribbon from some of her favorite dresses, now too old and ragged to wear. A poem I had written when I was eight. A silver-veined black stone I had found in the river and given her one day so many years ago I could not remember. A handkerchief with my initials on it, ripped almost in half and of no use to anyone. A sketch that nine-year-old Roelynn had made of me, that looked nothing like me, identifiable only because my name was written at the top of the page. A broken brooch that had belonged to our mother. A buckle from one of our father's shoes.

Silly, pointless, sentimental reminders of friends and family and intimate history. You would never have expected to find such things among Adele's possessions. Or maybe you would. You certainly would not have expected to find them among mine.

I had almost given up when I thought to look under her pillow. I myself can't abide a lumpy pillow, so it would never have occurred to me to hide something under my head, but it was clear Adele had different notions of comfort and importance than I did. As soon as I slipped my hand under the cotton slipcase, my fingers encountered the smooth feel of a richer fabric. I tugged, and out came a flat, slim parcel of satin about the size of my hand. I could feel small objects tucked inside but could find no way to get at them, since all four edges of the bag were sewn shut.

I crossed the room, pulled my scissors from a drawer, slit one seam, and dumped the contents of the bag on the top of my bed.

Four items fell out, and I examined them one by one. The first was a hollow gold heart hung on an incredibly fine chain. I pursed my lips into a soundless whistle, for this was a rather expensive piece—not the sort of thing our parents could afford to give us or that Adele or I could buy for ourselves. It had been a gift, then. And it took no kind of genius to realize that it was a lover's token.

Adele had a secret beau. Who in the world could he be?

The second item was a beautiful, heavy envelope with "Adele" written on the front of it. I looked inside—she had not saved the letter, or if she had, it was somewhere else in the room—but clearly she had not been able to throw away this memento that featured her own name written in her beloved's handwriting. I studied the script; not a hand I knew. I sniffed at the open flap. No scent. Nothing to indicate the person's identity.

The third item was a length of ribbon, thin and dainty, an iridescent white shot through with threads of silver and gold and turquoise. This was a piece I recognized—she had used just such ribbon to trim the Summermoon dress she'd worn three years ago. I hadn't been with her when she bought it, so I couldn't guess why it was so significant that she had saved a scrap of it with her most precious treasures. Perhaps her young man had helped her pick it out; perhaps he had paid for it. Perhaps, the day she had worn the dress, he had told her he loved her.

The last item in her hoard was a round flat disk of white stone, worn through in the center so that it formed a fairly symmetrical circle. Unlike the other things in the packet, it was not in pristine condition. It was blackened with soot as if it had been rescued from a fire; a small scrap of singed ribbon was still wrapped around one portion.

I held this between my fingers for a long moment, frowning. It looked familiar, but I could not at first say why. A white stone hung on a fancy ribbon that had been thrown into and then saved from a fire. . . .

"A lover's quarrel?" I said out loud in a very quiet voice. "A gift from him that she tossed in the flames and then rescued when she repented? But everyone knows that stone won't really burn. Wouldn't you throw it into the ocean if you really wanted to get rid of it? But maybe she didn't want it to burn. Maybe she threw it for luck into a Wintermoon fire. . . ."

As soon as I said the words, I remembered. Wintermoon, two years ago. Micah and Roelynn bringing Melinda back to our house, and staying for the burning of the wreath. Micah pulling this white stone from his pocket, claiming it offered the gift of a complete life. Adele offering him a ribbon to tie it to the greenery.

Had this been one of the years Adele and I had gotten up early the next morning to sift through the cinders of the Wintermoon fire? I couldn't remember. But she at least had made her way to that cold bonfire the next day and poked through the ashes till she found the piece she wanted.

Micah's stone. Adele was in love with Micah Karro.

Micah Karro was drowned.

I knew now why my sister's heart was breaking.

~ ✺ ~

We had guests at the inn, so the morning was busy. There were beds to strip, piles of laundry to do, grates to clean, and all sorts of preparation to be done for the next few meals. We had fed lunch to our guests before any of us had a chance to take an afternoon meal, but then I wheedled for a treat.

"It's such a beautiful day," I said to our mother. "Can't Adele and I eat outside? We'll come right back in to help with the afternoon chores."

"Yes—fine—but I'm going to make a new recipe tonight, and I'm going to need your help in the kitchen," Mother said, already distracted by the next task on her agenda. "Come back in as soon as you're done."

I organized bread and cheese and dried meat while Adele filled a jug with water. She was gathering up some stained linen napkins, suitable for outdoor dining, when I headed out the back door with a blanket over my arm. I spread it out under the silent green leaves of the kirrenberry tree.

When Adele stepped outside and saw where I was, she hesitated just a moment before coming over to join me. I waited till we had arranged our feast and built our sandwiches before I spoke.

"If you don't eat every bite, I'm going to tell Mother and Father," I said calmly. "If you get up in the middle of the night and throw it all back up, I'm going to tell them. If you try to leave the house without me, I'm going to follow you. If you walk anywhere near the harbor and look like you're going to jump in the water, I'm going to grab your arm and haul you back. If you so much as glance at a knife, I'm going to scream as loud as I possibly can, and everyone will come running."

She looked at me. Even her hands, folded in her lap, looked parched and thin. "I'm not trying to kill myself," she said.

"You're not trying to live, either."

"I don't feel like living."

"How long have you been in love with Micah?" I asked.

Now she looked away, but she didn't try to lie. "Forever. As long as I can remember. Except when we were children, it didn't feel like love. It just felt like—" She made a small gesture and then instantly stilled her hand again. "It was just that we were friends, and no one else was such a good friend. It's just been the past few years that I've thought— that I've known—that I knew to put the word to it."

"How does he feel about you?"

She gave me a quick look, for the tense I had used, I suppose. "The same."

"Does his father know? Does Roelynn?"

She shook her head, then shrugged. "Roelynn has guessed, maybe, by now. Neither of us ever told her, and we wouldn't think of telling Karro. There was never any chance that Micah would be allowed to marry me. I knew that. His father would have made a grand match for him, as he is trying to do for Roelynn. I never thought we had any future." She dropped her head in her hands, and her blonde hair spilled across her cheeks to cover her face. "I just didn't think the future would be so completely empty of everything," she whispered.

I moved over and put both my arms around her. I could feel her shoulders shaking. The imperturbable Adele was sobbing.

"I know," I said, whispering into her hair. "I know. I know." Useless words, of course, but at least they were true. I couldn't think of anything else to say.

CHAPTER TEN

I didn't tell our parents what Adele and I had discussed under the kirrenberry tree, but perhaps our mother, at any rate, suspected some of it. Over the next few days, I noticed her gazing at Adele with a narrow attention, making sure she had an extra piece of bread on her plate at dinner or a cup of hot chocolate before we went to bed. It was possible she took her cues from me, for I watched my sister all through the day and at random intervals through the night for the next ten days.

Adele tried very hard during that time to get better. I can't say she succeeded particularly well, but at least she got no worse. She ate a little more; she slept a little longer. If I insisted she go for a walk with me, she obediently got to her feet and followed me out the door. She did not recover to the point that she was lively or amused, but I didn't expect that.

I found myself hoping that Melinda would come to Merendon soon, for I knew what I would wish for if she did. Some way for my sister to be happy again. Something to take away the heartache. While I was at it, I would wish the same things for Roelynn, who had grown just as haggard and waifish as Adele.

It was not a dream that I could expect to come true. So, in the absence of miracles, I made a great but human effort to see that my sister and my best friend survived their grief. Mostly this meant spending as much time with them as my duties at the inn and classes at school allowed—but I would have done that anyway. Perhaps I did nothing to ease their lives at that point except exist and remind them that I loved them. Perhaps that's all anyone can do at such a time.

One day about six weeks after Micah had disappeared, Adele and I went over to Roelynn's house as soon as school let out. Karro's rules had grown lax in this past month and a half. He didn't care so much these days that an innkeeper's daughters ate in his dining room or played in his orchards, and Roelynn liked to have us over to fill up the empty days. The three of us went directly to the kitchen, where we snatched hot pastries straight from the pan and made the head cook smile. She was a kind, ample, older woman who had clearly been doing her best to take care of Roelynn during this bitter time, and she always greeted Adele and me with heartfelt welcome.

"Don't burn your tongues now," she admonished. "That filling is hot! It's good for you, though. Each of you eat two or three of those."

"Don't you have to save some for dinner?" Adele asked.

The cook shook her head. "No company tonight, and there's plenty here for those who have any interest in eating." She looked meaningfully at Roelynn and then glanced up at the ceiling, where Karro's office was one floor above us.

"I'll have another, then," I said.

The three of us withdrew to a small table in the corner to consume our tarts and drink glasses of fresh milk. Karro's kitchen was an inviting place, huge and high-ceilinged, with three stoves and two fireplaces and all sorts of interesting pantries and cabinets. Hanging from the exposed beams of the ceiling were copper-bottomed pans and sprays of dried herbs, and jostling between the tables and the stoves were usually three cooks and two or three assistants. And nothing—not the fancy restaurants of Wodenderry, not the streets of Merendon on Summermoon Eve—smelled as wonderful as Karro's kitchen on baking day.

"How's your father today?" Adele asked eventually.

Roelynn shrugged. "About the same."

"Is he getting any business done?" I asked.

"A little. He met with a couple of ship captains yesterday, and I think he signed another contract. I only know what the steward tells me."

"Your father doesn't talk to you?" Adele asked.

Roelynn shrugged again. "He never talked to me much. He really only talked to Micah."

We were all silent a moment. "What about Summermoon?" I finally said. "Is your father going to do anything?"

Roelynn shook her head. "I don't think he'll be able to summon the strength. And I think—I can't either. I can't help plan a dinner or a ball, and greet people at the door, and laugh, and pretend I'm happy." She looked out the window. "I don't even know how I'm going to get through the day," she whispered.

"You can come to the Leaf and Berry on Summermoon," Adele said. "We can always use extra hands in the kitchen. You can put on a plain white apron and serve dinner to the guests."

I was scandalized, but Roelynn was smiling. "Can I wear a little lace cap and speak with a country accent?"

"I'm sure people will expect it," Adele said.

"I hope Melinda comes for Summermoon," Roelynn said. "She doesn't always."

"I heard a story the other day," Adele said. "That Melinda had been in Tambleham shortly after a woman there had a baby girl. And the woman was moping around the house because she was so depressed. She had wanted a baby boy instead. And then Melinda passed through town. And the next time the woman went to change the baby's diapers—" Adele paused for effect. "—the girl had changed into a boy!"

"No!" Roelynn exclaimed.

"Yes! That's what I heard, anyway," Adele said.

They were both smiling—the first time in weeks—so I didn't bother to point out that the story was patently false. I had heard the tale, too, from a traveler who'd had one too many glasses of ale in the taproom, and I hadn't believed it for a second.

"I heard that when Melinda left Thrush Hollow, a troupe of mimes and jugglers came to town," Roelynn said. "And they'd never been to Thrush Hollow before. And some little boy—ten years old—had wished for that every day since he was five years old. No one else cared that they were there, but he was the happiest boy in the kingdom."

"I think maybe we should ask Melinda about some of these stories," I said dryly.

"Why?" Roelynn said. "She'll tell you herself, she doesn't have the power to choose which dreams come true and which ones don't. She just has this—magic—in her body that sometimes works and sometimes doesn't."

Roelynn fell silent. We all knew what she would be wishing for right now, and what Melinda would most decidedly grant, if the Dream-Maker had the power to make such decisions.

"So!" I said, just to be saying something. "Do you think your father will be taking you to Wodenderry anytime this year?"

"I don't know. He hasn't mentioned it. I know he wants to renew his shipping contracts with the queen, though, so I expect he'll have to go to the royal city sometime."

"Would you want to go?" Adele asked.

Roelynn made an indecisive gesture with her hands. "Maybe. I don't know. A trip like that would be good for me—give me something to think about."

"Maybe you could come to school with us," I suggested, trying to come up with practical distractions. "We're studying foreign history right now."

"Thank you, I'd rather be trampled by horses from a runaway carriage," she answered politely.

135

"Work in the dress shop," Adele suggested, getting into the spirit. "Wait on haughty and indecisive customers who always ask you if you can give them a better discount."

"Or the stables," I said. "You're good with animals."

"And you like the grooms and the coachmen," Adele murmured.

That actually made Roelynn laugh. "All excellent ideas," she said. "I have to come up with some kind of activity, I suppose. I haven't wanted to do much of anything since Micah died."

"He's not dead," I said absently. I was trying to think of an even more outrageous pursuit to suggest.

It was a moment before I realized that Roelynn and Adele were staring at me in utter, shocked silence. It was another moment before I realized what I had just said. I put my hands across my mouth, as if to check for untrue words, but my lips were blameless. I felt that pressure against my chest, diamond-hard and just as precious, that always signaled absolute certainty.

"He's not dead," I whispered. "You know I can't say the words if they're false."

"How do you know?" Roelynn whispered back. I had thought she was pale before, but her face was completely bloodless now. "Please don't—if you're not sure—please—"

"I just know," I said. "I don't know where he is. But he's alive."

Roelynn put her head down on the table and started sobbing. The cook bustled up, concerned and motherly, and put her arms around Roelynn's shoulders. The look she split between Adele and me said she would never welcome us back in her kitchen to upset her darling again.

"I'm sorry," I said, my tongue tripping over my words. "I said something—I didn't mean to make her cry—just give me a few minutes to explain. . . ."

"I think it's time for you and your sister to go home now," the cook said in a severe voice. "I think I'll just put Miss Roelynn to bed now. Maybe you'd better not come by tomorrow."

"But I—" I started, but Adele grabbed my hand and rose to her feet. "Tell her to come to the inn if she wants to talk later," I called over my shoulder as Adele towed me past the stoves and tables and out the back door of the kitchen.

We had walked through the vegetable garden, past the orchards, and down to the street before Adele relaxed her grip on my hand. She hadn't said a word since I had made my startling pronouncement, though her face had looked as pale as Roelynn's. I glanced over at her now, as we wove through the pedestrian traffic on our way back to the inn. Her face was composed and unreadable as ever, but flushed with a delicate color. She looked pretty, and she hadn't looked pretty for weeks. She looked happy.

"It has to be true," I said, "or I couldn't say it."

She gave me a radiant smile, then leaned in to kiss me on the cheek. I swear she actually skipped a few steps down the street. "I know," she said. "I believe you."

Every morning for the next week, I woke to find Adele lying on her bed, watching me. Every day, as soon as she saw me open my eyes, she said, "Micah is coming home today."

Every morning for the first six days, I replied, "That isn't true."

The seventh day, I said, "That's true." I felt an insistent tension in my heart, an excitement and a conviction both impossible to ignore.

We were both on our feet and dressed within minutes. It was a school day, so we left a vague note for our parents saying that we had had to leave but would come back later with good news. We ran through the streets to Roelynn's house, slipping like ghosts through the early morning fog. At the kitchen door, we managed to convince the cook that we really had to see Roelynn, it was terribly important, and she assigned a young abigail to lead us silently upstairs to the room where Roelynn slept.

She wasn't sleeping. She was watching the door, as I imagined she might have been watching it every day for the past week. "It's today?" she said, sitting up in bed.

"It's *now*," I confirmed.

Soon the three of us were racing toward the harbor as fast as our feet would take us. We could see the ocean from almost every vantage point, count the tall masts of the docked ships—and spot the potbellied white sail of the small merchant vessel that was coasting toward land on a die-away breeze. We ran even faster, till our lungs burned and our legs ached and our cheeks were red with exertion. We arrived moments after the anchor had been let down, and the gangplank had been lowered to the pier. We were there in time to see a tall, thin figure come limping off of the deck and make its way carefully, painfully, down the swaying surface of the wooden walkway.

Roelynn shrieked and flung herself at him with such force she almost carried both of them into the water. Adele and I were only a few steps behind, but we hung back once we had reached them, not wanting to intrude on their reunion. I could hear Roelynn's voice, sobbing into his shirt, "You're alive, you're alive, you're alive," and Micah's voice in astonished counterpoint, "But how did you know I would be here? This morning? On this ship?"

And then he looked up, and he saw me, and by the expression on his face, I knew that he understood the role I had played. He thanked me with his eyes while he kissed the top of his sister's head. I was shocked at how emaciated his body looked, how drawn his features were. Wherever he had been, he had suffered greatly. I felt a sudden great wave of affection for him, this man I had always thought so dull, so uninteresting. What a tale he must have to tell of terrors he had survived! And what a good man he must have been all this time, though I had never known it, if two of the people I loved best in the world had been made so happy by his return. I found myself studying his face and finding in it all sorts of virtues I had never realized he possessed—strength of will, and courage, and kindness. It was the face of a decent man, I realized, one who could be trusted never to fail you. His face was lovable, even if it would never be handsome.

And then he looked at my sister, and his face changed, and I realized I had been wrong again. At that moment, he was beautiful.

~ ℘ ~

Micah's return was a nine days' wonder in Merendon. Karro could not very well decree a holiday in honor of the event, but it was clear to everyone that Summermoon would serve as a de facto celebration. Never was the town to see such a festival! Karro had engaged entertainers from all over the kingdom to come to Merendon. He had bought out the cellars of the vintners and ordered half the livestock of the county to be slaughtered to serve his dinner table. I never laid eyes on Karro between the day of Micah's return and Summermoon Eve, and yet it was impossible to escape the sense of his joy. His son had returned. Karro was Karro again.

And Roelynn was Roelynn and Adele was Adele, though for each of them their happiness was tempered with the remembered horror of loss. So easily this story could have ended another way—so likely, they knew, that sometime in the future it would. They were deliriously happy now, but they were both haunted; they would not forget to be grateful for this remarkable bounty, and they would not forget that it might be snatched away again at any moment.

Adele never shared with me what words passed between her and Micah when they finally got a chance for a private conference. If Micah swore that his brush with death had made life more precious to him—if it had made him realize that he could not give up Adele, no matter what his father demanded—she did not mention it to me. As far as I knew, nothing had changed between them.

But Adele had changed. It was difficult for me to say

exactly how. She had always been quiet, so her silence was nothing new. She had always been self-possessed and hard to ruffle, so her deep, unshakable tranquillity did not particularly excite attention now. But something had happened to her, laid its mark and color on her soul. I think it might have been merely the fact that she loved him, and he was alive. Perhaps she simply became an adult that summer, learning to handle an adult's fears and rewards, the truly terrible and truly wonderful things that children never have to endure.

Her experience put her a year ahead of me, but I was not far behind, and neither was Roelynn. The very next year, all of our lives changed forever.

Part

Two

CHAPTER ELEVEN

he year that Roelynn, Adele, and I turned seventeen, we prepared for the grandest Summermoon festival that Merendon had ever seen. Adele and I were particularly happy because we had graduated from school in the spring; Roelynn's parade of private tutors also had come to an end. We were all very certain we were young ladies now, the kind who could be expected to enjoy themselves at Summermoon. Indeed, the whole town braced itself for a rare and brilliant celebration as Karro began planning for his now-traditional ball three months in advance.

Word soon spread that Karro had invited seven families from Wodenderry to attend the ball, and six had accepted. All six were blessed with beautiful young daughters of marriageable age, so it was not hard to see what Karro's intentions were. If Adele minded the intrusion of such competition, she did not say so. Roelynn herself thought it very funny that her father would think any highborn young lady could be induced to believe that Micah was excellent husband material.

"For I love him very much, you know I do, but he's not a courtier," she told us one afternoon in spring. "He is not the sort of man a girl pines for and sighs over. I'm sure all of these girls are very put out to be forced to come to Merendon for a provincial ball when you know the queen will be having her own much more elegant affair in the royal city."

"I thought the queen had been invited to your father's ball, too," I said.

"Well, of course, she's been *invited,* but she declined most graciously," Roelynn said.

"And the prince?"

Roelynn giggled. "Oh, he was invited. But it turns out he's already accepted an invitation in—where was it? Oakton." She named a rather unfashionable town on the west edge of the kingdom.

"That seems unlikely," Adele said.

"*Most* unlikely," Roelynn agreed. "So I can't help but think he's going off with his cronies somewhere on some disreputable jaunt. One hardly likes to speculate what it might be."

Of course, we did speculate for a few moments, but since the three of us had all led rather sheltered lives, we were fairly sure we had not come up with anything depraved enough. When we ran out of ideas, Adele asked Roelynn, "So who will you be dreaming of come Summermoon? Are

any of these highborn Wodenderry ladies bringing along an attractive brother or two?"

Roelynn shook her dark head, her eyes wide with innocence. "No! I am quite fancy-free at the moment and determined to stay so. Men are more heartache than they're worth, I've decided."

Naturally, what this really meant was that Roelynn would be ripe for falling in love with the next unsuitable man who came along.

He happened to be the dancing master's apprentice.

The dancing master and his young assistant arrived at our inn one night most romantically, in a driving rain. Father ran out to take their coal black horses to the stables down the street, while Mother and Adele fetched them towels and blankets to dry their hair and faces and soak up the excess water from their cloaks. I stirred up the parlor fire and scurried back to the kitchen to see what we might have on hand so late at night, for it was almost eleven. All the other guests (musicians) were sleeping, and the four of us had been getting ready for bed when the urgent pounding had come at the front door. Adele and I had hurriedly thrown patched cotton gowns over our thin nightdresses and run down the stairs to discover the cause of the commotion.

Two late travelers, arriving in a storm. Two attractive young men, I might add. Well, this was certainly worth staying awake for.

By the time I came out of the kitchen with a tray of

hearty snacks, the new guests were ensconced in big cozy chairs before the fire and looking rather more comfortable. Father was back, totally drenched but appearing genial as always, and he was asking them questions about their trip as Adele and Mother set up small serving tables beside each chair. I put plates of food on each table, then stepped back beside Adele to lean against the parlor wall. Both of us were trying to turn invisible so that we would be allowed to stay up as long as possible. Both of us were staring at the new arrivals with frank curiosity.

One of the men had dark curly hair and a dark curly beard and snapping blue eyes that looked as if he thought even this wet ride had been a fine adventure. He was eating with gusto and paused every once in a while to toss Mother a word of praise for the taste of the roasted chicken or the fineness of the bread. Meanwhile, he answered all my father's questions about the condition of the roads behind and volunteered comments about the lodgings they had sampled while they traveled. He might have been in his mid-twenties, though the beard made it hard to be sure. His clothes, now steaming a little before the fire, looked as if they had once been very expensive but had been used so long and mended so often that now they betrayed a sort of faded gentility. Of course, they could have been just travel clothes; he might have much more splendid outfits in his luggage. His hands were large and blunt, but well cared for; he wore a large ruby ring on his left hand but no other sign of wealth.

It was impossible not to write him down as a member of the gentry who had fallen on hard times.

His companion ate just as heartily but hardly said a word. Still, he was so beautiful that even in his silence he drew the greater portion of our attention. He had fine, straight, ash blond hair; it probably fell some way past his shoulders, though it was difficult to tell, since it was tied back with a plain black ribbon. His cheekbones were amazingly sharp and his eyes were a mossy brown, and the combination of colors and angles gave him a somewhat elfin appearance. When they had come in, it was obvious that both men were tall, but when they were seated, the fairer one looked slim and delicate. I thought he was a few years younger than his companion, perhaps a few years older than Adele and I. His clothes, too, were fine but faded. If he wore any jewelry at all, it would have to be a pendant under his shirt where no one could see it. Though he did not look as if he could particularly afford such adornments.

Father finally got tired of inquiring about the condition of the roads and asked the only questions that Adele and I were really interested in. "So! What brings you to Merendon? And how long are you staying?"

The dark-haired man looked at the fair one. "We've heard there's to be a big ball here at Summermoon," the older one said. "Organized by some rich merchant in town."

Father nodded. "Yes, Karro's held such a ball for the past few years. A great event it is."

"I'm a dancing master from the royal city," the guest continued. "And this is my apprentice. We thought there might be some young ladies—and possibly some young gentlemen—who would appreciate a chance to brush up on

149

their skills. Unless balls are commonplace here and every-one feels quite secure in their waltzes and their cotillions," he added.

Adele squeezed my hand, but neither of us looked away from the two men in the big comfortable chairs. Dance instructors here at our inn! The Leaf & Berry would be the most popular destination in town.

"A dancing master!" our mother exclaimed. "Bless me, I don't think I've ever met such a person. And all you do all day is teach other people how to move their feet?"

Adele gripped my hand again, this time in mortification. Our mother was a wonderful woman, but she didn't always see the point in frivolity. It would be a dreadful thing if she offended these elegant creatures and sent them off to look for accommodations elsewhere.

But the curly-haired stranger was laughing. "Yes, that's all we do. Quite a ridiculous waste of time, wouldn't you say? But it makes our patrons happy, and it allows us to spend time more agreeably than we would pursuing an income through hard labor. We always practice indoors, so we can work whatever the weather, and we're usually well fed and well treated. Now and then our grateful clients toss an extra gold coin our way or hand down a fine garment that no longer fits them. . . ." He gestured at his own silken clothes. "It is a life just this side of elegance, and it suits me admirably."

His companion gave him a droll look out of his dark eyes, and the dancing master laughed. "Alexander finds different aspects of the life to be more enjoyable," he said, but did not specify. Adele and I could figure that out for ourselves, however. Alexander was so handsome that there was no doubt half of his customers fell in love with him, certainly the young girls whose mamas were trying to teach them the finer points of etiquette on the dance floor. I imagined he might be quite a dangerous man to invite into certain homes. I hoped the dancing master was able to keep his assistant more or less in check.

"Well! Would you be wanting to set up classes here at the inn?" Father said, glancing around the room with a measuring eye. Now Adele and I clutched each other with joy. "If we moved the furniture out . . . how much space would you need?"

The dancing master looked around the room with great interest, his blue eyes bright with calculation. "It's a little smaller than we're used to, but—yes, I think it would do quite well. Sessions of, say, six students at a time, plus my assistant and myself. I think we could manage to move around the room with a certain amount of grace. What do you think, Alexander?"

Alexander looked up from his plate of food and grinned. It was hard to believe, but he was even more good-looking when he smiled. "I think this will do excellently well," he said in a melodious drawl.

The dancing master nodded decisively and braced his hands on his knees as if planning for negotiations. "Then we'd like to engage your services for the next few weeks," he said to Father. "Two bedchambers and this parlor, for our exclusive use. We will advertise and schedule our classes, but we want this room to be available to us at any time we might wish."

"There'll be a fee, of course," Father said.

"Of course."

Mother and Father withdrew a few moments to confer. Alexander finished the meal on his plate, then sopped up the extra sauce with his bread. For such a slender man, he seemed amazingly capable of eating; he looked as if he could have started over from the beginning and consumed another complete meal. Then again, perhaps his gypsy life made regular mealtimes rare, and that fact actually accounted for his thinness.

Adele stepped forward. "There's more in the kitchen if you're still hungry," she said.

Alexander looked up at her, and a dazzling smile crossed his face. "No, this was just enough," he said in that beautiful voice. "But I was taught to let nothing go to waste."

His master snorted at that, so I guessed there was a story there, but not one I was likely to learn. I, too, stepped away from the wall. "More ale? Some water?" I suggested. "Or shall we clear the dishes away?"

As if for the first time, the two men seemed to see us both. I could see their eyes flick from Adele's face to mine and back again. "By the crown and scepter, you're twins," the dancing master exclaimed. Not a very original observation, but he seemed so delighted that I couldn't help but smile anyway.

Alexander was also smiling most attractively. "Identical twins," he added. "People must get you mixed up all the time."

"They do," Adele said. "It can be very entertaining."

The dancing master was scanning us with close attention. "But the eyes are different, aren't they?" he said. "And you wear your hair the opposite ways."

I had to admit I was impressed. Most people failed to notice those slight variations until they were pointed out, and even then they could not remember which twin was which. "We favor our opposite hands, too," I said, holding up my left hand while Adele extended her right.

"Still, that's not much help for a man who comes across you suddenly and tries to figure out which one you are," the dancing master said in a slightly dissatisfied voice. "How do people tell you apart?"

Adele, as always, was highly amused by the possibility of confusion. "They can ask us our names," she suggested.

"And those names are?"

"I'm Eleda. She's Adele," I answered. "But sometimes Adele answers to my name. I never answer to hers."

The dancing master divided a look between us again, seeming thoroughly intrigued. He was the sort of man who liked a puzzle, I supposed, and there couldn't have been too many puzzles to solve on the wet road to Merendon. "So you must have very different personalities as well," he speculated.

"Very," I said rather shortly. Adele merely offered him her mysterious smile.

"Hmmm," the dancing master said. "I wonder if

we will be here long enough to sort you out?"

"I don't mind confusing them," Alexander said. "They're both very pretty girls."

This made me smile and Adele laugh. "So what brings you to Merendon?" I asked, just to have something to say.

"I thought we already said. The famous ball at Mr. Karro's house."

I tilted my head a little, my senses alert. True—and yet not entirely. "There must be important balls in Wodenderry during the summer season," I said. "Why not stay there and run your lessons?"

The two men exchanged rueful glances. "There was—a reason—we needed to escape the city," the dancing master said at last. "Something quite minor, you understand, but— potentially unpleasant. Merendon seemed just far enough away to provide us a place to . . . relax. Think things over. Decide our next course of action."

Adele was nodding, but I frowned a little. It was clear he was not being completely honest, and yet he really hadn't said much of anything, so it was hard to judge. My quick suspicion was that Alexander had romanced a young noble-woman and an irate father wanted them out of the city. "Well, I hope our little town lives up to your expectations," was all I could think to reply.

Alexander grinned. "It has so far."

I didn't have a chance to respond to that. Father returned at that moment, a sum of money written on a piece of paper. "This is the price we've come up with," he said, showing the dancing master. "It covers your own meals as well as refreshments that might be offered to your patrons. Is it agreeable to you?"

The dark-haired man barely glanced at the figure and thrust a hand into his breeches pocket. "Most agreeable. How much of it would you like in advance?"

"The first week," my father said firmly.

The dancing master produced a roll of gold coins. "This should cover us. If you find we are more expensive than you bargained for, talk to me again at the end of the week and we'll discuss the matter."

Such open-handedness was unheard-of among our guests. I could see my father wishing he had asked for more money and then silently admonishing himself not to be greedy. Before he could say anything, our mother came hurrying up with the guest book in her hand. "Here, which of you would like to sign the book?" she asked. "And I'm sorry, I didn't catch both your names."

"I'm Alexander," the blond young man said, bowing from the waist as he sat in the overstuffed chair. I could only imagine how gracefully he would perform such a maneuver if he were standing and really trying to make a good impression.

"I'm Gregory, and I'll sign your register," said the dancing master, taking the book from my mother's hand.

I was staring at him, but he did not notice. His head was bowed over the page as he signed his name with a bold flourish. I could see the word *Gregory* taking shape only seconds after the syllables had come left his mouth. But every instinct in my body told me that he was lying, and that that was not his name at all.

CHAPTER TWELVE

I would say that it was barely noon the next day before every single resident of Merendon had heard the news about the dancing master and his apprentice. And this was even before my father and the man who called himself Gregory had hand-lettered a sign and attached it to a stake in the front lawn. "Available here: DANCING CLASSES, first come, first served." By evening of that first day, we had two dozen residents signed up for the first week of classes and more who had come to inquire. It was clear the dancing master and his apprentice were going to be a rousing success.

Roelynn was one of the first to stop by. "Dance instructors from Wodenderry," she breathed in a voice of undiluted delight. "But how utterly thrilling. And they've come to Merendon because of my father's ball! At last I have a reason to be grateful for my father's ostentation. I must sign up for classes."

Adele glanced over at her. "I hardly think you need them. You're a better dancer than anyone in Merendon."

Roelynn laughed. "But I *want* them. Think how much fun! And there will be no problem convincing my father they're necessary. He would not want me to be embarrassed by being less skillful than the young women from Wodenderry who are coming to town for the ball."

Indeed, the very next afternoon Roelynn returned carrying a roll of gold coins to pay for her lessons and bearing instructions from her father: She and Micah were both to take lessons with the new arrivals. But they were to have their own private sessions that were not to be intruded on or observed by any of the lesser townspeople.

"Though I'm *not* twirling around your parlor every day for two weeks in my brother's arms," Roelynn told us with a little sniff. "So one of you will just have to come in and work with Micah, since I can't imagine the dancing masters will want to take a turn with him."

"We'd be happy to help out any way we can," I said very gravely, though I was laughing inside. Adele, who could always control her features perfectly, seemed to show the faintest pink. "When do your lessons start?"

"Next week, in the afternoon," Roelynn said. "Better buy yourself some dancing shoes."

So it came about, several days later, that Roelynn and Alexander, Adele and Micah, and Gregory and I formed three sets of couples to tread out the figures of the waltz in my parents' parlor. If that had not occurred, I often ask myself, would everything else have followed? Would the events of Summermoon have unfolded differently, less dramatically, had we never paired off to practice the minuet, the quadrille, the country reels? Impossible to know, of course. I tend to give all the blame to the polonaise.

In the days before Adele and I began to take our dancing lessons, we became quite familiar with the routines that governed the parlor, now empty of all its furniture. A group of young women (and occasionally a young man or two) would arrive a few minutes before their scheduled hour and stand giggling in the hall. Adele and I would take their hats and offer them refreshments and usher them into the room when it was ready. Gregory would greet everyone with warm enthusiasm; Alexander would manage to bestow a private smile on each blushing girl. First they would review the steps that had been covered in the previous lesson, then they would demonstrate the movements that were to be learned this day. Finally, one of them would wind up the large, ornate music box and the whole group would begin to dance.

I had wondered, till I first heard the tinny tinkling of that box, who was going to supply the music for the lessons. The inn had no piano or harp, and none of us could play an instrument, anyway. Unless Alexander or Gregory planned to sing aloud while they went through the figures of the dance, I could not imagine how they expected to find their beat. But the music box was a delightful little invention. It came with ten or twelve long cylinders of metal, each one of them capable of producing a different tune. Once the cylinder was inserted and the box was wound up, the music would play for a full two minutes. I swear, I could never get that music out of my head, even when I left the inn to run errands. My dreams were haunted by those light, merry tunes, made no less appealing by the strange acoustics and metallic precision. Even in the days before I knew the formal steps, my feet were engaged in dancing. It was that kind of music. It was that kind of summer.

Within two days, it felt as if Alexander and Gregory had always lived at the inn. I'm sure that was because, for noble folk, they seemed most unpretentious. Everything pleased Gregory, and most things made Alexander smile. They were polite to my mother, respectful to my father, and completely at ease with Adele and me. They didn't flirt with us, exactly—they treated us more like mischievous little sisters who could be counted on to enliven any situation.

As you might imagine, Adele responded more favorably to such treatment than I did.

It was not long before Adele and Alexander, in particular, developed a bantering relationship that delighted them both. I was cooking in the kitchen one day while Alexander sat in the dining room and Adele brought him various ales to try with his dinner. "These are all good," he said, sounding genuinely appreciative. "Better than much of the beer I've been served in Wodenderry. Does your father brew any of it?"

"No, but the supplier has been a friend of my father's since they were boys."

"Well, I'll take a glass of the lager, and Greg will probably prefer the stout," Alexander said. "I have to thank you for allowing me to sample them."

"Of course."

A pause. "Now which sister are you?" Alexander asked cautiously.

No hesitation. "Eleda." I looked up from my frying pan and stared at the door in some resentment, not that either of them could see me.

"The left-handed one? Write your name for me."

A laugh. "No, I'm Adele."

"The devious one." A note of satisfaction in his voice. "I thought so."

The softest voice imaginable. "Devious, sir? How cruel."

"Oh, well, if we're to talk of cruelty, let's discuss lying to poor weary travelers who try in good faith to learn the identities of their hosts."

"I would think dancing all day would exhaust you more than trying to learn four simple names."

This time he laughed. "Dancing all day with blushing, giggling, smiling, beautiful young girls? You must have a strange idea of the ways of young men if you think that's a tedious chore."

"For some men it would be torture."

"Well, I suppose I am more dissolute than most."

He was not, though. Dissolute, I mean. I never saw him or Gregory take more than two glasses of ale at any one meal, and they didn't go out carousing in the evenings at the excellent pubs of Merendon. They often played games of cards or chess in the dining room (there being no place left to sit in the parlor), and then retired relatively early to their rooms. While they might have flirted outrageously with the young women who came for lessons, they did not seem to be bent on seduction. They appeared, in fact, to think of very little except dancing.

During this first week before our own lessons began, Adele could think of very little except how to trick Alexander. She spent hours up in our room practicing writing my name with her left hand, but she never mastered the skill well enough to deceive anybody. If Alexander commented on some item of clothing I'd worn, Adele would be sure to put it on the very next day. If he was within view and someone called my name, she would turn and respond. If I was nowhere in sight, she would ask, "Where's Adele?" Once we had explained to the two of them our roles as Safe-Keeper and Truth-Teller, she would go sit under the chatter-leaf every time she had a free moment.

I don't know if Alexander was ever truly fooled, but he pretended to be often enough to make them both erupt into gales of laughter. For myself, I could not understand what was so funny, and I spent much of those first few days seething with a silent irritation.

Gregory seemed to find my anger as amusing as Alexander found Adele's antics. He was coming in one day as I was flouncing out, having overheard my sister tell our guest that it was impossible for her to speak a lie. "Well! You're in a hurry," Gregory observed, holding the door for me as I stalked out to fetch more wood for the kitchen stove. "What's put such a scowl on your face?"

"Irrational behavior," I said shortly, and headed for the woodpile. He followed me, which surprised me, and loaded up his own arms with fuel. No guest had ever done such a thing before.

"How much do you need?" he asked. "Is this enough?"

"Yes—plenty—thank you," I stammered. He followed me back into the house, too, and arranged the logs precisely in the carrier.

Then he pulled up a chair at the kitchen table and seemed prepared to sit and talk. "So who's being irrational?" he asked. "I don't suppose you could spare a cup of tea, could you? I'm thirsty."

I could hardly tell him to get out of the kitchen, though I couldn't imagine why he would want to sit there and converse with me. So I set the kettle on to boil and got out one of the stained old earthenware cups we used just for family. If he was going to sit in the workers' quarters, he was not going to be treated like a guest.

"My sister," I fumed. "Playing games with your apprentice."

Gregory laughed softly. "I think my apprentice quite enjoys the games."

"But it's so ridiculous!" I exclaimed. "Why would that be any fun at all? Who would want to pretend to be someone she's not?"

Gregory cocked his head to one side. "Someone whose ordinary life is hard or full of trouble. That person might like to escape into someone else's personality for a while."

That brought me to a full stop. "Adele's life is not so hard," I said stiffly.

He shrugged. "Maybe not, but she's a Safe-Keeper. If the

Safe-Keepers I'm acquainted with are any guide, Adele knows some dreadful tales, and some of them may haunt her from time to time. It would be a relief to be careless and silly now and then."

In fact, I could not dispute this. I knew only a few stories Adele had kept secret that had later come to light in some public way, but they had been brutal enough. If she harbored many of these, her thoughts must always be hemmed about with shadows.

"You might be right," I said grudgingly. "But I don't think that's Adele's motivation. She just likes to see what happens when things are stirred up. She's like a cat sitting on the corner of a dresser, pushing at some little china dish. Pushing it to the edge. Just to see what happens when it falls to the floor."

Gregory grinned. "And never in your life have you pushed a china dish off the edge of the dresser."

The kettle sent up its hysterical whistle, and I hurriedly poured a cup of hot water for Gregory. He steeped his tea and watched me with bright blue interest. Clearly, he still wanted an answer. I made a mug of tea for myself as well, and stood there sipping it as I thought the situation over.

"I think there's enough trouble in the world already without stirring up more," I said at last. "I don't understand why things have to be so tangled. I don't understand why people go around confused, and don't ask questions, and get things muddled up. I don't understand why everyone isn't just absolutely honest all the time."

The answer seemed to please him, though I was not sure

why. As if he liked the way I saw the world, all sharp edges and simple lines. "I think the truth is that most people are afraid of absolute honesty," he said. "They're always hoping against hope that what they know as reality in fact can be changed by pretending the world is otherwise. If they say they are rich, or handsome, or clever, perhaps those things will come true. Not many people have the strength to stand before the mirror and see themselves as they truly are."

"I just don't see the point in deception," I said.

"I know," Gregory replied. "That's what I like about you."

I gave him a keen look. I was remembering that the name he claimed was not, in fact, his own. "It is something you have some experience with, I'd wager," I said rather dryly.

He grinned. "Oh, I do. Any man or woman who has spent some time in noble circles will tell you the same. You must always lie and flatter and swear promises you cannot possibly keep, all to make sure the queen is happy or your own political position is secure. You must make alliances with men you positively hate, and flirt with the ugliest women in the kingdom. Think of my own position! Servant to the gentry! Can you imagine any situation more bounded by deceit? 'You dance most excellently well, my lady.' 'Ah, your daughter is the very picture of grace.' 'You will win the hearts of all the young men tonight, I am sure of it.' It is by charm alone that I make my way in the world—and charm, you know, is merely duplicity wrapped up in an irresistible package."

My one experience with charm made me wholehearted-ly agree with that. "Well, you needn't waste any effort trying to flatter and compliment me," I said. "I prefer to hear the truth—in fact, I usually know when I'm being lied to."

He toasted me with his cup of tea, now nearly empty. "I know," he said. "I wouldn't even try."

"You already have."

He tilted his head, interested but hardly alarmed. "Really? When?"

"When you said your name was Gregory," I said, and then held my breath to see his reaction.

He burst out laughing. I had not expected him to be amused; my scowl came back. "Ah, but that was before I knew you were a Truth-Teller," he said gaily. "I would not try such tricks now."

I waited for a moment. "Then you'll tell me your proper name, I suppose?" I asked politely.

He was still smiling. "If the occasion demands. Oh, yes, I will be perfectly forthright with you then."

I turned away and began noisily piling dishes in the sink for washing. "I can hardly guess what occasions *you* consid-er to require the utmost honesty," I said.

He came to his feet and set his cup on the counter next to me. "Well, then," he said, "I suppose you have a great deal to learn."

Only later did it occur to me that Gregory might be more adept at spotting the truth than speaking it. For instance, never once in the following days did he mix me up with my sister, and she tried to trick him with the same methods she used on Alexander. I don't know if, that very first evening in our house, he had memorized the slight physical differences between us or if, like the people who knew us best, he thought we were so dissimilar that he really never experienced any confusion. I did know that it was gratifying to be viewed as an individual, myself, not just one of a set of interchangeable servant girls. I did know that, false name or no, the dancing master was one of the most appealing men I'd ever met.

CHAPTER
THIRTEEN

wo days later, Roelynn and Micah arrived to begin their private dancing lessons. At first, everything seemed wrong. Adele and I knew how to perform various country jigs, and we even had some rudimentary knowledge of the more formal dances like the minuet, but I at least felt clumsy and stupid when it came time to try most of the other complicated steps. I was used to hauling wood and shaking out wet laundry and scrubbing the stains off the good carpet; I was not used to putting my hand on a man's shoulder or setting it on his sleeve and moving my body through a precise series of movements.

Micah was exceptionally patient with me, constantly reassuring me that I had not hurt him when I crushed his toes with my heel, but that only made me feel worse. I wasn't quite sure how I had drawn Micah as a partner, anyway. Well, yes, I was. Adele, whom I had expected to link hands with Micah herself, had made certain she was standing by Alexander when the first bright notes of the music sounded. So she had been paired with Alexander; Roelynn, who had no intention of ever dancing with her brother, had turned naturally to Gregory; and that had left me to stumble through the figures with Micah.

It was just the sort of behavior I had come to think of as typical of Adele. I knew she wanted to dance with Micah. It was obvious, by the quick and hopeless looks he sent in her direction, that he wanted to dance with her. Roelynn, who had frankly told us she thought Alexander was the most handsome young man she'd ever seen, clearly would have preferred him to Gregory. And, well, I would not have minded learning some of these intricate steps while being lightly held in Gregory's arms. Thus Adele must make everything impossibly difficult by ensuring that the longed-for combinations did not occur. Another instance of pushing over the china bowl to shatter on the floor.

But I was supposed to be dancing with Micah, and so dance with Micah I would, if I could catch the knack of it. He was not particularly skilled at the pastime himself, for he was such an earnest young man, but he knew enough not to disgrace himself with titled ladies in his father's ballroom. So he corrected me in a grave voice when I missed a step, and pulled me gently in the proper direction when I tried to twirl away. When I nearly brought us both crashing into the pointed edge of the mantel, he turned his shoulder sharply into the corner and took the brunt of the impact. You would not think that learning a dance was the best field in which to come to appreciate another person's character, but in this case it was. After we had completed a half hour of clumsy dipping and swaying, I was half in love with Micah myself, just for his invariable kindness. If his other virtues were half so steadfast, he was a rare prize indeed.

"There, that was much better," he said as our latest trial ended. "A little practice, and you'll be very good."

"After this, you'll be well prepared to squire the rawest young girl around your father's ballroom," I said, trying to make a joke of it. "No one can possibly step on your feet more often than I did."

"You're so light that I hardly felt it," he said gallantly, and we both laughed.

Roelynn pushed her dark hair back from her face and smiled at all of us. "This is so much fun," she said. "Better than a full orchestra and a hot ballroom on a summer night."

"Let's take a break for refreshments, and then change partners for the second half of the hour," Gregory suggested.

I found myself interested to see what would happen when it came time to pair up again. Would Roelynn's determination outsmart Adele's subtlety? We all stood around sipping lemonade and munching on sweet cookies, and I watched as Roelynn edged toward Alexander and Adele made conversation with Gregory. I hid a smile in the yellow swirls of my drink. I would probably be poor Micah's partner for this second round as well.

"Everyone rested? Good," Gregory said, and wound up the music box again. He set it on the mantel to play, and then calmly pushed through the small knot of dancers to take my hand. "Pair up," he said.

Roelynn turned instantly into Alexander's arms, and

Adele had no choice but to accept Micah's courtly and humble bow. I ducked my head to hide a laugh.

From the very first measures of the music, it was clear that this was the way the six of us were meant to dance.

Adele and Micah moved smoothly into the first figure of the waltz, catching each other's cues with the ease of long friendship. Her hand rested so lightly on his shoulder that I was sure her fingers did not crease the fabric, and his palm was placed at her waist with such formal correctness that he could have been dancing with the queen herself. But there was something about the way they responded to each other, something about their parallel rhythms, that made it obvious they were no strangers to embracing. Nothing in their faces gave them away. Adele did not blush or giggle. Micah's expression did not relax into a foolish grin. But they knew each other; they loved each other. I did not see how words or expressions could have made it any plainer.

"Ah," I heard Gregory sigh in my ear, and I knew he was seeing what I saw. But I did not respond. I merely turned my gaze to assess the other couple in the room.

Alexander and Roelynn, it appeared, had just this very instant invented the delights of dance. No silly restraint here, no pretense of indifference. They held each other rather indecently close and twirled around the room with a gait that was perilously close to romping. He gazed down at her with that alluring smile on his face, all-melting brown eyes and sensuous curved lips. She was laughing up at him with a face so pretty and so inviting that I could hardly believe he did not kiss her on the spot. She was a hoyden and he was a rogue, and it was impossible to believe either had ever had a more perfectly suited partner. They were so engrossed in each other that I was willing to believe they did not even hear the music, that they merely kept to the beat because it matched the frolicking cadence of their hearts.

"*Ah* again," said Gregory, who apparently could always tell what I was seeing and what I was thinking without any hints from me.

"It is proving to be a most interesting dance lesson," I said, my voice very low.

"Yes, but at least *you* were expecting it to be," he replied, his tone as quiet as mine. "I had no idea."

I risked a quick look up at him. He was smiling down at me, his teeth very white against the dark curls of his beard. "With Roelynn, you never know what to expect," I said.

"But you are not surprised about your sister."

I did not answer.

One thing did surprise me, however, and that was how immeasurably my dancing had improved once I was partnered with Gregory. Perhaps, because he was a professional, he was just much better at this particular pastime than Micah was. He knew what kind of mistakes an inexperienced girl was likely to make, and he gently guided her feet in the proper direction. Perhaps he just held me a little closer, so that it was easier for me to anticipate his actions, move left when his body moved right, dip when he wanted me to bend. Perhaps the previous half hour's practice had taught me more than I realized at the time. Perhaps—oh, perhaps I merely liked him better, wanted to please him more, and felt lighter in his arms.

Though that was ridiculous, and I had no interest in falling in love with him and inevitably breaking my heart and feeling as if I wanted to die once he and his handsome companion rode out of Merendon in a few weeks' time. So I schooled my features into a serious expression and paid closer attention to the music so that I did not miss the signal to reverse directions.

"What? Why are you frowning at me?" Gregory asked immediately.

"I'm not *frowning*. I'm concentrating."

"It will be much easier if you merely follow my lead. No concentration required."

"I don't know if it's possible for me to do that."

He laughed softly. "No, I suppose not. But you're managing very well despite the fact that you're thinking about it too hard."

"I imagine everyone dances well with you," I said, and I could not keep the slightest note of despondency out of my voice.

He laughed again. "Now, how shall I answer that without lying?"

"Don't even try. It's obvious you're such a gifted dancer that you make every girl seem skillful in turn."

"I've always liked to dance," he said, releasing my hand so that we promenaded side by side for one turn around the room. When the music gave its notice, we faced each other again and I replaced my hand on his shoulder. He continued as if there had been no pause. "But I don't believe I have ever enjoyed any dance as much as this one with you."

I waited for that clarion blast to sound in my head, the insistent bleat of *liar, liar*. But it did not come. Odd as it must be to him as well as to me, Gregory was speaking the truth.

The dancing lessons continued on exactly this way for the next full week. Every session would begin with us paired up in some way that suited none of us, and Adele was usually the reason for that; every session ended with the arrangement of partners that seemed to make everyone happiest. I don't know what the men discussed among themselves, but never, not once, did Adele or I make any comments about our dancing partners.

That left Roelynn to rhapsodize about Alexander's multiplicity of charms. He was handsome; he was funny; he was graceful; he was generous. Generous? How did one discover a trait like that on a dance floor? It turned out that she and Alexander had spent some time together, on the odd afternoon here or the cool evening there, as the week unfolded. "And he bought me some flavored ice at the booth that's gone up at the edge of town, and he paid to gain us admittance into the tent where the singers were performing," she said. "Oh! And he bought me the sweetest doll with a painted porcelain face and hair that I think is *real* hair. I hope it didn't come from a dead person."

"Generous indeed," Adele said, predictably amused. "Just how much money do you think a dancing master's apprentice has to waste on pretty girls? Not much, I would think."

"No," Roelynn said sunnily. "Which makes me think he is spending it on no one but me."

It was clear that Roelynn had fallen in love with yet one more ineligible young man. I was in no position to criticize the time she spent with him, however, since I seemed to be committing the same indiscretion myself. Not that I was off dallying with Alexander—oh no. I was spending pleasant hours outside the makeshift ballroom with the dancing master himself.

It seemed strange to me, considering how many hours of his day were booked with lessons, how much free time Gregory managed to find. When I was working in the kitchen, he frequently came in for an informal cup of tea. When I was bringing in wood or weeding the garden, he joined me more often than not and contributed his own strength to the chore. Many times when I had errands to run, he found some excuse to come along, and then he carried my packages home or sometimes—like Alexander— treated me to some sweet offered by the streetside vendors.

I particularly remember one stroll down the main boulevards of Merendon after we had had six days of lessons. The town was not yet as crowded as it would be in the final days before Summermoon, but it was starting to fill up. Jugglers practiced their routines in the green spaces; singers offered up their voices on the street corners; vendors set up carts in any convenient cul-de-sac and sold everything from meat to ale to pastries. The weather was so fine and the collective mood was so good that it seemed as if the festival had already arrived and merely stretched itself out to accommodate a season instead of a day.

I was accosted probably eight different times during the hour we took to pace down one street and up another.

First I was approached by a clutch of young boys, maybe eleven or twelve, who came running up and calling my name. "Eleda! Eleda!" they cried. Children this age never bothered asking tricky questions to discover which twin was which. They just grabbed my fingers and squeezed to see how much power I could put in the return grip, or tossed me a ball to see which hand I instinctively used to catch it. This always satisfied them. They were always right.

"Eleda, he was cheating!"

"I was not!"

"He said his marble knocked mine out of the circle, but it *didn't*. He moved it with his foot."

Disputes of this nature, I'd found, were always glaringly obvious to me. As soon as their voices sounded, the timbre of the lie jarred against my internal sensors. "Robbie didn't cheat, but Martin did," I said coolly, causing howls of fury to be directed at Martin. "You'd better take back your original marbles and replay those last few games."

There were a number of harmless blows rained on the unrepentant Martin, and then the whole group moved off like one migratory swarm. We hadn't gone more than half a block down the street when a woman named Constance hurried out through the door of our finest restaurant.

"Eleda! Wonderful! I was wanting to talk to you. I need

to—" She paused and gave me a doubtful look. "That is, is it safe to tell you something in confidence?"

I laughed. "No!"

Constance broke into a smile. "Oh, good. It *is* you. Come inside and tell me what you think of this. I want to start serving it during Summermoon week, and I think it's quite tasty, but you will tell me if it is or not."

"I'll give my opinion, too," Gregory volunteered.

She gave him a rather harried smile. She was about my mother's age, though she had grayed earlier, and her face was perpetually flushed from hours spent in the kitchen. "Naturally, I'd like to hear what you think," she said politely. I didn't think she had the faintest idea who he was.

We followed her through the darkened front room with its carefully set tables and went back into the hot, crowded, extremely aromatic kitchen. "I like the way it smells, anyway," I said, taking a sniff. Beef and onions and bread. Constance appeared to have made some kind of meat pie that was more sophisticated than the traditional dish.

"Yes, I got the recipe from my sister, who lives in Wodenderry. Here's a small portion for each of you."

We serve fairly plain fare at the inn, so I don't know much about fancy foods, but I instantly loved the mix of flavors that exploded on my tongue. I could identify wine and a few spices in addition to the main ingredients, and the bread of the crust was rich with butter. "Constance! This is delicious!" I exclaimed.

"Oh, good, you like it."

"You got this from someone in Wodenderry?" Gregory

asked, holding his plate out for another taste. "Not from any household or restaurant I was ever invited to."

"So you like it, too?"

"I'll come back tonight for a full portion if you're going to practice the recipe again."

Constance laughed, her pink cheeks even pinker with pleasure. "What do you think I should call it—the Royal Dish? The Perfect Pie? Can I tell everyone you gave it your approval?"

We discussed possible names for the new menu item, I gave permission to use my name, and Gregory and I were on our way again.

"This is proving to be even more enjoyable than I thought it would," he said, amused. "Though I find myself wondering how the promenade down the street would differ if I was with your sister instead of you."

I laughed. "Oh, people would be creeping up from the sides of buildings, having waited in the shadows for her to walk by. And then they would tug surreptitiously on her sleeve, and whisper something in her ear, and she would nod and whisper back. Tell them a time and place to meet her, usually, though sometimes she'll go off with them right that very moment if their story is desperate and doesn't take much time to tell."

"And she never repeats the tales?"

"Never a word."

"That's a hard job," he commented.

I grimaced. "I couldn't do it."

We stopped next at the dressmaker's shop. I was sure

Gregory would wait for me outside, because it wasn't the sort of place a man usually likes to enter, but he stepped right through the door behind me. When I gave him a look of surprise, he grinned.

"I thought I might order a new waistcoat," he said. It was a lie, I could tell, but a harmless one. I shrugged.

I was here to pick up the frocks my mother, Adele, and I had ordered for Summermoon. Even though Summermoon was a working holiday for us, it was a holiday nonetheless, and my mother firmly believed that everyone deserved new clothing on such occasions. Every year for as long as I could remember, all three of us had gotten new wool or velvet gowns at Wintermoon, and cotton and linen dresses at Summermoon. My father, less interested in fashion, consented to a new vest or jacket about once every five years. This was not one of those years.

I had barely stepped three feet inside the door when Eileen Dawson and her mother came up to me. Eileen was a much more sober girl these days than she'd been a few years ago, but in some ways kinder. At any rate, she was always friendlier to my sister and me than she had been back when we were in school together. I suppose personal tragedy often has that effect—it makes you think more carefully about the way you treat other people. Or it makes you hate everyone else more than you ever thought possible. One of the two.

"Eleda," she said. "Or is it Adele?"

"Eleda," I answered, but the shopkeeper called to us from across the room.

"That's not the right question to ask!" Lissette said.

"You must ask her if she would keep your secret!"

Eileen looked at me, her eyebrows arched over her beautiful face. I sighed. How much easier my life would have been if Adele had not been so capricious. "No," I said. "I wouldn't."

"Eleda," Eileen said, satisfied. "What do you think of this material? My mother wants to buy it for my wedding dress."

She extended her hands, buried in a length of cool, watered silk. Eileen was even fairer than I was, with extraordinarily blonde hair and pale, pale skin. Her eyes were a blue so light that at times they seemed colorless. She was so delicate that she possessed an ephemeral quality; you could imagine her vanishing into moonlight even as you watched.

"Hold it up to your face," I said, though I didn't need to. I already thought it was a dreadful fabric for her, and the juxtaposition of skin and cloth only confirmed my impressions. I shook my head. "I think it makes you look like a ghost," I said. "You need a fabric with a rosier tone to it."

Her mother was instantly antagonized. "It's the most expensive silk in the shop!" she exclaimed. "Eileen deserves the best!"

"Eileen deserves to look her best, too," I said quietly. "But buy what you want."

Eileen instantly laid aside the fabric and turned to Lissette. "I don't like it, either," she said. "Let's look at that figured silk again."

The Dawsons moved up to the front of the store to confer with Lissette. Gregory sidled my way. "And now I'm almost afraid to ask what you think of this green satin," he said in an undervoice. "I'm certain you'll say it's too showy for Summermoon. Should I opt for blue instead?"

I glanced at the bolts he indicated and smothered a laugh. They were both ghastly, the kind of cheap material you might use to line a cloak or a portmanteau, but not something most people would consider wearing. While his clothes were a touch outmoded, it was obvious they had once been of the highest pitch of fashion. I knew he was teasing me. "Why don't you buy some of each?" I said warmly. "Then you'll have a spare to wear if you spill something on one."

He grinned, but before he could answer, another young girl came out from the back room where I had once hidden while Roelynn and her father brangled. She was a year or two younger than I was, awkward and gangly, but her father was a wealthy Merendon landowner, and I knew she had been invited to Karro's ball. I couldn't remember her name, but I more or less liked her. She wore now a wide smile and a hopeful expression as she paraded up to me in a gown so new that it still had pins holding some of the seams together.

"It's Eleda, right? That's what you told Eileen?" she asked. I nodded in confirmation, and she pressed on. "What do you think of my dress? Isn't it beautiful?"

It was, in fact, hideous. The cut was wrong for her, accentuating her bony shoulders and long, skinny arms, and the broad sash at the waist ended in a bow over her backside that did not enhance her body in the slightest. Her mother came trailing out behind her and cast me a rather frightened look. I read into that expression that she had tried to talk her daughter into something that would suit her better, but that her daughter had insisted on this cut, this color, and would be heartbroken now if anyone told her she had chosen wrongly. Plus, of course, the dress was nearly finished; there would be a great deal of expense involved if it was deemed improper now.

"What beautiful fabric," I said in an admiring voice, reaching out a hand to touch one of the ruched shoulders. It was a gorgeous fuchsia that went well with her rich coloring. "And look what highlights it brings out in your hair! I can tell you are very happy with this dress."

She laughed excitedly and spun around. Her mother mouthed the words "Thank you" at me. The girl said, "I'll be the belle of Mr. Karro's ball, don't you think?"

There was not a chance of that. Scores of young ladies would be at the ball, most of them more beautiful and sophisticated than this country nobody, but I had learned how to speak the truth with a modicum of tact. "I think there will be a lot of belles at this particular ball," I said with a laugh. "But I'm sure plenty of young men will notice you."

"It's my first ball," she said.

"I hope it's wonderful," I replied.

I managed to pick up my purchases and get out of the shop before one more person approached and asked for an opinion. "Nicely done," Gregory murmured as he took the bundles from my arms. He directed me toward a street vendor selling watery and rather warm lemonade. But the day was hot and I was thirsty and I was glad for the treat. Clearly in no hurry, Gregory then plopped down on a nearby bench, the parcels piled up next to him, so I perforce took a seat as well.

For a moment, we sipped our drinks in silence. Then he said, "I can't help but notice that your friend Roelynn has taken rather a liking to my young assistant. What do you think of that?"

CHAPTER
FOURTEEN

laughed and then I sighed. "Well, it was inevitable that Roelynn would fall in love with Alexander," I said.

"How so?"

I gestured with the hand that wasn't holding the lemonade. "Roelynn always falls in love with the most unsuitable men in the vicinity. Grooms, coachmen, impoverished noblemen from Wodenderry whom she'll never see once the season is over—it's all the same to Roelynn. She falls in love with them all."

"It seems like a very uncomfortable way to live."

I laughed again. "Indeed it does! But I think Roelynn sees these forbidden romances as her one chance at—oh—rebellion and excitement. She knows that fairly soon her father will marry her off to someone important and titled, and she imagines her future as being insipid and circumscribed. So she's wild now while she can be."

Gregory took a meditative swallow. "Does her father

have any particular important and titled man in mind for his daughter?"

"How can you have lived in Merendon even two weeks and not heard that gossip?" I wondered. "Practically since she was born, Karro has wanted to betroth her to the prince."

Gregory's blue eyes grew very wide. "The prince? Prince Darian?"

I nodded vigorously. "Yes. Karro and the queen have been in business, oh, five or more years—I believe she has granted him the largest shipping contracts in the kingdom— and ever since they first signed a paper, Karro has been scheming to get Roelynn engaged to Darian. None of us is privileged to hear the queen's side of the story, of course, but in Merendon, speculation is that she is strongly considering the match. She's invited Roelynn to the palace several times and been very attentive to her. Although that could just be because she is generally very kind, for a queen," I added.

He was instantly diverted. "You've met Queen Lirabel?"

I nodded. "Yes, right after Princess Arisande was born. Adele and I were among the Truth-Tellers and Safe-Keepers who were allowed to come to the royal city and make our observations."

"And what did you think of the princess?"

I laughed. "Well, she was a baby, after all. But I thought she seemed like she would grow up to be a very sweet girl. Has she?"

"So far. She's still pretty young, and very much indulged. But she seems most easygoing."

"Unlike the prince," I said, remembering what I had said during that memorable audience.

"You met Darian?" he asked, surprised.

"Oh, no. He wasn't there. I just go by general reports. And the fact that the queen's advisor seemed amused when I said the prince might cause his mother some anxious moments. He seems to be full of deviltry."

"Yes, but for all his faults, Prince Darian is considered rather a beautiful young man," Gregory said, returning to the main topic. "Roelynn has met him several times and *still* decided she'd rather marry an ostler or a guard?"

"Not at all! They've never met! It's the funniest thing. There have been three or four times the prince has been scheduled to be at an event, and some—some improbable excuse has kept him away. Roelynn is convinced he has a secret lover of his own and has no more desire to meet her than she has to meet him. I must say," I added rather severely, "I don't understand why Karro *or* the queen can't let their children figure out for themselves whom they want to marry."

"The price of great power and riches," Gregory said with a grin. "You represent not just yourself, but the hopes and dreams of your household or your kingdom. It's one of the few reasons I've always been glad I wasn't a very important man."

"I suppose. So even if this match with the prince doesn't work out, Roelynn is fairly certain her father will want her to marry someone else dull and respectable. So she has her fun now."

"Roelynn doesn't seem the type," Gregory said cautiously, "to be forced into a marriage with anybody, no matter what her father says."

I laughed again at that. "You're right. So maybe she's just wild because she's wild, and she'll never marry to oblige her father. And Alexander is just one in a long line of harmless flirtations that she enjoys before she does something *truly* disgraceful."

"I have to think," said Gregory, "that a girl so flighty would not be the most appropriate person to marry the prince. And be queen someday."

"Oh, she'd be a wonderful queen," I said. I'd never really thought about it before, but the words came out of my mouth with conviction. "She's run her father's household since she was a little girl—and you should see the place, it's spotless and so well organized. All her servants love her, all the tradesmen in Merendon love her—she has such a gaiety that it draws people to her, but she's not . . . she's not cheap about it. She doesn't just pretend to like the people around her, she really does like them. She remembers birthdays and favorite colors. She's incredibly loyal. She's a good person in this sort of frivolous package. And she's so beautiful. I think she'd be the most popular queen this country had ever had."

Gregory cocked his head to one side. "So, then, we should find some way to promote the match. We should thwart her romance with my apprentice."

"I wouldn't worry about it," I said. "You'll only be here a few more weeks, and then you'll be gone. Roelynn will sigh

for a month or two, and maybe send Alexander a few per-
fumed notes, and tell us how much she misses him, but—"
I shrugged. "You'll never come back here, she'll never see
him again, she'll move on with her life. Fall in love with a
farmer, maybe, or one of the jugglers who comes to town for
next Summermoon."

He was watching me now, those bright eyes narrowed in
speculation. "What makes you think we'd never come back
to Merendon?" he asked.

I was surprised. "I don't—I just thought—won't you be
returning to Wodenderry whenever your current troubles
are solved?"

"Certainly, but that doesn't mean we never plan to leave
the city limits again," he said. "Why shouldn't we travel
back here? We have a growing list of clients. They may need
to refresh their skills before next Summermoon. Their sons
and daughters who are too young to need instruction now
may require some guidance in a year or two. And the queen
is always importing new dances from foreign kingdoms," he
concluded with a smile. "Won't the folk of Merendon want
to learn those before they go off to the royal city and show
themselves up as provincials?"

Strange, it had not occurred to me that, once this season ended, I would ever see Gregory again. I had realized
with some resignation that I thought him a delightful man,
most entertaining and indubitably attractive, and I realized
that I would be hard-pressed not to develop a hopeless
affection for him. But I had not supposed it really mattered.
He would leave Merendon, I would—like Roelynn—sigh for

a few weeks, be convinced my heart was broken, wallow in a period of despair, and then eventually shake myself out of it and move on with my life.

I had not contended with the thought that I might have to see him every year for an indefinite span of time, live under the same roof with him if he stayed at our inn, and watch him charm the young girls and put the young men at ease while the bouncy, tinny strains of the music box plucked out their melody behind him. I thought that might end up being a little too much for my heart to bear.

It was now even more important that I not allow myself to fall in love with him.

"Well," I said, and my voice sounded a little scratchy and stiff. "I'm sure you're right. I'm sure most of the people of Merendon would be happy to have you back again."

He grinned at me as if he realized just how close I skated to a lie. "So tell me," he invited. "What marvelous new sartorial creations did we just pick up at the dressmaker's shop? What will you be wearing to the Summermoon ball?"

I hate to admit it, but I tittered. I hate people who titter. I even hate the word *titter*. But there was no other appropriate response. "Oh, I'm not going to the ball!"

He stared. "Not? Of course you are. You and Adele are Roelynn's best friends."

"We're an innkeeper's daughters," I explained. "Only the landowners and the merchants and their families will be going. And the wealthier families from nearby cities and a few visitors from Wodenderry," I added.

Gregory was outraged at my words. I was astonished at

his outrage. "But that's—that's ridiculous! That's so elitist and pointless! Perhaps he might not invite every trades-man's daughter in Merendon, but—and, damn it, why *shouldn't* he invite every trademan's daughter in Merendon? Every one of them ought to be allowed to attend the ball! To dress up as fancy as she pleases and look absolutely beautiful—every young woman deserves a chance for that."

"And every young man," I added a little dryly, "or there will be no one for the girls to dance with."

He seemed truly angry now. "I mean, who is this Karro, anyway? He's just some backwater shipping merchant who's got more money than the queen herself, but that doesn't make him better than his fellows and neighbors. And he thinks his daughter deserves to marry the *prince*? And he can't even show a little generosity to his city?"

I was laughing. "It's not worth all this posturing," I said lightly. "None of the tradesmen's daughters expect to be invited. We have more fun, anyway, during Summermoon, visiting the fairs and hearing the singers and going to the plays—" I had to stop for a moment and collect myself. The words almost scalded as they came out of my mouth. Well, I had once enjoyed going to the plays, but I hadn't attempt-ed such entertainment in two years. Couldn't imagine I would want to any time in the near future. "We don't expect such honors," I resumed quietly. "We understand our place in the city. In the society."

"Well, it makes me furious," he said, and crossed his arms on his chest.

I could not keep a sardonic note from my voice. "Oh, and I suppose, there in Wodenderry, you and Alexander get invited to all the queen's events," I said. "I suppose all the great ladies you instruct in the quadrille and the polonaise want you at their parties to mingle with their guests as equals."

For an instant, his face wore a startled expression, and then his eyes narrowed. I saw a look of extreme wariness settle over his features. I knew instantly that he was trying to decide how to phrase something so that I wouldn't think he was lying.

"I've been at some events hosted by the nobility," he said carefully. "I have—it seems as if I've fallen on harder times now, but I have some connections. My relations are not wholly despised. If someone needs an extra man at the table or someone has found me entertaining enough, I am invited to attend some fairly grand functions."

I listened carefully, but nothing in his reply sounded false. But I could tell he was picking his way around pitfalls. "Then I suppose you've been invited to Karro's ball as well?" I asked sweetly.

"Oh, no!" he said cheerfully. "Though Alexander seems to think that Roelynn will try to wangle us invitations. But I don't want to go."

"Why not?"

He grimaced. "Too many people from Wodenderry there. Exactly the people I least want to see. Roelynn provided a guest list the other day, and Alexander and I were both horrified. Though Alexander," he added in some bitterness, "seems to be ready to throw caution to the winds. I think if Roelynn secures him an invitation, he'll go, whether or not it means he'll spend the evening ducking the most unpleasant set of pompous fools you'd ever hope to meet this side of Lowford."

"And now that you put me in mind of it," I said in a scolding voice, "I don't know why you should be calling Roelynn flighty when your own apprentice is at least as unsteady as she is."

He grinned unexpectedly. Really, he was a handsome man in general, but when a smile lit his face, he was almost irresistible. "Alexander is a scamp," he admitted. "No harm in him that I've seen, but not much seriousness either. He's as bad as Prince Darian, and I'm sure you've heard tales about *him*."

"Indeed, we all have."

"Alexander's mother is in despair, wondering what reckless thing he'll do next."

"Is that why she apprenticed him to you?"

"Oh, she thinks I'm responsible for half his misdeeds, which I assure you is not true! I've pulled him out of more scrapes than she even knows about. But she's not entirely thrilled to see him spending so much time with me. I only make her worry more."

"Perhaps if you had a profession more—substantial—than dance instruction," I said.

"More respectable, you mean? What would you suggest?"

"Well, I have to confess, I'm not really sure what

noblemen do to earn money. I thought they always just inherited it."

"I could gamble for a living," he said, seeming to think it over. "That's considered respectable. All the nobles gamble, and most of them are disastrous at it. But I don't win as often as I'd like, in general, which is why I haven't really pursued it as a career option. I could mark the cards, maybe. That would give me an edge."

"I can't imagine that Alexander's mother would think that was an improvement over dancing."

"No," he agreed. "And I've no head for figures, so I could hardly be some rich man's bookkeeper. And my handwriting isn't legible, even to the people who love me most, so I could hardly be a great man's secretary. Not interested in commerce. Fatigued by the very thought of farming." He shook his head. "No, my list of choices is very short."

"I'm beginning to think you're as given over to triviality as your apprentice," I said with mock sternness.

He smiled down at me. Devastating. "You know what I'd really like?" he said, and he actually sounded sincere. "I'd like your father's job. Running some sort of lodgings in a big town like Merendon. Making people feel welcome. Offering a valuable service and doing it well. I've stayed at more than a hundred inns from one end of the kingdom to another, and I've never liked one half so well as the Leaf and Berry. You can ask Alexander. More than one morning, I've gotten up and said, 'I'm not leaving this place.'"

I glowed a little to hear the compliment directed at my parents, but my practical nature couldn't resist seizing the opportunity. "Do that, then," I encouraged. "Find some of your wealthy relatives who will invest in your enterprise, and build an inn on one of the main posting roads. I'm sure my father would be happy to tell you everything you need to know."

"Maybe he'd give me a job," Gregory said thoughtfully. "I wouldn't even have to go back to Wodenderry."

At that, I just stared at him, feeling my blood turn to seawater.

He smiled at me, just the slightest touch of malice on his face. "Wouldn't that be fun?" he said softly. "If I were to live here year-round? You could see me every day. Wouldn't you like that?"

I could hardly think what to say, since the truth was ineligible and a lie would not pass my lips. He knew it, too. He knew I nursed a slight *tendresse* for him, and he had deliberately laid a trap with bland, harmless words.

"It might take some getting used to," was all I managed. "Having another person at the inn. But of course, so far it's been quite pleasant having you around. And Alexander, too, naturally."

He laughed out loud, wholly amused. I came to my feet, not amused in the slightest. "I think I might talk to your father this afternoon," he said cheerfully, grabbing my packages again as he stood beside me. I was already in motion, so he had to take two or three long strides to catch up with me. "I'd be interested to hear what he had to say."

And because I could not think of an answer to that, either, I merely walked on in silence.

CHAPTER FIFTEEN

he next week passed in much the same manner. In and among our usual chores of cooking food, cleaning rooms, weeding gardens, and waiting on guests, Adele and I continued with our dancing lessons in the afternoons and our flirtations during what opportunities offered. Roelynn, perhaps, didn't have the same chores to complete as Adele and I did, but she more than anyone appeared to enjoy both the dancing lessons and the random moments of dalliance.

She told us of some of her encounters with the young apprentice. He had gone riding with her when she carried messages from her father to a merchant in a nearby town. He had bought tickets to a comedy playing on the outskirts of Merendon, and pleaded till she accepted his invitation to accompany him. He had sat her down in the dining room of the Leaf & Berry one afternoon and taught her how to play two of the most notorious card games popular among the aristocracy (notorious because large numbers of young men lost half their fortunes through these games every year).

I suspected there were assignations she did not tell us about. She knew better than to lie to me outright, but her silence spoke eloquently enough to give Adele some idea of what was going on. I was sure there had been meetings by moonlight, kisses by starlight, teary partings at the first hint of sunlight. I started to notice that every day she wore the same gold chain barely visible at the neckline of her dress. I didn't know what pendant might be attached to it, but I was fairly certain that the piece had been a gift from Alexander and that she had vowed to never take it off.

For his part, Alexander seemed equally smitten with Roelynn. I could not help but think that such a beautiful, indolent, and no doubt spoiled young man had had more than his share of romances with gullible girls, and my first thought was that he was merely indulging in a flirtation in order to pass the time. But he seemed so happy when he was with her. I studied him as we stood in the parlor waiting for Micah and Roelynn to arrive. The expression that crossed his face the first time he saw her, every time I watched him, always stopped my heart. It was as if he had been touched by pure joy, visited by magic. It was as if he loved her.

The town was abuzz with rumors of the romance, for it was occurring so publicly. The dressmaker whispered to the brewmaster who whispered to the chef who whispered to the butcher. *Miss Roelynn is in love again, with that young dancing fellow. He seems nice enough, don't you think? Her father will never allow it, but it's a treat to see her so happy, I say.* Constance repeated it to Lissette who repeated it to Mrs. Haskins. *Miss Roelynn was here again today with that boy from the city. I swear they were holding hands till they caught me looking. Never heard a pretty girl laugh in such a pretty way.*

Everybody knew, and everybody gossiped, but no one repeated any of the tales to Karro. I knew that was true, because none of the townspeople had ever betrayed Roelynn in the past, and there had been more than one illicit adventure that had unfolded under their noses.

I also knew it was true because the romance continued, and if Karro had even suspected such a thing was going on, he would have put a stop to it on the instant. There would have been a scene such as none of us had ever witnessed before. But there was no such commotion. The affair progressed in secret, after a fashion. Summermoon drew closer every day.

Gregory wanted me to accompany him to one of the entertainments held every night on the outskirts of town during the days leading up to the festival night. He did not seem picky about which one—he was willing to see singers, jugglers, acrobats, actors, anything I would happen to choose.

"I'm much too busy," I told him, for perhaps the thirtieth time, as he once again sat with me in the kitchen, watching me chop vegetables. He and Alexander had started to have more free time now that Summermoon was almost upon us and their clients turned to other important duties: trying out new hairstyles, going for final fittings on their gowns, and choosing their accessories. They still gave

lessons most mornings but were idle almost every afternoon. Gregory could usually be found somewhere around
the inn, usually tormenting me; Alexander was nowhere to
be seen. One could only guess where he might have gone to
find amusement.

"You can't be busy every minute of the day," Gregory
objected.

"Yes, I could. At an inn there is no end of work," I
informed him. "That's something you should know if you
decide to open your own establishment. There's always
laundry to do and food to prepare and fires to make up and
baths to draw and—oh, it's endless. We only have nine
rooms, and they keep the four of us occupied from sunup till
sundown."

"But once it's sundown," he said, "can't you get away for
an hour or two? Won't Adele cover for you one night if you
do her work the next? She gives you a night out with me,
you give her a night out with Micah. It seems like a fair
trade."

I gave him one repressive look, for it was an understood
thing that we never spoke of Micah and Adele in the same
breath. He rolled his eyes and offered an amendment. "Oh,
very well. You give Adele a night out with *some of her
friends*. How's that?"

"I'm too busy," I repeated.

"Are you afraid that your parents might object to your
attending the fair with me?" he inquired. "I don't know
what kind of rules you might have about keeping a formal
distance between you and your guests. And of course, I'm a

stranger from the royal city—they might find me an unacceptable escort for you for that reason alone."

It was one of the times I really wished I could tell a lie. "No," I said honestly, if a bit resentfully. "My parents think you're charming. You and Alexander both. 'So polite and well behaved,' I think was what my mother said. They wouldn't mind at all."

"Well, then," he said, sounding pleased with himself. "Let's see what our choices are." He had some playbills that he had appropriated from various posts around town, and he now flattened these on the table before him. "'Cozie Fleurs and His Amazing Acrobats,'" he read. "Seriously, how can you not want to go watch someone named Cozie Fleurs? 'They leap! They spin! They appear to fly!' They do sound most amazing."

"Yes, they've been here before, and everyone said they were impressive," I said.

"What about singing instead? We've got the Maritime Rhymers, who I believe are quite bawdy—I saw them, or some group with almost the same name, a few years ago. I thought they were quite funny, but you—hmmm, maybe the madrigal singers instead. Lovely music, so it says here— eight-part harmony performed by classically trained voices."

"I think I'd rather see the acrobats," I said.

"Yes, or—I know! Here's a theater troupe performing *The Princess in Love; Or, The Royal Mix-up*. I'm sure it's very light—no one wants to see high drama at Summermoon."

He paused, and I realized he was waiting for me to answer. "I don't care much for theater," I said finally.

He leaned back in his chair, his hands still pressed to the playbills. "But that was two years ago," he objected. "Surely you can stand to see a play again? If you go with me?"

I had been standing at the counter, dicing carrots and onions, half turned so that I could carry on a conversation with him. But now I spun all the way around to stare at him, the paring knife still clutched in my left hand. "What did you say?" I demanded.

He didn't drop his eyes or sit up straighter or look sorry or embarrassed. He kept his blue gaze on me and repeated, "That was two years ago. Aren't you over him by now?"

For a moment, conscious of the knife in my hands, I seriously wanted to throw it across the room so it landed somewhere in the vicinity of his heart.

"You have no right to know that," I said in a shaking voice. "And it's cruel of you to mention it now."

He shrugged and tipped his chair back, but kept his eyes unwaveringly on me. "You can guess who told me, and no cruelty was intended," he said. "If you like, I can make everything equal by listing for you all my own failed romances. They are not many, but one or two are spectacular. I am sure you would start to feel better immediately."

I turned back to the counter and began chopping again, though my hands were unsteady enough to make this a rather dangerous enterprise. Roelynn, of course, had told the tale, since Adele would never repeat such a thing. And she probably had not even told Gregory; she had probably whispered it one night to Alexander as the two of them watched a group of out-of-town actors perform some farcical play. *Eleda was almost betrayed by an actor once— she loved him, and he pretended to love her, but Adele protected her and someone else was hurt instead.* How exactly had the story been told? I found that I didn't want to know which details Gregory knew and which he did not.

"No, thank you," I said stiffly. "I find I don't have much taste for tales of love gone awry."

"Well, then, we can scratch theater from our list of possibilities," he said. My back was to him, but I could hear him crumpling up one of the cheap posters. "That leaves singing and acrobatics. I'm more inclined to the acrobats, aren't you?"

I opened my mouth, then shut it with a snap. Once again, he had laid a trap for me. If I were merely to answer the casual question, then truthfully I would have to admit that, yes, I preferred acrobats to singers. If I were to answer the deeper question, I would either have to perjure myself with a lie—*I have no interest in seeing any performers of any persuasion while in your company*—or confess that I would love to go with him to any entertainment he might devise.

Silence, as my sister had learned so long ago, was the only option.

"Tomorrow night, then?" he said. "Then the night after that, Adele can be free. The night after that is Summermoon, and who can guess what riches that particular evening will hold?"

"I don't know that I will be able to go with you tomorrow night," I said in a low voice, and that was certainly the truth.

"I think you will," he said comfortably. "I'm counting on it."

The only person I could reasonably discuss all this with was my sister. Adele herself had been more unreadable than usual these past few weeks—though perhaps that was my own fault. Perhaps she had been just the same as ever, but I had been too wrapped up in my own story to pay any attention to hers. It had been an exquisitely painful kind of rapture for her, I knew, to spend so much time dancing in Micah's arms. There surely had to have been a way for her to excuse herself from the sessions if she really wanted to—if nothing else, she could have faked a twisted ankle, an act she would have been able to pull off so well even I would have had trouble knowing it was a lie. But she had wanted to dance with Micah at least as much as she had not wanted to dance with him, and every day, just a minute before the Karro siblings had arrived, she had stepped into the parlor to await them. She had appeared, always, wholly serene, but I could see the faint pallor of excitement pearling her cheeks. I could see the tension in the hands that she kept so carefully at her sides. I knew that she was anticipating delicious torture, but she could not make herself leave the room.

It was time for a heart-to-heart between sisters.

I waited till that night, when we had finished washing up and putting on our thin summer nightdresses. I climbed into my bed first. I saw Adele blow out the candle and heard her settle on her mattress. I waited till she had stopped arranging the pillows and sheets and lay quiet.

"Adele," I said in a low voice.

"Yes?"

"I think this is the most dreadful Summermoon ever."

I heard her laugh and then move about on the bed again. I knew she was sitting up now, her spine against the headboard, her knees drawn up, her hands linked around her ankles. I knew, because I was taking the same position. So we had talked, quietly and in the dark, since we were very small.

"The most dreadful, the most wonderful," she said with a sigh. "I don't know how we'll manage once it's over."

"Roelynn and Alexander," I said.

"You and Gregory."

"Micah and you."

Silence for a moment, and then she said, "At least the dancing lessons are over. That's been the hardest part."

"And the best part."

The cottony sound of her head nodding against the pillow propped behind her on the headboard. "I don't know any terrible secrets about Gregory, if you were wondering," she said. "I couldn't tell you if I *did*, but I can tell you that I don't."

"He wants me to go with him, tomorrow night," I said. "To see some players. I told him I couldn't get away— too busy—but he thought we could trade nights off, me tomorrow and you the night after."

"Do you want to go with him?" she asked.

"Oh—I do, I don't. One more memory to store up later and spend a lot of time trying to forget."

"I think you should go," she said. "I can take care of your chores for one night. But only if you want to."

I sighed. "I don't suppose it matters. He'll be gone once Summermoon is over. Better that way, of course, and I know it, but I will be so dejected when he's gone."

"Better that way," she echoed sadly. "Than to see him every day and think—and wonder—" Her voice stopped abruptly in the dark.

"Micah loves you," I said. I could hear her nod again. "Does he want to marry you? Does he even talk about such things?"

"All the time. He wants to defy his father and elope. But I—it would be—I would be the cause of a rift between him and his father that would last for their lifetimes. How can I do such a thing? How can I be such a barrier? I have told him I will not marry him without his father's blessing."

"Well, that must throw him into despair on a regular basis!" I exclaimed.

She made a sound that was almost a laugh. "Oh, he thinks that if Roelynn ever does marry the prince, Karro will be so delighted he will let Micah wed where he will."

I thought of Roelynn and Alexander, and the light in Roelynn's face that I had not seen during any of her other disastrous liaisons. "I don't think Roelynn will be marrying the prince anytime soon," I said.

"No, and who would want her to?" Adele agreed. "Like the rest of us, she deserves to be happy—and to choose her own way to achieve that happiness. I could not want her to sacrifice her joy in order to guarantee mine."

I sighed again. It was a night made for sighing. "I no longer even know what to long for," I said, sliding down a little in the bed. "I think, 'Melinda will be here soon, and then I will make a wish that she will make come true.' But I don't know what that wish would be. So many other lives seem tangled up with my own hopes and wishes. I would want all our dreams to come true."

I could hear Adele moving, too, stretching back out on the bed and pushing her pillow into a more agreeable shape. "Yes, I have been thinking about Melinda, too," she said. "I know what I would wish for—just this one time, just for this Summermoon. I would wish that you and I would be allowed to go to Karro's for the ball. I don't even want to be invited to dance. I just want to stand in the shadows and watch. I have the feeling that everything would be solved then—if we were there, in the house, on Summermoon night."

Personally, I couldn't see that such a wish had much value—if you were going to expend the energy to fashion a dream that was not going to come true, it might as well be a grand one. "I guess my wishes are a little more vague," I said. "I want us to be happy and have love. All three of us."

"All six," Adele murmured.

I laughed, and snuggled my cheek against the pillow. "Everyone," I whispered drowsily. "The whole world."

"I would settle for us," she replied, yawning through the words. We were silent a few more moments, and then we slept.

CHAPTER SIXTEEN

n the morning, in the middle of a rainstorm, Melinda arrived. She was astonished and a little put out to discover that there was no space left at the Leaf & Berry. "What? You've given away my room to some vagrants from Wodenderry?" she demanded as she sat in the kitchen and had tea with my mother, Adele, and me. Alexander and Gregory had vanished for the afternoon, and the house was curiously silent without the bright music percolating in from the parlor. "You have *always* had a place for me! I can count on you absolutely!"

"Indeed, and I feel most dreadful about turning you away," said my mother, who had agonized over this issue for the past three days. "I don't know what we were thinking when we booked the inn to these young men for such a long time! But now that they're here, we can hardly turn them out—"

"And I suppose I am to go from door to door, in the rain, to see if I can find anyone willing to take me in," Melinda said. I thought she was amused rather than offended by the situation, particularly since my mother was clearly so distraught, but she couldn't help teasing just a little.

"No, no, we have found a place for you already," my mother said eagerly. "Constance has just begun to rent out her top room—really, it's charming, and the street is quieter than ours. I've already reserved it for you, for you know how crowded Merendon gets on Summermoon. But she was delighted to think the Dream-Maker would be her guest. I hate to send you there. You'll like the place so much you'll never come back to the Leaf and Berry."

Melinda blew on her tea, then took a cautious sip. "So, Hannah, who are these young men who have ousted me from my place? Do I know them?"

"A dancing master named Gregory and his apprentice, Alexander," Mother said.

"Alexander has long fair hair that he usually wears tied back. Aristocratic features. Handsome," I said. I was trying not to pile on too many adjectives. "Gregory is dark, blue-eyed, has a beard. They both seem well born but not very well off."

Melinda looked thoughtful, then shook her head. "I don't know anyone with those names who answers to those descriptions. But I'm hardly acquainted with every fallen nobleman in the kingdom. I take it they've been popular additions to the cultural scene?"

My mother threw her hands in the air. "Oh, Melinda! This is the first time the inn has been quiet since they arrived! That music never stops! I hear it when I'm dreaming."

Melinda smiled. "Well, I'm sorry to miss them. Maybe I'll catch them some afternoon when I come over to have tea with you. Though the next few days look to be very busy, and with Summermoon the day after tomorrow—"

"I'm sure you'll meet them one day or another," Adele said softly. "It seems like everyone has."

It was still raining when I gathered Melinda's bags and escorted her to Constance's house just two blocks off High Street. In fact, the Dream-Maker quite liked the cozy little room on the second floor with its ruffled lace curtains and fluffy white bedspread. "Though it's not quite the Leaf and Berry," she said, smiling at me. "I would tell you to wait here until the rain lets up, but I don't think it's going to."

"I've got to get back anyway, whether I'm wet or not," I said. I had to work ahead on tonight's dinner since I wouldn't be there to help serve it. Of course, if it kept raining, not even the amazing acrobatic troupe would be able to perform. Now there was a discouraging thought. "It's just not the same without you in the inn on Summermoon!"

"Remember that next year before you give away my room."

In a few moments, I was back out on the street, holding a heavy shawl over my head in a rather feeble attempt to keep the rain from my face. The cobblestones were slick with mud, water, and the occasional unwary worm; the world smelled like hot, wet brick. The faint breeze was cool enough now, but once the rain stopped, the air would heat up to a sultry pitch, uncomfortable for as long as the sun stayed out. Still, there was an excellent chance that the temperature would be tolerable by nightfall.

I splashed along as quickly as I could, turning the corner onto our street and making for the inn, only a few blocks away. A dark and rather broad man, head down and shoulders hunched against the rain, headed directly for me, and I stepped closer to the buildings to try to keep out of his way. A pointless civility—he caught my arm as I hurried past, and peered in under my shawl to try to identify me. It was Roelynn's father.

"You—you're that girl from the inn, aren't you?" he demanded. "My daughter's friend?"

Imprecise but true. I nodded. "Yes."

"I need to tell you something."

I glanced quickly over both shoulders, looking for shelter, but he shrugged off such inessentials. "It'll be quick," he said. "I just—this has been weighing on me. I want—I had to tell someone, and who better than you?"

"What is it?" I said cautiously.

"I sent a cutter out," he said flatly. "To intercept one of Mac Balder's ships. He's got a fresh cargo from a foreign port, or he says he has, coming in within the next two days. I don't want—damn it, *I'm* the one who brings in the exotic merchandise! *I'm* the one who makes the best deals with other kingdoms! So I sent a ship out to commandeer his freight. You know his men will fight—*my* men would, under the same circumstances. I'm afraid there might be—well— who knows how it will end? Not well, that seems certain."

I was staring at him from under the awning of my shawl.

Gaping, more like. I could feel the rain beating against my dress from the knees on down, soaking the fabric, soaking my shoes. None of that seemed to matter at the moment. "You wanted to tell me that?" I demanded.

He shrugged. "Dreadful, I know. The things a man does to stay in business! The stories I could tell you of my last thirty years would turn that yellow hair of yours pure white. Never thought I'd have anything to say to a Safe-Keeper, but it's true what everyone claims. I feel better having gotten all that off my chest."

"I'm not—" I began, but he interrupted me.

"I know," he said. "You're not going to tell anyone." He shook his head. "What a strange day this has been," he said. And without saying another word, or giving me a chance to say one, he turned away and plunged back into the pouring rain.

More slowly I walked the final yards to the Leaf & Berry, letting my shawl fall over my head like a limp mantle, so wet now it did not seem worth the effort to try to keep my face dry. Clearly Karro had confided in the wrong sister; he had failed to ask the crucial question about my identity. But his confession was more shocking than his lapse of judgment. He had sent out a team of pirates to steal another man's cargo— and, perhaps, to kill another man's crew! It was heinous. It was unforgivable. I should be running even now to go pounding on Mac Balder's door, to inform the harbormaster and Joe Muller and the other key townspeople of Merendon that this outrage was being enacted even as we spoke. I was a Truth-Teller; they would believe me without proof.

But. My essential honesty forced me to wrestle with this dilemma: I had been told his secret under false pretenses. I had done nothing to deceive him, but he had acted in accordance with the rules as he understood them. If it had, in fact, been Adele to whom he told his secret, no force in this world would have made her repeat his words. Did I not stand in for Adele, in this instance? Did I not owe him the courtesy of the covenant? Was not the role of a Safe-Keeper merely to listen, and to know, and to keep silence?

Only one person in the world could answer these questions for me, and she was gone when I came panting into the kitchen.

"Where's Adele?" I asked my mother as I vigorously toweled off my hair and tossed my sodden shoes into the corner. "I have to talk to her. Right now."

From the other room, I could hear the tinkling sounds of the music box plucking away at one of its melodies. The kitchen itself smelled like baking ham and cooling cobbler. My mother looked up from the table, where she sat staring at a pile of silver coins. "She's not here right now," Mother said in a strange voice.

I threw my shawl over a hook and sat at the table beside her. "Where did she go? Why do you look like that? What's all that money for?"

Mother stared over at me, her soft blue eyes a little dazed. "It's from Karro," she said. "Can you believe how much? It'll pay to fix the roof and refurbish half the rooms!"

"Karro!" I exclaimed. He must have been coming from the Leaf & Berry even as I encountered him in the street.

"What did he want? Was he looking for Adele?"

My mother shook her head, then nodded. "He was looking for both of you, actually. He said he wanted to hire your services on Summermoon night. One of his kitchen girls was called away because her mother's dying and another one had to be let go just yesterday because he caught her stealing. He has all those people coming for the ball—he wants you and Adele to work for him, just that one night." She fingered the silver coins spread on the table. "And he paid us all this money."

I felt a little shiver go down my back. That was what Adele had wished for—to be at Karro's on Summermoon. "But you need us on Summermoon," I said slowly. "It's our busiest night of the year."

Mother nodded. "Oh, but this is enough to hire Lissette's cousin—and Lissette, too, if she wants the work. You know the dressmaker's job is finished the minute the ball begins."

"So you told him yes?"

"Well, I didn't see any reason to tell him no! Unless you don't want—I mean, I suppose it's one thing for you girls to work at our place, it's a family business, but perhaps you don't want to be treated as servants at another man's house. And Roelynn is your friend, after all. If you don't want to— I'll give the money back. I'll understand."

She sounded so resolute and so kind that I had to lean over and give her a damp kiss on the cheek. "I can safely speak for Adele when I tell you we'll both be happy to go," I said. "But where *is* Adele? I really have to talk to her."

"She went with your father to the orchards for a few

more bushels of fruit." The orchards, with their ordered rows of delicate trees, were some miles away out the western road. "She won't be back for two or three hours. Maybe longer if the rain doesn't stop."

Two or three hours. Could I really keep a secret that long? Should I? I could feel the words jumbling around in my mouth, begging to be spoken. I pressed my lips together to keep them in.

Mother roused herself from her fascination with the money. "Well! As long as you're so wet anyway, could you run down to Lissette's shop and ask her if she and her cousin will come work on Summermoon? But come back as quick as you can. I haven't even started the laundry, and there's two pies still to make. . . ."

I divided the rest of the morning and the early part of the afternoon into three activities: completing a wide range of chores, watching out for Adele's return, and keeping an eye on the weather, which gradually began to clear. Flocks of gaily dressed dancing students blew through the front door like jeweled birds turned rather bedraggled by the rain; the accented triplets of the waltz and the mazurka followed me whether I was upstairs or down, inside or out. I had not yet had a chance to tell Gregory I would accompany him that night. I wondered if I would have even more startling news to impart before the day was over.

The sun had just begun to break through a sullen mass of clouds when I saw Adele's bright hair as she arrived at the front door of the inn. I was upstairs in a guest room, but looking out the window for the hundredth time. She was alighting from the inn's little gig, which my father then drove off toward the stables. I dropped my pile of dirty linen to the floor and headed straight for the hall. I was halfway down the stairs, close enough to call Adele's name, when I saw someone hurry in the front door after her and stop her in the foyer.

Thick, dark, hunched over a little as if to shield himself from rain or merely to brace himself against the onslaught of trouble. Karro.

I halted on the steps and tried to twist myself over the railing in such a way that I could see the two of them talking without revealing that I myself was present. Karro didn't bother to glance up or around or anywhere except at Adele's face, but Adele knew I was there, I could tell. She instantly turned her back on me and addressed Karro in a low voice, as if she didn't want me to hear. It was an instinctive gesture on the part of a Safe-Keeper, I knew, but still it was annoying.

"Good afternoon, sir. Is there something I can help you with?" she asked.

His voice boomed up the stairway, and I could hear him as clearly as if he stood right next to me. "Yes. I spoke to your sister Adele this afternoon and now I want to talk to you. There's something you have to know."

Adele laid her hand on his arm and very gently steered him back toward the door. "Let's go outside where we might find a little privacy," I heard her say, and then the door to the kitchen closed and shut off all other sounds.

Furious, I raced into one of the bedrooms that over-looked the back lawn so I could see where she led him, and

then I gasped aloud. To the chatterleaf tree! She had the
nerve to pretend that she was me, and that whatever he was
telling her was something she would then attest to if anyone
ever pressed him for the truth! I fumbled with the sash and
eased the window open, leaning far out over the wet case-
ment, but I could catch nothing of their conversation. Karro
was a bellower, but Adele had managed to convince him to
keep his voice down, and naturally she was not the kind of
person who would ever permit herself to be overheard. I
could see him gesturing, could watch her head bob up and
down, but I could not even guess at their conversation.

Whatever his story was, it did not take long to tell. A
very few minutes passed before Karro was on his way again
and Adele was calmly stepping through the back door into
the kitchen. I had flown down the stairs, and I grabbed her
arm before she had even closed the door.

"I have to talk to you," I hissed.

She nodded but put a finger to her lips. Down the short
hallway, the music had come to a syncopated conclusion,
and there was the sound of sudden laughter and conversation. Lesson over; in minutes, this particular class of students would be pouring into the hall. I nodded my head
toward the steps and pulled Adele all the way to the third
floor before I released her arm.

"What did he say to you?" I demanded as soon as we
were safely in our own room. "He stopped me on the street
this morning, and he thought I was you, and he told me—"

Adele reached up and put her hand across my mouth.
"Don't," she said rather sharply. "Don't repeat it."

I jerked my head away. "But it's terrible! Even you— how can you know things like this?—I can't keep it a secret."

This time she laid a single finger against my lips and made a *shushing* sound. Incredibly, she was smiling. "And he has told *me* something, believing I am you," she said. "But I think it is not so terrible a thing, this once, that I am you and you are me. I think, for a few days at least, you can safely keep this secret."

Adele could lie to anybody, but she wasn't lying now. "Is that the truth?" I whispered. "Because my silence could mean that people will get hurt—maybe killed—"

"Wait until Summermoon," she said. "And then we'll see."

"You know something," I said.

She nodded. "I always know something."

I took a deep breath, looked away from her, and slowly released it. If I trusted anyone in this world, it was Adele. If she said to wait, I would wait. "I bet I know something that you don't," I said.

"I suppose that could happen," she replied, and I could hear the smile in her voice. "Is it something you can tell me?"

"Karro has requested that you and I come work at the mansion on Summermoon, to replace two servants who have been called away." I turned my head back to look at her, and I saw the color fade from her face. "So we'll be there for the ball."

Quickly, the blush returned to her cheeks, leaving them

pinker and rounder than before. She looked both pleased and slightly apprehensive. "My wish come true," she said lightly.

"I wonder what else people have wished for lately that is about to be granted that night?" I asked.

Adele laughed soundlessly. "It seems like that kind of season," she admitted, "when a lot of dreams will fall due."

CHAPTER
SEVENTEEN

ate a hasty dinner, then left Adele to do all the cleaning up. In our room, I put on my new Summermoon frock, a light, sleeveless dress whose colors of blue and green and yellow matched my eyes and hair. I wore the thinnest pair of flat shoes and threaded a blue ribbon through my hair.

This was about as beautiful as the Truth-Teller from the Leaf & Berry was likely to get.

I made my way downstairs just as all the clocks were striking six, and found Gregory waiting for me in the small foyer. I had never told him I would accompany him, and we certainly had not set an hour to meet. But there he was and there I was, and he smiled to see me descending.

"Don't you look like the very spirit of summer," he greeted me. For himself, he was wearing a royal blue shirt that made his eyes look like a noon sky, and pale pantaloons tucked into calf-high brown boots. I thought the silver buckle on his belt looked very fine. He had trimmed his beard and combed his hair, and it was clear that, like me, he had made an effort to appear to his best advantage. "I like that dress."

"I like it, too."

He crooked his elbow, and for the life of me I could not forbear resting my fingers on his arm. In this formation we swept out the front door and down the street, heading for the sounds of revelry.

It was truly the most wonderful evening of my life. The temperature was warm but not unbearable, and a light breeze meandered through the town as soon as the sun dropped toward the horizon. Every few minutes we stopped to sample some of the food or drinks being offered by the itinerant vendors—sausage on a stick, fresh fruit, cheese, dill bread, sweet confections, lemonade, wine, flavored water. One merchant was selling necklaces of white flowers so powerfully fragrant that their scent overcame almost every other odor. Gregory bought one for me and dropped it over my head, lifting my hair from the back of my neck so the blossoms would lie against my skin.

We stopped at the booth where people could test their skill in throwing a blade into a target, and Gregory won a prize, a cheap bracelet hung with dangling charms. He presented it to me and I wore it for the rest of the evening. At other booths we played ringtoss or tried to determine the number of beans in a jar. They would not allow me to guess the ages of the three crones sitting on bare stools at another booth. "Not the Truth-Teller, *she's* no fun at this game!" the barker cried, but he was smiling, and he made me laugh. Gregory speculated that they were each fifty years old or less, which won him no prizes but made the women blow him grateful kisses.

We listened to singers on the street corners, flutists in the parks, harpers hidden under the low-slung awnings of shops that had been closed for the evening. We ducked into the red tent of a fortune-teller who read our palms and guessed our futures. "You will find love and contentment in the unlikeliest of places," she told Gregory. To me she said, "Everything you have ever wished for will come true." I found myself ruing the fact that I had not been more prodigal and specific whenever I had made a wish in the past.

It was dark by the time we made our way to the small arena where the acrobats were performing, and we stood in back of the large crowd that had gathered to watch them. I spent most of the hour we were there clutching Gregory's arm and mute with horror, expecting at any moment one of the tumblers would fall to his death from a high wire or a swooping swing. Everyone survived, however, and their flawless arabesques through unsupported air were truly amazing to see. I applauded madly once the performance was over, and Gregory handed me a few coppers to toss to the stage in appreciation. There were so many coins of every denomination being flung at the acrobats that the whole arena appeared to be under a deluge of metallic rain.

"I have never seen anything like that," I exclaimed as the crowd began to disperse and we strolled away. "I can't imagine that even Wodenderry has anything more thrilling."

Gregory laughed. He had taken my hand to guide me out of the press of people, but once we were free of the crowd, he did not release me. "I've seen acrobats in Wodenderry, but they were no better than these fellows," he said cheerfully. "Can you figure out why they aren't all dead?"

"Witchcraft, most likely," I joked. I did not believe in witches. "I can think of no other answer."

He made as if to speak and then paused, cocking his head to one side. "I hear music," he said. "Dance music. Is someone holding a ball?"

I pointed. "Sometimes they set up a stage on the east edge of town, and use it as a dance floor," I said. "They don't do your fancy numbers, though! Reels and country dances, mostly."

He tugged on my hand to pull me in that direction. "Oh, but we have to go investigate this," he said. "We have not danced together in a very long time." Micah and Roelynn had stopped coming for lessons three days ago.

"You have a strange notion of time," I commented, but I let him tow me through the streets.

He grinned down at me. It was very close to midnight now, so the city should have been quite dark, but every window was filled with candles, and special torches had been lit along all the major thoroughfares. His face was perfectly plain to see. "Some days seem a lifetime long," he said. "Others only last an hour. Tonight, for instance. Already it is too short, and it's not over yet."

"I shouldn't be out more than another hour," I said, conscientiously remembering what my mother had told me when she agreed to give me the night off.

"It will seem like a minute," he said.

I did not answer, but privately I agreed.

Soon we arrived at the makeshift dance hall, a thick wooden floor laid over a sturdy frame and open to the night sky. The railing that enclosed it had been gaily festooned with knots of ribbons and bunches of flowers, but that was not its most impressive decoration. All around the square of the floor were hung brightly colored globes, filled with flickering interior candlelight. They threw a muted, multihued illumination across the square of the dance floor and provided a most festive air.

Four musicians sat in a tight group in one corner of the floor, sawing away at stringed instruments that I couldn't even identify. The music was lively, and the couples galloping around the dance floor looked breathless and delighted.

"Oh, what fun!" I exclaimed without thinking.

Gregory pulled me up the three steps that led from the ground to the wooden platform. "Then let us join in," he said.

And we did. Until this summer, I had never been too comfortable participating even in the simple dances, for I was never sure of my steps and could not always catch the cues of the music. But after the last couple of weeks of instruction— and with Gregory's sure arm around my waist—I felt completely confident in my ability. We waited for a break in the whirling circle and then smoothly stepped in.

Later, I could not remember every dance that we performed. As I had warned Gregory, very few of the sedate formal dances were offered at such a venue, but the musicians did rollick through a couple of reels and an extremely vigorous waltz. Every once in a while, indifferent to his audience, Gregory would guide me through some rather dashing move—a twirl under his arm, a quick lift that caused my feet to flare out behind me—and we began to hear a few appreciative murmurs from the crowd. Gradually, as the hour progressed, the other couples began to pull back, giving us more room to show off our maneuvers, until finally we had the whole platform to ourselves. The musicians, on their mettle, launched into an energetic redowa that had us skimming across the whole stage in a dizzying crisscross of patterns. As the music came to a triumphant and somewhat discordant close, Gregory surprised me by dipping me backward over his arm and then gathering me back up in a flourish that had me squeezed tight against his chest. We stood there for a moment, gazing at each other, panting into the sudden silence.

"Well, kiss her, then, boy!" one of the watchers called, and the hearty mutter of approval that followed indicated that the whole crowd was in favor of this notion.

"No help for it," Gregory said, and bent down to brush his lips against mine. The touch was as warm and unalarming as summer rain. Almost immediately, he released me, still keeping his hold on my hand. He made me a great sweeping bow, and I responded with the best curtsy I could manage. The crowd offered a light ripple of applause.

The musicians took a moment to retune their instruments, and the other dancers drifted back onto the floor to await the next number. I suddenly noticed how high the moon was, two days away from full and spilling silver into the sky. "It's late," I said reluctantly. "I have to go home."

"One more dance?" Gregory begged.

"Oh—I probably shouldn't—"

But then, simultaneously, the musicians struck up a slow lover's waltz, and all the globes of colored light winked out. The crowd sent up an astonished gasp. In a second, our eyes adjusted. We saw that the lights had been merely muted when a series of metal hoods had been dropped over the lamps. The effect was to bathe the whole dance floor in a wistful, romantic glow.

"Ah, this one you cannot refuse me," Gregory whispered, and pulled me back into his arms.

How could I resist? I let him hold me closer than he had ever dared during our lessons in my parents' parlor, and I rested my head against the soft cotton of his shirt. The music seemed wrought by enchantment, coming from hands that were fey, not human. Like the other couples, we moved with a slow, intoxicated dreaminess, gliding soundlessly across the floor in small, precise circles. Only if you have ever been in love will you know what I mean when I say I wanted that dance to continue forever. I did not want to have to lift my head, drop my arms, walk back down the street to my prosaic house and my ordinary life. I just wanted to be this girl in this man's arms, unchanging, unchanged, and pooled about with music.

Naturally, the song came to an end, and hope made everyone stand absolutely still for the longest moment. But there was no second plaintive melody to follow the first; the musicians were tuning their instruments again and joking with one another about some note someone had missed in a disputed measure. Gradually, the couples pulled apart. The women shook their hair back, the men smoothed down their sleeves. The hoods were snapped back from the colored globes, which now seemed oddly garish and overbright against the darkness.

"I really have to go home now," I said to Gregory, my voice both urgent and despondent. "I promised."

"And I would not be the man to have you break a vow," he said. He took my hand again and led me down the three steps. I tried to pull my fingers free, but his grip tightened, and so I acquiesced.

Hand in hand we walked the mile or so from the dance stage to the inn. We did not speak at all, but our progress was accompanied by small sounds, both near and distant—music from some other venue, conversation and laughter from three streets over, the clatter of chimes in the trees when the wind pushed hard enough. It seemed that, in every other doorway we passed, couples stood embraced together, kissing passionately. I remembered Gregory's light kiss, and touched my hand surreptitiously to my mouth.

We were not far from the inn, and passing the darkened mouth of an inset doorway, when Gregory suddenly pulled me into the shelter of the building's front entrance. I looked up to ask an indignant question, but he put his fingers across my lips and peered out onto the street we had just left. At first I could see nothing except inexact shadows interlaced with brittle moonlight a few yards in either direction. Then

I made out two figures standing so close to the fabric shop that I had taken them to be dressmaker's forms set in the window. They were just stepping apart from an embrace that seemed to have shaken them both, for they stood there a long moment, staring at each other, hands clasped chest-high between them, saying nothing. After a long silence, they turned our way and began slowly pacing down the street, their hands still tightly locked together.

When they were a few feet away, I identified Roelynn and Alexander. It was clear Gregory had recognized them first—recognized, too, the reckless, abandoned quality of their stolen kiss. Even by moonlight it was easy to read the wildness on Roelynn's face as they passed by, the determination on Alexander's. Impossible to guess what such expressions portended, except calamity.

"Well. There's more trouble than I thought to borrow when we rode into Merendon," Gregory breathed in my ear when they were far enough away that we could risk speaking again.

"Maybe you should go back to Wodenderry as soon as possible," I whispered back. "Tomorrow morning."

He looked at me a moment by imperfect moonlight. "Leaving aside the fact that I don't want to go back to Wodenderry tomorrow," he said, "I think I would find it difficult to persuade Alexander to agree to such a course of action."

"You're his master. Doesn't he have to do what you say?"

Gregory laughed softly. "Curiously, no. At any rate, he never does. And I cannot imagine that he will heed me at all on the morrow."

We had stepped out onto the street and were making our own way slowly down the last stretch of cobblestone. I said nothing until we had arrived at the inn and crept around back to where the kitchen door had been left unlocked for us. "Then there is nothing to be done?" I asked.

Gregory seemed to debate. "Only one thing that I can see," he said.

"And that is?"

"Follow Alexander's example."

And he pulled me into his arms and kissed me again. This time his mouth was heavy on mine, and I felt the rough texture of his beard scrub against my skin. He held me so close to his chest that my garland of white flowers was crushed between us, washing us both in perfume. I felt my breath falter and my heart revolt. It was a shock when he finally released me.

For a moment, we watched each other like strangers set to duel. "So tell me, Truth-Teller," he said at last in a low voice. "What did you think of this night?"

My hand was on the latch; I considered entering the house without replying. But at last I shrugged and shook my head. "I will never have another like it," I said. And then I pushed the door open and slipped inside the kitchen. There were two candles burning on the counter, one for me, one for Gregory. He remained outside, as if he had something to think about and only night air would make it clear. I took my candle and stole up the stairs to the room where my sister lay sleeping. Five minutes, and I was undressed and lying in bed.

Where I lay for the next three hours, lost in remembrance, music echoing in my ears, the scent of white flowers clinging to my skin.

CHAPTER
EIGHTEEN

he next day was hot and balmy, which may have explained my lethargy. I could have blamed it on the fact that I'd slept only a few hours, or on the fact that, when I woke, I was depressed. Kisses by moonlight were all very well if they didn't matter to you, if you didn't care that you were likely never to see your kissing partner again, if you could be lighthearted and nonchalant about their sudden and random occurrences. I didn't think I'd be able to manage such a thing. I was fairly certain Roelynn wouldn't. And if, as I suspected, Adele and Micah had progressed at least to the stage of kisses, I didn't think they would be able to shrug off such tokens of affection either.

Which made it seem that kisses by moonlight might better be avoided altogether.

There was much to do in the kitchen and the garden, so, once I forced myself out of bed and got dressed, I was able to keep myself busy all through the day. Adele, who could pass whole weeks without speaking, seemed desperately silent this day, as if she knew secrets so explosive merely to open her mouth would be to detonate them. She had never told me in so many words that, in trade for my night off with Gregory, she would take this evening and spend it with Micah, but her troubled urgency led me to infer that this was the case.

We did not see Gregory or Alexander all day. The Summermoon ball was tomorrow night, and a few last clumsy souls were trying to learn in one day all the rhythms and graces they had not been able to master in the previous three and a half weeks. The sound of the music box never stopped; the door to the parlor never opened except to admit new students. We left trays of refreshments on a table in the hall and picked up empty plates later. I imagined all parties would be exhausted by day's end and ready to vow they would never dance again.

Adele stayed long enough to help me serve the evening meal to the other guests, but I cleaned up dinner on my own. I assumed she had slipped upstairs to change clothes, but if she did, she didn't pause in the kitchen on her way back downstairs to show me what she had chosen to wear. It crossed my mind that she might not have left the inn at all, merely hidden herself in some hall closet or attic corner to wait for the night to pass. It would have been just like her.

It was somewhere between nine and ten that night before everything dirty had been washed, everything fresh had been put away, and everything that could be prepared for the morning had been diced, mixed, or started. "Well!" Mother said, surveying the orderly kitchen. "I believe I'll find your father and see if he would like to stroll out and sample what delights might be available at this hour of night. You'll stay?"

"I'll stay," I confirmed.

She took off her apron and hung it on a hook. "Bob!" she called, pushing through the kitchen out into the hall. "Where are you? Let's walk down to the pub."

There was always more to do, of course, so I polished good silver and ironed napkins and looked over a recipe that Constance had lent me. I was tired enough to go straight up to bed and fall asleep, but generally we tried to make sure that one of the family members was awake till midnight, particularly during holiday seasons, in case a guest needed something. I could hear occasional noises from the second floor, and the sound of voices as people came back through the front door.

No one came looking for me till almost midnight, when Gregory stepped through the door that connected the kitchen to the dining room.

"Oh, good," he said in the most casual voice, and pulled out one of the chairs around the table. "I was hoping some-one would be here. Is it too late to get a cup of tea?"

Wordlessly, I shook my head. I had been standing by the pantry, debating which spices needed to be replenished and which we wouldn't need to restock for at least two weeks. Five steps, and I was at the great stove, moving the kettle over to the heat.

"And one of those cherry tarts, if there are any left," he added. "Now *that's* something they don't know how to make at the bakeries in Wodenderry."

I assembled a plate, a mug, and the foodstuffs to go with the crockery, then set them all down in front of him. I still hadn't spoken, and I kept my eyes mostly on my tasks.

"I hope you'll sit here with me while I eat," he said in a wheedling voice.

There was no way to refuse. I couldn't very well leave my post until my parents or my sister came home. I might as well have tea. I poured myself a cup, decided I wouldn't be able to choke down a tart, and sat down at the table across from Gregory.

He lifted the mug to his mouth and studied me over the rim. "Or am I wrong?" he teased. "Is this the silent sister? The one who keeps all her thoughts to herself?"

I found my voice. "Now would be an awkward time to begin to get us mixed up," I said.

He laughed and took a sip. "Perhaps I have had you confused all along," he said. "Perhaps I have been courting Adele on half the days I thought I was courting Eleda."

Courting. A strong word. "She wouldn't be the one to tell me if that were so," I said.

He smiled and took another sip of his tea. "Isn't it strange to you," he said, "to live in the same house, share such a small space, such a confined life, with someone who is so exactly your opposite? We all know people who are more like us or less so, whom we feel comfortable with because their beliefs are similar to ours or whom we don't entirely trust because they are so very different from us. And yet Adele is your sister. You are closer than any two sisters I've ever seen. How do you manage that, I wonder?

Does it ever make you despise each other? Try to change the other?"

I shook my head. "No. I understand what you're saying, but no. I can't explain it."

He hitched his chair closer. "I think I've figured it out, though," he said. "You're halves of the same whole. Night and day, sun and shadow, earth and sky. Most people cannot stand perfect truth, you know—and very few people can truly keep a secret, and even then, it's usually only one that matters to them personally. Most people are a mix of the two of you, in some degree or another. They tell a polite lie when the situation requires—they speak out if justice is called for. They cannot adhere so fanatically to one course or another. It's beyond them. That's why we have Safe-Keepers and Truth-Tellers—to make sure ordinary folk see the proper examples, even if they can't live up to the model."

This was giving me a headache. I didn't care much for philosophy at this point. I was wondering why he'd kissed me last night and avoided me today. "Then, I suppose, like most people, you're as happy with the fiction as the truth."

"Lord, I am so sick of lies," he burst out, and his voice blazed with grievance. "At court, it is nothing but equivocations and half promises. *I will do this for you. I will do that for you. No, you misunderstood me. I never said that. I never meant that. I have too much honor to agree to such a scheme.* Bah!" He waved a hand as if to sweep all the intrigue away. "I told myself if I ever met an honest man, I'd go into business with him, and if I ever met an honest woman, I'd marry her."

Now my eyes snapped to his, but I had absolutely nothing to say.

He leaned back in his chair and stretched his legs out under the table. "So what do you envision?" he said. "For the rest of your life? You'll live in Merendon forever? Travel? Raise horses, raise a garden, raise children? What do you want, when you look ahead?"

My voice was small. "I want not to be unhappy."

He shook his head. "That's no wish. Everyone's unhappy at some point. Dreams go astray, people you love die, war comes, or famine comes, or drought or plague. But what do you hold on to through all that? What keeps you going?"

I shook my head. I had never thought to put it into words. I had just always thought happiness would make itself known to me when it arrived, introduce itself like a long-awaited guest. "I suppose you could answer the same question if someone asked it of you," I said.

Now he tucked his legs back under him and leaned across the table, intense. "Can you keep a secret?" he demanded.

I just looked at him for a moment. "Not really, no."

He laughed. He looked delighted. "Then you can repeat it if you like," he said. "I don't think I'll be going back to Wodenderry after all. I'm falling in love with you."

Heat coiled through me as if spiraling up through a spring. The same energy drove me to my feet and I stood there, my hands in fists at my sides, my face damaged with a blush. "I don't know about love," I said very rapidly. "I don't trust it. It would be easier for me if you went away."

He settled back in his chair and smiled up at me, seeming in no way perturbed. "You think it would be," he said.
"But you're wrong. You're not lying—you're just mistaken."

"I don't want to love anybody," I said in a subdued voice.

He tilted his head to one side. "Then tell me this," he
said. "Have you had any luck at keeping yourself from
falling in love with me?"

I could not possibly give him a truthful answer to that.
With shaking hands, I gathered up the dishes on the table
and carried them to the counter to be washed in the morning. There was a laugh outside, and then a set of footsteps,
and my mother and father came in through the back door.

"Oh! That was a lovely night!" my mother exclaimed,
tossing her hair back and smoothing her skirt. "Eleda,
Gregory, did you see the jugglers when you were out yesterday? I swear, they were throwing fifteen plates into the air
at once. Never dropped one of them!"

"I liked the acrobats," my father said. "Can't understand
why they're not all dead, though."

Almost exactly what Gregory had said. I forced a smile.
"Yes, the acrobats were wonderful."

"I liked the dancing best," Gregory volunteered. "And
the food."

"Oh, well, food, you can get that anytime," my mother
said. "But those performers, now, they're worth waiting for
a whole year."

"I'm going to bed now," I said, rather abruptly, edging
toward the door.

"Is your sister back?" Mother asked.

"No. Not that I've seen," I corrected myself. Adele could have come in through the front door if she wanted to avoid any questions I might have.

"Then we'll leave a candle downstairs," Mother said through a yawn. "Gracious, but I'm tired, too. And tomorrow the longest day yet! Come on, Bob, up to bed with us."

Gregory preceded us up the stairway, turning off on the landing to the second floor while we all continued up another story. Adele was not in her bed when I entered the room, and I was asleep within minutes of lying down. I did not hear her creep in during the night, but she was there in the morning, appearing to sleep peacefully on her side of the room. I supposed it was possible I would never know whether or not she had spent the evening with Micah. Then again, I had not exactly given her all the details of my outing with Gregory.

I sighed. It was Summermoon, and a sigh seemed like the most appropriate greeting for the day.

CHAPTER
NINETEEN

dele and I arrived at Karro's mansion a little before noon on the day of the ball and expected to be there till almost dawn. We had brought two changes of clothes, in case we spilled things or encountered other mishaps, and our most comfortable shoes. The round, red-cheeked cook greeted us with devout thanks and instantly set us to doing chores. Five other women worked beside us in the kitchen, and even so I wasn't sure we could possibly finish everything that needed to be completed.

Making cakes, baking bread, basting turkeys, chopping vegetables, folding pastry, filling pies, frying meat, churning butter, melting cheese . . . and more tasks that I cannot even call to mind. There was no end to it. I was used to cooking for anywhere from four to twenty-five people, but I was not accustomed to making a meal for a hundred. No, preparing a *feast* for a hundred. It was a different enterprise altogether.

Roelynn came dancing down an hour or two before the first guests were due to arrive, when we were at a fever pitch of activity and could not spare five minutes to talk to her. But her face was so alive with mischief and her hands on our elbows were so insistent that we put down our knives and our platters and followed her to the far corner of the kitchen.

"What have you done?" I asked with some misgiving.

She giggled and leaned forward to whisper. "Alexander and Gregory are coming to the ball."

I had edged forward to hear her, but now I jerked back. "No! As—as who? Itinerant dance instructors?"

She shrugged. "As friends of one of the noble couples who have been invited by my father. There will be so many people here, my father cannot possibly speak to all of them. And Alexander and Gregory are so well mannered that they will seem to fit right in. Even if my father happens to run into one of them, they'll talk about horses or commerce, and my father will never know that they weren't supposed to be here."

"That seems like a dangerous charade," Adele commented.

Roelynn lifted her chin. "I don't care. I want Alexander here. It's Summermoon, and I want to dance with him. Yes, and I wish both of you were at the ball as well, instead of laboring back here in the kitchen like hired help. Next year, I swear to you, you'll be in formal gowns on the arms of handsome men when my father holds his ball. All of our dreams will come true by next year."

"I don't know that that's exactly my dream," I said dryly.

Roelynn laughed and kissed me on the cheek. "It's my

dream for you," she said gaily. "I wished it for you, and so it must come true."

"Tell Melinda that," Adele said with a smile.

"Oh, I already have."

The cook called our names impatiently. "We have to get back to work," I said. "Come down and show us your gown when you're dressed."

"Oh, there's a place you can watch the ballroom and not be seen," Roelynn said, waving at the cook with an impatient hand. "I'll show you."

So we stole another five minutes to follow Roelynn down a servants' hallway, up a half stair, and into a small pantry that overlooked the dance floor. Indeed, a few perfectly placed eyeholes permitted an excellent view of the room, where even now servants and hired decorators were hanging banners and arranging vases of flowers. "Micah and I used to come here all the time when we were children, before we were old enough to dance," Roelynn whispered. "Back then, it seemed very exciting to watch grand parties!"

"Now it's more exciting to attend them," Adele said.

Roelynn gave her a mischievous look. "Well, this year it will be more fun, when Alexander's here."

"Adele! Eleda!" The cook's voice came again, slightly frantic.

"We have to go," I said. "Your father's paying us high wages for our skills. Have a wonderful time."

And we both hugged her before hurrying back to the kitchen. Where we worked without another moment's pause for the next four hours, preparing and serving the banquet.

In truth, Adele and I did not carry the tureens and platters into the dining room; other, more experienced girls had the responsibility of serving the guests. But we filled the bowls and plates, and we put the final touches on the cakes and cobblers while the guests were eating the main portion of the meal. And then we began stacking and cleaning the dirty dishes as they were brought back into the kitchen—mountains of them, so many dishes I thought we might as well take them down to the harbor and wash them in the big tub of the sea. It would be dawn before all this china was scrubbed and dried.

We were still piling dishes around the counters when we heard the music start from three rooms over. Adele and I exchanged one quick, smiling glance. It was a waltz we recognized from Gregory's music box, though as performed by a full orchestra, it sounded almost nothing like the tinny little tune we were familiar with. Daintily, Adele extended her right foot and tapped out the first few measures of the dance. I sketched a curtsy as if to a noble partner. Then we both turned back to the dishes and smothered our sighs.

About an hour after the dinner had ended and the music had begun, the intense pace in the kitchen slowed down. All the used plates had been brought in from the great dining hall, and a light snack had been laid out on the sideboard in a smaller dining room adjacent to the dance floor. There was still a great deal to do but less concern about deadline, and the cook and her assistants all collectively relaxed. People took a moment to eat, sampling an untouched turkey breast or the hind end of a crusty loaf of bread. I was starving, so I ate scraps from almost every serving platter, and all of them were delicious. The cook seemed quite pleased when I complimented her on several recipes.

I was finishing a bite of pigeon pie when a change in the music signaled another waltz we knew. "Oh, let's go watch this," Adele said in a low voice.

I glanced at the cook for permission. She hesitated, then smiled and nodded. Wiping my fingers on my apron, I followed Adele down the hall and up the stairs to the lookout room. We each found a convenient eyehole in the wall and bent over a little to gaze out.

What a magical sight the ballroom appeared to be right then! It was hung with great swaths of green and yellow silk, and ropes of bright flowers were twined over every doorway and window frame. There must have been a hundred candelabra spaced around the room, and overhead three wheeled chandeliers held another thirty or forty candles each. In this warm light, Karro's guests danced and talked and laughed and moved like a restless and colorful painting. A hundred people had been invited to the dinner and another hundred to the ball, but it seemed as if twice that number swirled around through the gorgeous room, a living pageant of beauty.

I observed the dancers eagerly, looking for the people I knew. There was Micah, holding what looked like a stilted conversation with a very beautiful young lady; her flaming red hair was exaggerated by the striking color of her emerald green gown. There was Karro, dressed in black, standing in a circle of formally clad men who all appeared to be discussing commerce. There was Gregory, dancing most elegantly with Melinda. He was laughing, of course—the man always laughed—but Melinda appeared to be delivering a very serious lecture. Interesting. As far as I knew, she had not met our dancing master or his apprentice since she had been in Merendon, and she had not seemed to recognize their names when I described them. One rarely lectured complete strangers, however.

I remembered something that I had stupidly forgotten during these last wonderful weeks: Gregory was here under a pseudonym. Perhaps she knew him very well under his proper name.

I was still considering what this might mean when Adele gasped and reached over to grip my arm. I instantly tore my gaze from Gregory and looked around for the source of her astonishment. It wasn't hard to find. The crowd of dancers had parted a little, just enough to show off the couple on the center of the floor. Roelynn and Alexander. She was dressed in a magnificent gown of deep rose, square-cut at the neckline, hung with falls of lace at the sleeves, the bodice, and the hem. Her hair was swept back and knotted on top of her head, braided with snippets of more lace and pinned here and there with diamonds. More diamonds glittered around her throat. She looked like a princess or perhaps an apparition—the very incarnation of a fairy-tale enchantress.

But I had seen Roelynn look lovely before. It was Alexander who drew my attention.

He was dressed in smartly cut black velvet with a foaming ivory-colored cravat at his throat. His fair hair had been pulled back and tied with a velvet ribbon, and the style exposed all the sharp angles of his cheeks and chin. Perhaps it was the severity of the hairstyle or the somber color of the suit, but Alexander had never looked so serious before—so stern, so unsmiling, so noble. So absolutely beautiful. He held Roelynn very correctly, arms extended stiffly till his hands rested at her waist and on her shoulder. They were gazing at each other as if there was no one else in the room.

However, there were a fair number of other people in the room, and most of them were staring at Alexander and Roelynn. I identified the handful of strangers present—the couples from Wodenderry that Karro had invited to give consequence to his ball—and I saw all of them watching Alexander with troubled, speculative eyes. Not for the first time, I wondered about the precise nature of the scandal that had sent Alexander and Gregory running from the royal city in disgrace. One of these Wodenderry visitors could fill me in on the details, I had no doubt.

I wondered if it was perhaps my duty as Roelynn's friend and Truth-Teller of Merendon to find out.

"Has Karro seen Roelynn dancing with Alexander?" Adele asked in a whisper. There was no possible way anyone on the dance floor could overhear our conversation, but there was something about the very act of spying that led us to speak in low voices.

"I don't know. He seems very absorbed in his own conversation."

"Why can't she have more discretion?" Adele demanded. Because discretion was something she herself had in abundant supply, it was hard for her to understand why other people lacked it. "If she's going to dance with an uninvited guest, at least she should do it in a less spectacular way."

I was still watching Roelynn and Alexander watch each other, intent, absorbed, oblivious. I remembered seeing their fervent embrace two nights ago. "I think they've reached the point where they don't care who sees them or how spectacular their behavior is," I said.

"Karro will care."

There was no answer to that except the obvious. Karro would very certainly care.

Finally the music stopped and all the couples disentangled, some more reluctantly than others. While we watched, Melinda and Gregory materialized beside Roelynn and Alexander. A smiling Gregory took Roelynn's hand as the orchestra pattered into another melody; a frowning Melinda appeared to launch into a furious scold of Alexander. So she knew him, too! The fair-haired young man merely gave her a deep bow and held out his arms to escort her into the polonaise. Within a few moments, the movements of the dance had separated the couples.

I pulled away from the eyehole and backed against the wall, needing the support. "Well," I said. "We'll have to count this as a successful evening only if it doesn't result in bloodshed."

Adele gave me a sober look, clearly not thinking my comment was funny. I shrugged, she spread her hands in resignation, and without saying another word, we headed back to the kitchen.

It was perhaps an hour later when Melinda came to find us. Another tedious hour of scraping food into garbage pails, dipping plates into soapy hot water, leaving pans to soak in oversize sinks. I tried to remember the generous pile of silver coins on our own kitchen table, but that amount seemed to shrink to a paltry sum as the wearisome evening wore on. One of the house servants, a girl who couldn't have been more than fourteen, took five minutes to rest her sore back against the wall, and fell asleep there standing up. Even the cook didn't bother to reprimand her, so she stayed there until her head jerked forward hard enough to wake her up.

When Melinda appeared, dressed in gold and white, it was as if some kind of rare fabled bird had alighted among the common crows and sparrows of the countryside. The cook and most of her assistants drew back, in awe of her elegance and station, though the girl who had fallen asleep crept close enough to brush her fingers across the back of Melinda's dress. A visit from the Dream-Maker; may as well take the chance of touching her in the hopes that she might make your dream come true.

"Eleda. Adele," Melinda snapped. "Come with me right away. I think—" And she turned away and fled back down the hallway before completing her sentence.

I think there's going to be trouble. No need to say it out loud.

CHAPTER TWENTY

dele and I followed Melinda down the corridor that led to the dining room, then down another hallway that paralleled the dance floor. Clearly Melinda had been in this house often enough to have a fair idea of where she was going. We could hear the music distinctly, though muffled somewhat by the thick walls, and the low soothing murmur of indistinguishable conversation. I hurried to catch up.

"What's wrong?" I demanded. "What happened?"

"I just saw Karro yank Roelynn off of the dance floor and pull her out of the room," Melinda said over her shoulder. "There's a little den right down this hall—the closest place for one to find privacy, I think, if one had just exited the ballroom."

"Did he see her dancing with Alexander?" Adele asked.

Melinda half turned to give Adele an unreadable look. "'Dancing with Alexander'?" she repeated. "That would be one way to put it."

I was about to ask for more details when our attention

was arrested by the noise of a choked cry. It sounded like Roelynn, and it sounded as if it had come from behind the closed door just ahead of us. Without hesitation, Melinda twisted the knob and stalked into the small room.

What greeted our eyes was a horrifying sight. Roelynn, in her rose and silver gown, was backed up against a dark-paneled wall, her hands flat to the wood behind her, her head thrown back as if to scream. Karro stood over her like some black bird of prey, a hulking, dangerous presence, reeking with fury. He had both hands around her throat and appeared to be trying to choke the life out of her.

"Delton Karro," Melinda snapped in a hard, authoritative tone. "Let her go!"

Karro whirled around to face us, but he did not drop his hands from Roelynn's throat. Consequently, she stumbled in a half circle around him in some grotesque parody of a maypole. He repositioned his arms and jerked her against his body so that she was suddenly standing with her back flat against his chest. He had one arm crooked around her neck—and a small silver dagger pointed at her throat. I was so shocked that for a moment I could not move or think, but I heard Adele gasp and I saw Melinda move closer.

"Step away from us, Dream-Maker," he warned, and it was clear by his voice that he was so angry he had temporarily slipped into the realm of madness. "This quarrel has nothing to do with you."

Melinda was enviably cool at the best of times, but now she was positively icy. "Drop your hands from that girl's neck and talk to me," she said. "Tell me what disaster has brought you to this pass. There must be some way it can be mended."

"It will be mended well enough!" Karro shouted. "When I have beaten her senseless and locked her in her room! Shameless, disobedient girl! She defies me at every turn— she flirts with every handsome commoner who comes her way—when she knows, she *knows* of the plans I have for her, the life I could make for her—"

"Father," Roelynn squeaked, but he uttered an inarticulate cry and seemed to squeeze his arm even tighter. She whimpered and lay still.

Melinda took a step closer, and now she tried a different tack. Extending a hand, she spoke in a coaxing voice. "What plans?" she said. "What life? I'm sure whatever you're angry about now is just a misunderstanding."

"A misunderstanding? A misunderstanding? Did you see her, dancing the night away with that lowborn boy, that man, that—that nobody! I asked someone, 'Who is it who has claimed my daughter's attention all night?' and I was told, 'Oh, he's the dancing master's apprentice.' *The dancing master's apprentice?* Some cast-off poor relation of a bad branch of someone's noble family, no doubt! When I had such dreams of her! When I was planning to marry her to the prince!" He contrived to shake her so hard that I was sure her very bones must be rattling.

"There's still plenty of time for your great dream to come true," Melinda said, still in that soothing voice. I wondered if Adele and I could tiptoe around her, sneak up to Karro, and assault him hard enough to free Roelynn. It seemed too risky, and yet I felt terrified and foolish, standing there doing nothing while Melinda tried to calm his rage. "She was just dancing with this young man. A harmless flirtation. Who's to say that she won't marry the prince after all?"

Karro shook his daughter again, growling low in his throat. "Yes, that's what she'll do if I have anything to say about it, but she—*she* has other ideas! 'I love him, Father,' she said to me as I dragged her off the dance floor. She loves him! She *thinks* she loves him! We'll see how much she loves him when she's been starved for a week."

"All girls talk that way when they've been dancing with attractive men," Melinda said in a dismissive voice. "Why, I'm sure tomorrow morning she won't even be able to remember his name."

To my complete astonishment, this was the moment Adele chose to speak up. "Anyway, even if she loves him, this young man does not love her," my sister said in a soft voice. "I know his secret."

Everyone in the room grew very still. Karro swung his heavy head toward Adele, and Melinda and I pivoted slightly in her direction. Even Roelynn, trapped in her father's brutal embrace, seemed to strain to hear what Adele might say next.

"What's that? He has a secret?" Karro cried. "Who are you then—oh, the Safe-Keeper. I know you. And you know a terrible secret about this young man? *Tell it to me now.*"

She couldn't, of course. A Safe-Keeper could no more

repeat a confidence than a Truth-Teller could speak a lie. But I saw her clench her hands and take a deep breath and seek the right words.

"Yesterday morning, I saw that man—Alexander—at the chapel with a young girl from Merendon," Adele said, speaking as calmly as if she betrayed secrets every day. Every word she said slammed like a stone against my rib cage, because I could tell that every word was true. "In stealth and secrecy, with only the pastor and one other for witness, they were married. You need not fear that Alexander will disrupt your plans for your daughter's future."

"Well!" Karro exclaimed, and his voice was richly pleased. I was sure he must be smiling, but I could not look at his face. All my attention was on Roelynn. Her cheeks had gone deathly white at Adele's words. She sagged in her father's arms, as if only his grip kept her on her feet, only his dagger against her throat reminded her to breathe. Alexander wed to another! It seemed absolutely impossible. But I could see that Roelynn believed Adele—as I believed her myself. "Well, this is splendid news indeed! Did you hear that, daughter?" he demanded, rattling her against him once more. "Yet again you've displayed the poorest imaginable judgment and chosen a man entirely unworthy of you. When will you learn? When will you realize you must be guided by me? Will I really need to beat some obedience in you—now, this very night?"

He must have relaxed his chokehold on her throat just the tiniest bit, for Roelynn managed to spit out an entire sentence. "The only time I will ever do what you want of me is when I am dead, and I lie in the grave you have provided," she said very fast and very hard.

He uttered another wordless cry and seemed swept with red fury. Making a quarter turn on one heel, he slammed her head twice against the paneled wall and pushed the dagger closer home. I saw a dot of blood form in the hollow of her throat above the lace-encrusted bodice.

Melinda called his name again, and the three of us moved closer, but now he brandished his knife in our direction and seemed quite prepared to use it on any of us. I could think of only one thing to do to calm him from his mindless rage and restore even a modicum of sanity to the scene. Promise him what he wanted.

"You need not worry for Roelynn's future," I said, raising my voice to be heard among all the oaths and pleas being loosed into the room. Everyone quieted down and looked at me, and I swallowed hard, hoping the words would allow themselves to be spoken. But surely if Adele could tell a secret, I could tell a lie. I had never done so. I could not be certain. "You know me, I think. I am Roelynn's friend Eleda. The Truth-Teller of Merendon."

"Yes, yes, speak then if you have anything to say!"

I swallowed again, my throat so tight it was hard to breathe. "All your plans for Roelynn will come true," I said, my voice sounding scratchy and strained. "She will marry no one but Prince Darian."

"Aaaahh!" Karro said, releasing a long, silky syllable of satisfaction. I kept my gaze on him, but I could see Roelynn close her eyes as if she had just been cursed, could see Adele staring at me in marveling disbelief. As for myself, I could scarcely believe I had been able to speak the lie, the first one I had ever uttered. My tongue did not choke me; my lips did not refuse the tainted words. I had not been brought down by lightning, or shriveled from within by the judgment of my own implacable conscience. A false word offered as a true one and the world did not end. I was as dis-illusioned by that as I was terrified by my present situation.

Karro was smiling widely now. "And if you say it, it must be true. My daughter will marry the prince after all. This dancing boy—all the other riffraff she consorts with—they all will amount to nothing. Her wild ways, her saucy man-ner—none of that will be enough to disgust the royal house. Roelynn will marry Darian."

"She will," I said, my mouth so dry the words would scarcely come out.

No one else had a chance to speak. There were sudden voices in the hall, mostly male, and the sound of jostling bodies. "This way!" someone called, and in a moment, the door burst open. Nearly a dozen people poured into the room. There was so much motion and commotion that it took a minute for me to sort out what was happening. I saw Micah charge through the throng of people and rescue his sister from his father's hold—I saw Alexander, a half step behind him, snatch her limp body from Micah and shield it with his own. Indeed, she seemed so frail and he so stricken that they sank in a double half-swoon to the floor. There, Alexander cradled her against him, holding her so tenderly and seeming so unaware of anything else going on in the room that I was afraid they might be trampled. Then I saw Gregory move over to stand between them and the milling crowd.

Watching the two of them together, I began to have my doubts about the veracity of Adele's story.

But she had spoken the truth. I might have been able to speak a lie, but I had not lost my ability to recognize a falsehood. Alexander had married a village girl yesterday morning.

Or perhaps . . .

Before I had a chance to work through it, there was another influx of angry men into the room. There were now maybe twenty-five people in the den that was designed to hold comfortably about a quarter of that number. Adele, Melinda, and I found ourselves shoved toward the wall across the room from where Gregory stood guard over the couple on the floor. I craned my neck, straining to see around velvet shoulders and starched collars to observe what was happening now.

"Delton Karro!" exclaimed one of the new arrivals. "You are accused of piracy on the high seas!"

"*What?*" bellowed Karro. He hauled the great bulk of his body around to face this new travail and seemed filled with so much force and energy it was as if he had not expended any of it on his daughter. "Who accuses me? What is the specific crime?"

"I accuse you!" cried another voice, and a second man stepped up beside the first. Finally, I recognized them both.

The first was the harbormaster, an old but iron-willed for-
mer sea captain. The second was Mac Balder, Karro's chief
rival, a cadaverously thin man with sunken cheeks and
wispy white hair. Around them crowded some of the richest
and most important men in Merendon, as well as several of
the visitors from Wodenderry.

"*I* accuse you!" Mac Balder repeated, shaking his finger
in Karro's face. Karro batted his hand away. "You sent one of
your clippers out to harass my *Melva Blue,* and now it's
missing, overdue in port by two days. Your men brought
down my ship! Massacred my sailors, I've no doubt—yes,
and stole my cargo, too! Do you think to sell it here in the
Merendon shops once I tell everyone that you're a thief and
a murderer? Do you think the queen will want to partner
with someone like you when I tell her what kind of man
you are? You'll be run out of Merendon, you liar, you
scoundrel—you— you—*killer.*"

Indeed, there was such a roar of outrage from the
gathering that it seemed likely Karro would be thrown out
of the city this very night. Bodies pressed closer to him;
hands reached out to cuff him across the face or shoulders.
I thought it possible that any number of people, myself
included, might be crushed underfoot by the reckless, furious crowd.

But two figures forced themselves between the angry
townspeople and the embattled Karro. One was the harbormaster, who held up his hands for quiet. The other was
Micah, who looked pale but determined.

"My father would not do such deeds," Micah called, his

voice barely audible above the boil of the crowd. "My father is an honorable businessman."

"I've never cared much for the cut of his honor!" someone shouted in response.

The harbormaster held his hands even higher. "Let us hear what Delton Karro has to say in response to these accusations," he commanded, and the noise around him subsided somewhat. "Let us hear his defense." He turned to look at Karro, where he hunched against the wall, defiant but just a little apprehensive.

"I didn't bring down the *Melva Blue*," Karro claimed, panting a little. "I admit it, I wanted to—but I didn't do it."

There was another swell of outrage at this acknowledgment, and then the harbormaster shouted at them all to be quiet again. "How can we know that what you say is true?" the harbormaster demanded.

Karro pushed himself away from the wall, scanned the room—and pointed straight at me. "There. That woman. The Truth-Teller. She'll repeat what I told her two days ago about Mac Balder's precious ship."

Now every person in the room had turned to stare at me. I couldn't help myself—I stole one quick glance in Gregory's direction, and found the encouragement on his face to be supremely comforting. I took a deep breath and stepped out a little into the mob of men. "Yes, indeed, you stopped me on the street in the middle of a rainstorm and told me a terrible thing," I said in a clear voice. "You told me you had sent out one of your own ships to intercept one of Mac Balder's, that you were jealous of his foreign cargo and you wanted your own men to bring it to port. You said you thought there was a good chance of bloodshed, too."

Now the noise in the room was deafening, men shouting and waving their fists, Karro hollering back with his face reddened by rage. I saw Micah wrestle his father to the wall as if to keep him from leaping across the assembled company to strangle me as he had strangled Roelynn. It was a good five minutes before the harbormaster was able to quiet everyone this time, and even then, Karro's voice could be heard in a manic rant. "She lies! She lies! The Truth-Teller lies!"

I waited till I thought people might be able to hear me, and then I spoke again, copying the cold tone Melinda had used earlier. "I do not lie," I said. "But I admit that when Karro told me these things, he believed he was speaking to my sister, the Safe-Keeper. He thought he was confessing to someone who would keep his dreadful secret."

"Ha!" Karro cried, straining against Micah's hold. "Then it was your *sister* I spoke to later in the day, when I came to your parents' house! I told her I had rescinded my orders. I told her that my heart misgave me and I had called my men back. I told her I could not do such a terrible thing, bitterly though I hated this man Balder. She knows—I told her. Ask that other girl!"

And now all eyes in the room turned toward Adele.

She stepped away from the wall with her usual poise and dropped a quick curtsy to the gathered crowd. The look on her face was grave and absolutely unreadable. The harbormaster said to her in a stern voice, "Is Karro telling the

truth? Did he indeed tell you these things? Did he counter-
mand his orders of piracy?"

"He certainly did speak to me that afternoon," she said,
her voice much steadier than mine had been. "But I am not
at liberty to repeat what he said to me. I am a Safe-Keeper,
and I do not reveal such secrets."

Karro howled with fury and frustration. The mob erupted
into fresh accusations of perfidy and surged forward again as
if to destroy him on the spot. I heard voices demand that
Karro be incarcerated, that he be forced out of town, that he
be hanged, that he be thrown into the ocean to drown. Once
again, the harbormaster was able to beat them back to a
state of semi-reason.

"We do not have proof!" the harbormaster shouted. "We
do not have definitive testimony! We cannot convict or punish the man based on the evidence of one missing ship!
Ships are late into harbor all the time!"

"He is still suspect!" Joe Muller called back. "He should
be dragged from his house and put in chains until we have
discovered the truth of the matter!"

"He's a damned unscrupulous man, is what he is!" cried
another voice. "Maybe he hasn't brought down Mac's ship,
but he's lied and he's cheated and he's bullied men before
this, and I say it's time the whole kingdom knows him for
the unsavory rat he is."

More men called out details of their own past dealings
with Karro, and I could see that, whatever else this evening
might bring, it would be the ruin of Karro's reputation. He
could see it, too. His face, so ruddy with rage all night, was

growing pale and lax; I could see a layer of sweat shining along his forehead. He tried to counter his neighbors' accusations with a voice that grew more feeble and unconvincing with every word. "No . . . you misunderstood . . . no, I never meant it that way . . . perhaps that was not quite fair, but we can work out a better deal. . . ."

Beside me, I felt Melinda shake out her gold and white skirts and then take a decisive step into the crowd. She had to push and tug a little, but as soon as all the men realized who moved among them, they hastily cleared a way for her. In a few moments, she was standing before Karro. She was not a tall woman, but at this moment she appeared to be gazing down at him.

"Delton Karro," she said, and her voice rang to all corners of the room, "you know that I have the power to make some wishes come true. For the past seventeen years, your one and only wish has been to see your daughter marry the prince. It has been the thing you have worked for above all others. Now, tonight, you may see a second dream present itself. You may wish to save your good name and rescue your business, both at dire risk right now. What shall it be? I cannot make both dreams come true. You must choose."

I held my breath to hear the answer. All around me, it seemed, the whole crowd similarly suspended breathing. No one spoke, no one moved, as we waited for Karro's reply.

At last he spoke, slowly, reluctantly. He was not a man used to being thwarted, not a man accustomed to giving up one thing to secure something else. He was a man who had always believed he could have everything he wanted. "I choose—I choose myself," he said heavily. "My daughter can marry whom she pleases."

"And your son?" Melinda added.

Karro dipped his head. "And my son. Let them wed where they will and be damned to them."

Melinda gave a brief, quick nod. "What I did not tell you," she said, "was that I would grant the wish you *didn't* choose. Your reputation is lost, but your daughter will still marry the prince."

There was a moment of stunned silence, then pandemonium. My heartbroken cry of *"Noooo!"* was lost in the general uproar. How could she do such an awful thing, how could Melinda snatch happiness away from both Roelynn and Adele, even to punish this terrible man? It was wrong; it was unjust; it was so unlike her. She might be granting Karro one of his wishes, but she had ruined the dreams of four other people in the room. Or three people, if Alexander really had gone off and married another girl yesterday morning . . .

The unruly crowd now rocked back and forth, calling for more penalties to be inflicted on Karro. I felt a hand close over mine and draw me back toward the relative safety of the wall. It was Adele, and she was smiling.

"Do not look so upset," she whispered in my ear, and even over the incredible noise in the room, I could hear her. "You'll see. Everything will turn out."

"What did he tell you?" I whispered back. "That day at the inn? What is the truth?" For emotions had been so high in the room that even I had had trouble telling when a lie was being spoken.

She smiled again and put a finger to her lips.

Just when I thought the noise level in the small room could not get any louder, there was an ear-splitting inhuman sound that made it seem as if the whole world was baying. I snatched my hand away from Adele's so I could clap both palms to my ears, and around me everyone else did the same. The noise came again, and I realized that it was the harbormaster blowing a foghorn, designed to steer ships away from trouble—or silence intemperate mobs. We all stared at him in stupefaction, and he pointed at the door.

There, unnoticed in the hubbub, stood a new arrival. He was not a man I knew, but it was clear he was a sailor of some sort, and the exhaustion on his face proclaimed he was the survivor of a very hazardous journey. When he saw every person in the room staring his way, he drew himself up stiff and straight and gave us all one smart salute.

"Jack Ailsley of the *Melva Blue,* just come into harbor," he announced. "Captain heard as there was some worry about our tardiness, so he sent me here to let you know we was all well."

CHAPTER
TWENTY-ONE

fter that, it was clear the room was too small to hold all the rejoicing, recriminations, and retellings that were necessary to make sense of this night. The whole crowd streamed out into the corridor and then down toward the ballroom—or, who knows, perhaps to the dining hall or some other chamber meant for large gatherings. I didn't know where they ended up. I didn't follow. Like my sister, Melinda, and Gregory—like Alexander and Roelynn, still embracing on the floor—I stayed in the little den as the room emptied out. When the last man had exited, talking volubly to his companion, Gregory closed the door behind them all and set his back to it.

"Now," he said, and his glinting blue eyes surveyed those of us remaining. "Will somebody please explain what just happened here?"

Melinda sank to a seat in one of the spindly upholstered chairs that were scattered around the room and that no one had wanted to take advantage of before. "Oh, my heavens," she said, and her voice was faint. "That's not a night that I'd like to live through more than once."

Alexander looked up from his position on the floor. I wondered how Roelynn could be so comfortable in his embrace when she had just learned that he had married another woman, but in fact, she seemed quite happy. For his part, Alexander seemed to be smoldering with a righteous fury. "That man," he said, in his low melodious voice. "Roelynn's father. He ought to be horsewhipped out of this town."

Melinda waved a languid hand. "Oh, he'll suffer some reverses of fortune, and the queen may break her connection with him, but he'll regain his footing, mark my words. He's too shrewd a businessman not to recover from this. He'll repair his standing. His real dream will come true after all."

That was too much for me. I propelled myself away from the wall and came to stand beside her chair, my whole body trembling. "How could you do such a thing?" I demanded. "When you knew—when surely you knew—oh, it's Alexander that Roelynn wants to marry, not that stupid prince! How could you destroy her happiness like that?"

Melinda looked up at me, the expression on her aristocratic face a little sardonic. "You realize, of course, that I cannot choose which wishes to grant and which to ignore. Whatever magic flows through my body makes its own decisions. I said all that merely to make Karro think. I said all that merely to force him to say aloud that he would give up his dreams for his daughter."

"Yes, but then you said that other thing!" I cried, knowing that I was not being entirely clear. I knew she understood me, though. "You said that Roelynn would marry the prince after all!"

Melinda shrugged. "Well, I wanted to disappoint Karro, at least for a moment. And besides, I wish my job as Dream-Maker was always so easy—to proclaim that I can make come true something that has already happened."

For a moment, there was absolute silence in the room.

Then I realized my legs would not support me anymore, and I sank to the floor in a puff of stiff black fabric. "What?" I finally said in a faint voice. But I was not looking at Melinda when I spoke. I was staring at Alexander. Roelynn, who had been lying so peacefully in Alexander's lap a moment ago, was also staring at him. Adele and Gregory were also staring at Alexander with oddly similar expressions of astonishment and amusement.

Melinda spoke into the stillness. "What your sister said earlier was true, you know. This young man did marry a girl of Merendon yesterday morning, and I was his witness. But the girl he married was Roelynn, not some seamstress he'd been flirting with on his free days. Adele told a secret, but it was not a secret from Roelynn."

"But—you said . . ." I whispered.

"That Roelynn would marry the prince? Well, of course. He's called himself Alexander for the past month, but his name is actually Darian. The queen's son. Heir to the throne."

This next silence was even more profound. This time

Roelynn was the one to break it with a single word. "What?" she squeaked.

I saw Alexander—rather, Darian—draw her closer when she seemed to be pulling back. "That was always my dream," he said in a serious voice. "To marry a girl because she loved me, not because she wanted to marry the prince. A girl who didn't care about pomp, who didn't particularly want to be royalty. My mother kept encouraging me to meet you. She kept inviting you to Wodenderry. But I didn't want to meet you as the prince. I didn't even really want to meet you at all. I was sure you would be ugly and squint-eyed and speak in a high, loud voice." He momentarily adjusted his own tones to replicate those of his supposed bride. Then he pointed at Gregory. "It was his idea to come meet you in disguise."

Now all eyes turned Gregory's way. If Alexander was really the prince, then Gregory must be . . . heavens, he could be anybody, but certainly not an impoverished dancing master. He was most likely both rich and noble.

And one of the biggest liars in the kingdom.

I dropped my gaze to stare at my clasped hands, but not before I saw the rueful expression that crossed Gregory's face as he watched me. "Yes, it was my idea, but I didn't expect things to go in such a spectacular way," he said in a pleading voice. "I thought we would merely meet the young lady and see if she was actually hideous. We'd stay a week or two and move on. We had plans to be back in Wodenderry on Summermoon, you know. We never expected to be detained here so long by—circumstances."

Roelynn's voice came again, still weak but growing stronger. "You're the *prince*?"

"I am," Alexander replied. "Sorry."

But Roelynn, of course, was laughing. She threw her arms around his neck and kissed him on the cheek and chin and forehead. "Oh, I'm so happy for you! I worried about you so much, and thought what a hard life you must have led, because you would never talk about it. I imagined your mother as this dreadful ogre and your father as cruel and cold. But I've met them several times and they're quite delightful people! Then you haven't suffered at all!"

"Well, I've suffered a little bit," he said in an unsteady voice. "Wondering what you were going to think when you found out how I'd tricked you."

"Oh, yes, I'm sure to be angry about that," Roelynn said in a mocking voice. "I thought I was marrying a charming but feckless ne'er-do-well who would always make me happy but never amount to much. And I find I've married the charming prince who will one day make me a queen. I don't know how I shall ever get over it."

Adele and I exchanged quick glances, unable to keep the smiles from our faces. Roelynn. So typical. How could he ever have worried? Of course, he had still behaved very badly. It's really not acceptable for anyone, royalty included, to go parading around the countryside pretending to be someone he's not. If it had been me, I would not have forgiven him quite so easily.

If it had been me . . .

I studiously did not look at Gregory as I spoke to

Melinda again. "So, then, I suppose you knew who Alexander really was the minute you laid eyes on him."

The Dream-Maker nodded. "But he made me promise not to give him away. I told him I would wait no longer than Summermoon, and then he must confess or I would do it for him."

"What about the others? There were half-a-dozen families from Wodenderry here for the ball. Any one of them could have betrayed him to Roelynn—or Karro."

Gregory answered, addressing me even though I refused to look at him. "When they first arrived in Merendon, it was just a matter of avoiding them. Simple enough to do, till Roelynn invited us to attend the festivities. Then we merely extracted the same promise from them—keep this secret till the end of Summermoon. They were happy to comply. Everyone likes to be on the receiving end of a secret. Most people just can't hold on to it for more than a few hours."

This made me turn to my sister again and give her a rather more searching look. She had been entirely too calm through this whole affair, entirely too certain that all would be well. "How long did you know this particular secret?" I asked.

"From the moment they arrived at our inn that night."

"No!" I exclaimed, and the others in the room echoed my astonishment.

"What gave me away?" asked Alexander—that is, Darian.

"I recognized your name," Adele answered.

"You knew Alexander was my secret name? How?"

265

"Fiona told me the day Eleda and I went to Wodenderry to meet your sister."

Alexander looked bewildered. "When did you and Eleda come to Wodenderry? When did you meet my sister?"

Adele waved a hand as if to indicate that that was the least important part of the story. "Five years ago. When the Truth-Tellers and Safe-Keepers were invited to the palace to see the princess. And Fiona told me Arisande's secret name, and then she told me yours." Adele paused to give him a rather stern look. "I didn't think it was very wise of you to use it in public that way. Then again, it kept Eleda from suspecting you. She knew Gregory's name was false, but she knew yours was a true name. It kept her from distrusting you."

"So then—so then—all along you knew Roelynn was falling in love with the prince," I said, stammering a little. "All along, tonight, you knew how things would turn out. You weren't afraid at all."

"I was a little nervous when we first walked into the room and Karro had his dagger out," she admitted.

Alexander put his lips to Roelynn's throat, where dried blood trailed toward the bright bodice of her gown. "If I had seen him holding a knife to your skin—"

Roelynn brushed this aside. "I wasn't worried. I didn't think he'd really hurt me."

"But how did *you* know?" Adele asked me. "When you proclaimed that Roelynn would marry no one but the prince. How did you know that was true?"

"I didn't know! I thought I was lying!"

"I thought you couldn't lie," Gregory said, sounding interested.

I gave him a brief, hot glance. "I can't. Unlike some people. So I spoke the truth without knowing it."

Alexander—I mean, Darian—was gazing at Adele. "But how did you know we were in the chapel getting married yesterday?" he asked. "We told no one but Melinda and the pastor. And surely they didn't betray us."

"Yes, Adele, how did you happen to be there to witness them being wed?" Melinda asked in a dry voice. I was fairly certain that she already knew the answer.

Adele, the most serene of women, was blushing a deep red. "We were—*I* was—I happened—"

"*We?*" Roelynn repeated, seeming to pounce on the word. "You were at the chapel with someone? A lover of your own, perhaps?"

"Oh, Adele," I breathed. "You wouldn't—you didn't—not without telling me . . ."

She stretched down a reassuring hand to pat me on the shoulder. "No, never. I would never think to marry without you present. I was just inquiring—we were just inquiring—we were looking ahead to Wintermoon, and wondering if that might be a good time—"

"So you're planning to marry," Gregory said in a hearty, congratulatory tone. "Anyone I've met since I've been in Merendon?"

Roelynn clapped her hands together in excitement. "Micah, of course!" she crowed. So much for keeping secrets from *her.* "And just tonight—you all heard him—just tonight my father said he would free me *and* Micah to make our own choices when it came to marriage. He cannot possibly renege on that now after such a public announcement."

Adele laughed, her face still pink. "Well, that's not what I was counting on," she said. "Earlier Micah had secured your father's promise that, if you married the prince, Micah could wed whomever he chose. And since I knew who Alexander really was, and since you had clearly fallen in love with each other—"

Roelynn clapped her hands again. "Happy endings all around," she said.

"It is a very good thing to be blessed by the Dream-Maker," Alexander said in a solemn voice.

Everyone nodded or murmured an assent to this, except for me. I was happy for Roelynn and my sister, of course— though my head was still in a whirl from all the precipitous events of the night—but I was not positive my own dreams had come true. I was not even sure I could identify my dreams.

Before anyone else could speak, there was a quick rapping on the door. Gregory stepped aside to open it, and we all gazed out, expecting Micah or the harbormaster or someone else with portentous news. But it was merely the cook, looking irate and determined.

"That kitchen's not going to clean itself, you know," she said in an irascible voice. "You were hired to stay till all the work was done, and there's a fair piece left to do. I'm not saying you weren't needed here for whatever that hullabaloo was all about, but everyone's gone back to the ballroom or gone on home, so I'm thinking you can get back to the kitchen where we need you."

Roelynn and the men protested—"I need them even more!" Roelynn exclaimed—but I jumped to my feet and Adele and I hurried to the door. We had been paid in advance, after all, and we knew very well the value of a good worker. Gregory caught my arm as I would have slipped past him.

"We must talk tomorrow morning," he said in a low voice.

I shook myself free and kept walking. "Tomorrow afternoon, more like," I said in a tired voice. "I'll be up till dawn."

"I have to tell you I have to explain—"

I shrugged. "You can if you want," I said, and followed the cook down the hall and back into the kitchen.

We spent a lifetime cleaning up the mess made at the Karro mansion on Summermoon.

CHAPTER
TWENTY-TWO

he day after Summermoon, the whole world slept late. Our guests were always informed that there would be no breakfast served that day, but they could help themselves to an assortment of fruits and breads left in the dining room. No carts or pedestrians ever clattered down the main street until nearly noon; no one was ever woken by loud voices raised in the early-morning hours. The sun would be well up in the sky and beating down with all its considerable might before the first soul was abroad in all of Merendon. Even the gulls and the crows seemed to take the morning off. Even the sea would lie quiet.

This morning, I woke up once, glanced over to see Adele still in bed, and promptly allowed myself to fall back asleep. When I woke a second time, a couple hours later, she was sitting up in bed and gazing around as if she couldn't remember ever seeing this room before. I could understand her sense of disorientation and displacement; I felt much the same way myself.

"Did all of that really happen?" I demanded, not bothering to specify.

She nodded. "The longest night of my life."

I swung my feet over the side of the bed and managed a
huge yawn. "And so you're really going to marry Micah?" I
said.

She smiled, and that flush came back. I imagined she
might have been blushing all through her dreams that night.
"Yes, I am really going to marry him."

"That makes me even happier for you than I am for
Roelynn."

"There's happiness enough for all of us to go around,"
she said. "For you, too."

I went to my armoire and tried to decide what to wear
for the day. "We shall see."

But of course, I saw almost as soon as I went downstairs.
Mother was moving slowly around the kitchen, fighting back
her own yawns and putting together a cold lunch. Father
was seated at the table, sipping tea as if he hoped it might
be the elixir of health and vigor or he had no hope of ever
standing up again.

My mother nodded toward the door. "You might take
your lunch outdoors," she said. "It's a fine day. And there's
someone waiting to share it with you under the chatterleaf
tree."

"Roelynn?" I said.

Mother gave me a quick disdainful look. "No, not
Roelynn. You know who."

I poured my own cup of tea and kissed my father on the

cheek. "Did you hear? The tales from last night?" I asked.

Father nodded. "Melinda came by this morning. The whole town's talking. To think we've had a prince under our roof all this time."

"A prince and his companion," Mother said in a meaningful way. "Now go outside and talk to him."

I put together a plate of bread and cheese and dried meat, balanced a mug of tea on the edge, and pushed my way out the back door. A few steps and I was under the spreading branches of the chatterleaf tree. Gregory was already sitting there, his own meal laid out on a gaily checked red gingham blanket. I dropped down next to him and arranged my food before me.

Then I gave him a very frosty look. "You lied to me," I said.

"I know it appears that way," he said. "And, in fact, I was prepared to lie to the whole world. It's something I've always found fairly easy to do. But I tried not to lie to you."

I took a bite of bread. I was actually starving. Last night's nibbles at the grand folks' food seemed a very long time ago. "You said you were a poor man with no family connections."

"I don't think I said I was poor, exactly, but I'm certainly not rich," he replied. "I'm a third son of a third son— hardly any prospects there, though there's always been plenty of money to support me. And I did tell you that I had some family connections. I just didn't tell you how high up those connections went."

"You said your name was Gregory."

"It's my uncle's name. Everyone says I look like him.

Sometimes my mother even slips and calls me by that name. It was a small lie."

"You said you had left Wodenderry to escape a scandal."

"Well, yes, that was a complete fiction, I suppose."

"You said you were a *dancing master.*"

He smiled at me and took my hand. "I'm a very good dancing master," he said. "Don't you think? Look how much you've learned from me."

I jerked my hand away. "I can never trust you."

"I don't know how you can possibly say that," he replied. "I've never done anything to hurt you. I helped your best friend find the man she'll love forever. I helped my own best friend find a girl who would marry him for love. I've helped make the Leaf and Berry a very profitable enterprise this summer. I've worked with you in the kitchen, danced with you in the parlor, and dreamed of you in the second-floor bedroom. And I never lied to you about how I feel about you. You should know that. You're the first girl who's ever inspired me to want to tell the truth."

I looked away, but he kept talking. "That was *my* dream," he said. "You've never lived at court—you have no idea how artificial it is, how it's all this elaborate pretense. My father tells me that my very first words were a lie, which lets you know how I was bred up in deceit from the cradle."

"What were your first words?" I said, but I still would not look at him.

He laughed. "'It's mine!' I can't even remember what I was laying claim to, but apparently it was somebody else's possession."

I couldn't help but smile a little at that. "And that was your dream?" I said. "To be forced to live a more honest existence?"

He took my hand again, and this time I didn't pull it away. "To be around honest people," he amended. "To stop always speculating on motives and jousting for royal favor. To just be. To just be happy." He squeezed my hand tighter. "I've been happier here. Happier than I've been anywhere. I want to hold on to that happiness as long as I can."

Now I turned back to face him. "You're the one who told me happiness doesn't last," I pointed out. "That dreams are disrupted and plans go awry."

"Yes, but you stand a better *chance* of being happy in some situations than others," he argued. "I want to be among people I like in a place that feels real. I want to stay here. I want to marry you."

I regarded him for a long moment, inspecting his face and weighing the echoes of his words. There was no doubt that he was entirely sincere. It was hard for me to hold on to my impassivity, but I was not entirely won over yet. "Who are you?" I asked. "What is your true name?"

"Tobin Virres Grayson Alain," he said promptly.

"Tobin," I said. "I'm not sure I will ever get used to that. I think I will always think of you as Gregory."

"Call me by any name you like," he said amiably. "I will answer to any hail from your voice."

I tried to frown him down, but his words made me smile. "And what is your station in life?"

"My father is brother to the king."

"*You're* the wicked cousin who always accompanied the prince on all his scandalous outings!" I exclaimed. "We've heard of Tobin for ages. He's a dreadful rake."

"Was," Gregory-Tobin said, bringing my hand to his mouth and kissing it. "*Was* a dreadful rake."

"How can you be sure you want to reform?" I demanded. "It's only been a few weeks. You may find country life and sheer respectability a little dull after another month or two."

"I don't think so," he said. "But set me a test, if you like. Make me prove that I can endure six months of a quiet existence in Merendon before you agree to marry me."

"A year," I said.

"Nine months," he offered.

I could not help smiling. "We'll start with six months," I said. "And go from there."

He still had my hand, and now he drew me closer, scattering the plates and teacups as he pulled me onto his lap. I was quite comfortable there, with his arms around my waist and his head bending over my head as he kissed me on my cheek. "So that is my dream come true," he whispered in my ear. "Life with a girl who loves me and will keep me on the straight and narrow way. I am so glad Melinda was here to grant me my wish. What is your dream, Truth-Teller? What have you always wanted above all else?"

I had to consider that for a moment, for I still did not have a good answer ready. It was very odd to think of oneself as the answer to someone else's prayers, and for a moment I wondered if that might be good enough, if to be a dream come true could be a dream of my own. But that could be only part of it, I decided. I had to have my own desires to work toward, my own goals to reach, though I had no objection to making them complementary with somebody else's goals.

"Happiness," I said at last, falling back on that single, great, unreliable dream that I had never been able to articulate any better than that. "I want happiness. Maybe in the coming years it will take a more specific shape. And maybe there are days it will waver and fall apart. But that's what I want. I don't know how to say it any more clearly."

"And does that happiness include me?" he asked.

I turned in his arms and kissed him on the mouth. He responded most enthusiastically. "Yes," I said, "it very definitely does."

And that was the truth of it. No need for lies or secrets between us, not now; for we had dreams, some that had been granted already and some that might take hold in the future. I was a Truth-Teller, and this was something I knew for certain: Happiness was a rare gift, and a precious one, and I would gather it close to me now and cherish it for all my days to come.

〜 ๑ 〜

HARON SHINN is a journalist who works for a trade magazine. She has won the William C. Crawford Award for Outstanding New Fantasy Writer, and was twice nominated for the John W. Campbell Award for Best New Writer. Her sequence of Samaria novels have been *Locus* best sellers, and her novel *Summers at Castle Auburn* was named an ALA Best Book for Young Adults.

A graduate of Northwestern University, Sharon Shinn has lived in the Midwest most of her life.